VIOLET'S MOUNTAIN

H.D. KNIGHTLEY

ISBN: 1519129637

ISBN 13: 9781519129635 (paperback)

Over Our Heads Publishing

Other titles by H.D. Knightley

Bright: Book One of The Estelle Series
Beyond: Book Two of The Estelle Series
Fly, The Light Princess Retold
and the upcoming Leveling

Hdknightley.com

For Dad

As we stood hand in hand
I found in the sky a soaring bird
High above the sand
Circling against the sun.
Her downward gaze perhaps
Picked us out
In the surge of surf
As we rode the waves
To the shallows.
The sun's rays dazzled our eyes
And she became magnified,
Her feathers outlined.
In the skies circling over ocean and land,
We felt its eyes sweep beyond us
Towards a large dune further down the beach.
Her circle included the dune,
Sand, ocean, and us,
Against the sun her black silhouette wheeled.

—D. C. Cushman

Part 1
FALLING

CHAPTER ONE
Better left unsaid

Violet watched the last sliver of sun collapse below the horizon as a tear rolled down her cheek. She hadn't cried at sunset for a while, so it was unusual—now, but not always—there was a time not so long ago when she cried through every sunset. "I miss you mom," her words floated out on her breath, mingled with the offshore breeze and swirled in her aural eddy, before flinging away behind her, headed who knows where. Traveling away.

This was Violet's nightly ritual and usually ended at the moment of the sun's last glimmer, but tonight she lingered. She looked to the north; her view stretching for miles. She wiped her cheek with the back of her hand and looked behind to the east and then up, the sky filling with stars as she watched, the night unfurling across the sky. Her gaze followed it's movement west, toward the ocean, and down, way way down below, to the sleepy beach town nestled in the dunes. There was a time, years ago, when she would go there, to shop, visit, play, but not anymore. Now she just...

"I wish something would change." As soon as she said it she regretted it. This wasn't a time for wants and wishes and dreams, for selfish thoughts, she had duties and musts and shoulds— "I wish something would change!" Her words echoed around in the upper atmosphere, better left unsaid, but she had said them. So there.

She was Violet Winslow and she had work to do and she would do it without grumbling but still, "I wish something would change, anything, maybe." She sighed and added, "Actually, forget I said anything Dear Sun, don't worry yourself on my account. You have plenty to do. Have a nice sleep and I'll see you tomorrow." She clicked on a spotlight, dropped her helmet's visor to shield her face, and ignited her welding torch. She aimed the tip of her flame at a point where steel met steel and an arc of sparks glittered away.

CHAPTER TWO
What an adventure

Edmund and Benjamin Hawkes checked the live-cams aimed at their favorite surf spot—conditions were perfect, so without uttering a word they implemented the Perfect Waves Contingency Plan—Edmund packed towels, wax, and wetsuits, and Benjamin raided the kitchen for food and packed a cooler. Then they met in the 'studio' to gather their boards, so that everything could be loaded into the van.

That's where they happened to be, waxing their boards, a surf video projected on the wall theater, talking excitedly about the day's plans, when their parents, Joe and Michelle Hawkes, swept into the room.

Joe asked, "Boys, where are you going?"

Edmund said, "Surfing, Dad, want to come?"

Benjamin said, "We have extra boards. We'd be happy to give you pointers."

"I can't, you know, it makes me feel sea sick, but never mind, why don't you both come to the house. We have some things to um, discuss."

Edmund asked, "Couldn't we do it here, we..." He looked down at his board, only half-waxed.

Joe glanced around the studio—at the towering boat, two jet skis, five paddleboards, two kayaks, twelve surfboards, refrigerator, couch, workhorses, shelves and shelves of camping equipment, and the blasted surf videos playing extra-large, running all day long and most nights too.

Joe said, "No, this conversation requires a bit more comfort."

"Oh." Edmund left his bar of wax on the board and followed Benjamin and their parents to the house and into the second parlor. The one decorated to seem casual, yet stuffy enough to impress guests, and way too grand to promote any comfort at all. Edmund began to sit, but Michelle tut-tutted and put a towel over the couch first.

"Mom, I'm not wet."

"Sand," she said pointedly.

"Sons, your mother and I have decided it's time for you to seek your way in the world."

This was a big declaration, a humongous declaration, and left Benjamin and Edmund staring confused.

Joe said, "We decided it yesterday, when we followed you to the beach to watch you surf. Your love of this water sport is positively ruining us."

"Look at us, I've put on ten pounds watching you splash around in the water," said Michelle. "I'm getting no exercise at all. I lie around eating, losing my figure."

"But Mom, there's lots of things you can do at the beach —"

"Oh please, you know I love lifting weights, how would I do that at the beach? Heavy things sink in the sand, and digging them out would ruin my fingernails. Think."

"But—"

"And your father loves rock climbing, he has filled the back acres of this estate with climbing walls, yet you boys go to the beach every day. Your father has nothing to climb at the beach, you know it's true."

Michelle continued, "I love you, I bore you, I fed you. I taught you almost everything you know, and now you're twenty, um something, Edmund, a month away from your birthday."

"Nineteen," said Edmund.

"Yes, yes."

Benjamin said, "I'm only just eighteen…"

"Edmund is almost twenty, and you're very advanced for your age. I've been aware of it since you were a toddler and playing with your little figure-thingies."

"What your mother is trying to say is we want the best for you, but it's also time for us to get our own lives back. It's not fair to expect us to lie on the beach reading books. I've read through every book on Naval history and your mother just hopes for a heavy piece of driftwood to wash up on the beach. We've decided you should seek your fortune starting tomorrow morning."

Edmund squinted his eyes, "I have a fortune. An enormous fortune. I'm to receive it on my twenty-first birthday, and then get the rest when you, my apologies Dad, die. What, exactly am I seeking?"

Michelle raised her hands. "You're seeking notoriety, celebrity, acclaim, of course! No one even knows you exist. How will you be memorable if you aren't famous for something?"

Edmund stared bewildered at Michelle, so Benjamin asked, "What are we going to be famous for?"

Joe said, "That's what you're seeking. You see, this is what we're talking about. I was watching you splash around in the water yesterday and realized you have no direction in your lives. Nothing you love to do."

Michelle said quietly to Joe, as if their sons had gone deaf and couldn't hear them, "Of course we have no one to blame but ourselves. We should have pushed them to be people of consequence. You let Edmund play around pretending to be a businessman. What does one do with that kind of education, I ask you?"

Joe said to Michelle, "And don't even get me started on Benjamin."

Michelle said with a well-practiced sigh, "I dreamt they would want to be sports stars, or rockstars, or models. Somebody important, who does things, and is recognized when they zoom by in their limos."

"Our limo windows are pretty dark," said Edmund. "You bought them like that precisely to keep us from being recognized."

Joe ignored Edmund's point and continued his sideline conversation with Michelle, "But the final straw was the other day. Edmund talked about opening a surf shop with his inheritance and Benjamin said he would work for him and in his own words, 'Teach surf lessons or something.'"

Michelle turned to her sons and said, "Teach surf lessons! Look at you Edmund, tall, lovely smile, the sun-bleached ends on your brown hair, those wide shoulders. I always assumed you'd be a rockstar."

"I'm not musical," he said. "Benjamin plays guitar."

"Well, the guitar players are never as famous as the singers. And look at you, so handsome! Go to the city and lead a band. I figure three years and you're playing stadiums. That's what we mean, seek your fortune."

Edmund and Benjamin conferred with each other silently.

Benjamin asked, "And what do you propose I do, carry Edmund's microphone around?"

Michelle said, "Not at all! You're taller by an inch and with your blonde hair and easy smile you should be a model. But you both need to wear something besides surf shorts and flip-flops."

"So Edmund is a rockstar and I'm a male model? I don't want to be a male model, I want to stay here. My friends are here."

Joe and Michelle glanced at each other. "This is what we mean, you boys need to find your own way, show some incentive. Plus, you aren't considering our needs. We haven't had a date in days and the last time we went away on a romantic vacation? Weeks."

Edmund blew out a large puff of air and attempted to understand from a different direction, he asked, "What were you doing Dad, when you were my age?"

"I moved into the new mansion that my father had built for me and—wait a second—that's immaterial. I worked hard for everything that was given to me. I worked at the company when I was of age."

Edmund said, "I'd be happy to work at the company. Can I start tomorrow?"

"No. No. No. There are people to do that for us. How would it be to have someone from the family working at the company? There's no need, besides it's a waste of your talents."

Benjamin and Edmund sighed, they weren't as practiced at sighing as their mother, but they gave it a good try. Benjamin said, "Edmund is an old guy, perhaps he could go on his own. I'm the baby of the family. I'm pretty sure you have to let me stay while I decide what I want to do. It's only fair."

"How will Edmund make it on his own? You're to accompany him while he seeks his fortune, it's your duty as a younger brother."

Edmund leaned forward. "What if we surfed competitively? We'll stay here and promise we'll get famous for surfing. It would be a win-win."

"Well, that's impossible, because we've decided to start a bed and breakfast here. The ladies at the club told your mother that B&Bs are very hip now, and so we've ordered the sign already."

Michelle said, "We're calling it The Home Is Where The Heart Is Bed And Breakfast. It's been a long dream of mine and this seemed like the best time to get started."

Edmund said, "You're renting out my wing of the house?"

"We have to redecorate first, but yes, ostensibly."

Michelle added, "You can visit anytime, call ahead for a reservation."

Benjamin and Edmund stared dumbfounded at their parents. Edmund wondered how he could talk them out of this, was it money they wanted? Or an agreement? What would make them reconsider? He wondered if he should call Anderson and Silvers the family's polite lawyers; perhaps they would step in with his parents, talk them out of this foolhardy plan?

Benjamin asked, "And you don't care what we do, where we go, or what we accomplish? We can go anywhere, do anything, just leave?"

Michelle said, "I don't know if I would make it sound quite so dire, but yes, you leave tomorrow morning. I'll have Mrs. Monroe pack your bags this afternoon."

The family continued to stare at each other for a few more minutes before Joe stood and said, "Okay honey, would you like to attend me out on the estate? I feel a climb is in order."

"Certainly dearest, I'll have Johnson carry down my new barbells, I could use a lift."

Michelle and Joe left the parlor with a sweep and Edmund and Benjamin remained sitting on their towel-covered chairs staring into space.

After there was no chance of their parents returning, Edmund broke the silence, "What brought this on?"

"I don't know, but we've been kicked out of our home. Could we not leave, just refuse?"

"No. We're going. I'm not someone to stay where I'm not wanted."

Benjamin said, "Damn, I guess today's surf is out of the question if we—do we leave in the morning? Where to?"

"They mentioned the city, but I'm going west. Straight to the coast, then we can head north. Along the beach." Edmund spoke in monotones, his body unmoving. "Pack your longboard. And your short. At least three boards."

Benjamin said, "Will we have a driver?"

Edmund said, "Not a driver. I'll see if I can find a truck. Bring your camping stuff."

He continued to stare into space while Benjamin said, "Okay" and walked upstairs to gather his things.

• • •

Edmund and Benjamin didn't see Joe or Michelle the rest of the day. Right before dinner their parents messaged that they had decided to "eat out that night with the Periwinkles" and "not to wait up" and they would "breakfast together before the boy's trip." Edmund and Benjamin dined and discussed their plans. Edmund had bought a truck. Benjamin had gathered the tent and chairs, and they debated all the other toys. Benjamin said, "We need our jet skis, how else will we tow in? And our boat? We're leaving it?"

Edmund took a deep breath. "Yep, it's time to simplify. Time to say goodbye."

They instructed Mrs. Monroe to unpack the businesslike suitcases she had packed and instead stuff their clothes into rucksacks. Mostly t-shirts. They promised her if they needed fancy going-out clothes they would call and have them shipped. Mrs. Monroe extracted a promise they wouldn't gallivant around the city in flip-flops and surf shorts, and they would dedicate their first song to her. She said a tearful goodbye to the young men she had known for almost a year.

* * *

The following morning Michelle greeted them warmly, "What an adventure you're embarking on today! I'm so happy for you both!"

Edmund and Benjamin stared at her stunned.

Joe said, "Have some eggs, you'll need your strength for your travels." Edmund took four heaping spoonfuls of scrambled eggs, Benjamin took six.

"So you're headed into the city?"

Edmund said, "Eventually, by way of Tunnels."

"What exactly is Tunnels?"

"A point break west of here. It should take us five days, scenic route."

"Well, that is not what your father and I had in mind. We thought you would go to the city and start a band. We talked it all through yesterday!"

"You talked it through yesterday. Ben and I decided we're going on one big surf trip. By truck. We'll stay in tents." Edmund chewed, eyes focused on the butter dish.

"How will you find yourself, seek your fortune, on a beach? You're wasting this opportunity we've given you. You'll only find a beach bum at the end."

Edmund stood, threw his napkin on the table, and said, "Father, Mother, we're off. See you someday. Hope your bed and breakfast is a smashing success."

Benjamin hastily threw his napkin down and pushed his chair back, as his mother protested to Edmund, "What about becoming a rockstar?"

"Oh, that's right—Ben, don't forget your acoustic guitar." Edmund stormed down the hall to the front door, Benjamin following with his guitar case in hand.

CHAPTER THREE
Future here we come

"So, that was it?"

Edmund glared at Benjamin over his driving arm. "What do you mean?"

"I mean, are we really homeless?"

Edmund sighed a deep, I-don't-want-to-talk-about-it sigh and said, "Don't start."

"But seriously, have you ever—"

"Benny I am not in the mood. I've got to get some distance."

"Okay, sure." Benjamin turned up the radio and pushed four buttons causing a high-pitched very loud static. He pushed five more buttons to make it stop. "Phew, I do not know how to work the new truck."

"Can tell." Edmund's silence descended and dampened the tunes satellite-streaming out of the speakers.

Benjamin jabbed another button, found a song he loved, and sang as he opened the small cooler between them and took out a jar of peanut butter, a loaf of bread, and some chocolate hazelnut spread, and with smears and flourishes created a triple-decker sandwich and licked the knife. Edmund raised a brow. "Seriously?" But Benjamin hummed and pretended not to notice.

Finally with his tongue poised a millimeter away from the knife, Benjamin asked, "Want me to make you one big brother?"

"Absolutely not. And seriously, that's junk, you should eat better."

"What, I should eat eight dollar, uber-organic, triple-washed-by-fairies apples like you?"

"Pass one, now you mention it."

Benjamin ate his sandwich and curled up against the door. "I'm going to sleep now, unless you want to talk about our current circumstances."

"Good night."

* * *

Edmund resorted to jerking the steering wheel every few minutes to keep himself from falling asleep. The desolate road was boring as hell and Benjamin had been asleep for hours, leaned and curled up against the passenger door—with a pillow, a mocking move if ever there was one. Edmund jerked the wheel again and chuckled because Benjamin's head lolled. "Benny, wake up, Benny."

"Wha? What?" Benjamin stretched and yawned. "Where are we?" He gazed around with bleary eyes. "Oh, same place. How can this crappy, boring landscape go on and on and on?"

"Boring? Try driving it, that's why I woke you up."

Benjamin said, "Why don't you let me drive and you take a nap for once?"

"Because I like to and it's hard to sit and relax when someone else is driving and—"

"Funny, you sound like mom and her control issues."

Edmund swerved the truck onto the shoulder. He climbed down the steps to the ground, walked around, and opened Benjamin's door. "Drive," he growled to Benjamin's smirk.

Edmund tried to nap, but found it impossible to get comfortable. He was decidedly uncomfortable and having been kicked from his home, uneasy and pissed. Staring at the never-ending, low-scrub landscape, watching the rocks slide by, wasn't helping. He readjusted his pillow turning his back to the window.

Benjamin said, "You could have bought a comfy, luxury ride, but no, you got a truck."

"A bio-diesel truck." Edmund opened one eye. "And I'd be able to sleep if you weren't such an erratic driver." They both knew he was joking, Benjamin hadn't deviated from the straight line of the highway.

"You know that's exactly why you're so universally adored, that enviro-preachiness thing you have going."

Edmund chuckled, "Just being a hero and saving the earth." He twisted and plumped the pillow.

"You are aware that you're the heir to a fortune made from oil extraction?"

Edmund humphed because it was true.

Benjamin changed the station, turning it to Jack Johnson and humming along.

Edmund gave up pretending to sleep. He stared out the front window at the long straight road ahead. Finally he said, "Our parents kicked us out."

"Yes, yes they did. Though I think they called it 'seeking our fortune.'"

"I already have a fortune, why should I go seek it? I wish Granddad was still alive. He wanted me to follow in his shoes, to work at the company. I've been training for it my whole life, and now Dad says I don't need to."

"He wants you to start a band."

"I know. They're completely delusional." Edmund glanced at his phone's map to find the directions to the campsite. "We have an hour before we get to the Blue Canyon campground."

Benjamin asked, "Why did they kick us out, really? I don't get it."

Edmund ran his hand down his face. "To start a Bed and Breakfast, but that's ridiculous, they don't like to work."

"Mom said it's been their dream, had you ever heard her mention it before?"

"Never."

They rode in silence to the campground, checked in, and then Edmund walked to the camp store for supplies. "Get marshmallows!" Benjamin called.

"Marshmallows? I have to buy *marshmallows?*"

"Live a little, I say. You can roll them in granola if you have to."

By the time Edmund returned, Benjamin had raised the tent, organized the beds, faced the chairs around the fire pit—and once Edmund dropped the load of wood—built a fire.

Edmund watched with his hands in his pockets. "How'd you get so competent, Benny-boy?"

"While you were studying to be a titan of industry and hanging with the prep school crowd, I got to go to summer camp." He blew on the minuscule flame causing it to cross to the larger log. "In ten minutes we should have a perfect fire for roasting."

"I bought those fluffy white junk pillows you asked for. I can't believe you made me."

"I'm going to turn you onto banana boats, it will be your favorite thing ever."

"I guess you haven't steered me wrong so far."

"Absolutely. I was right you would love surfing, remember? And now look at you, with your cutbacks and three-sixties. You'll be just as passionate about the gooey awesomeness of warm banana-chocolate-marshmallow goo."

"Will I?" asked Edmund, settling into a chair and allowing the heat of the fire, the warmth of their conversation and the gooeyness of the banana boats to lift his mood. By the end of the night Edmund had extracted a promise from Benjamin to teach him how to set up the tent and build a fire.

▲ ▲ ▲

On the trip they grew used to the truck's bouncing and rattling and jarring on even the smoothest roads. Edmund even learned to sleep in the passenger seat when he would deign to let Benjamin drive, almost comfortable. They rode in the shadow of the surfboards tied to the roof racks—three boards for each brother. The stacks of boards dwarfed the truck even though its big tires required small ladders to climb up and into it. The height of the surf truck gave them splendid views.

The brothers felt progressively better, friendlier, more human. In the evenings they ate banana boats and Benjamin played guitar and they talked and laughed. They created a whole standup routine that started, "This is such a fabulous idea to..." They would each finish the sentence: "Embark on a modeling career while eating 5,000 calories of marshmallows every night." Or, "Start a music career with two young men, one guitar, and a tent." Or, "Drive into the woods leaving our parents in charge of our family's fortune." Then they would laugh and laugh, every laugh getting them a step closer to their regular selves.

On Day Four, their route followed the coast north and they passed a few good surfing spots, marking them on a map in case they wanted to backtrack. The spots seemed fun and rideable, but they were nothing compared to Tunnels, and the brothers knew it. They chose to complete the mission—to keep going and stay out of the surf—but also, and later they agreed, they wanted to get as much distance as possible from their childhood home and the people currently redecorating it.

On a warm and sunny Day Five they reached the last stretch. The road turned away from the coastline and wound over a coastal mountain range and into glorious big trees. Trees so big Edmund had to pull the truck over. He tried to see up through the front window, "Whoa, check that out. Have you ever?"

"You are such a tree-hugging-granola-boy," said Benjamin.

"If you aren't amazed by these trees, then you aren't really seeing."

Benjamin popped the door latch, swinging his door open. "Okay tree-boy, you might be content to sit and stare, but I'm going to actually hug that tree."

He passed two towering trees and beelined to the tallest redwood with the biggest diameter trunk. "It's too wide!"

"That's because you're a little boy, clearly not competent in the hugging department." Edmund approached a different tree and threw his arms around. After years of surfing Edmund had ample shoulders and arms for the task, yet they still only went a tenth of the way. "Huugggggg, there, success. I have hugged this tree. Tree, I declare you hugged." He dusted his hands of the task.

A minivan carrying a family with a pile of giggling kids in the back pulled behind their truck. The father asked through the open window, "Do you need any help?"

Benjamin pulled his arms from around the tree and said, "Um, no."

Edmund said, "We're fine sir, my brother here is comforting a saddened tree. Brother, is the tree happier now?"

Red creeped up Benjamin's cheeks. "Definitely."

"Good. We have a lot of trees to get to, so we'll be going." Edmund climbed into the truck, Benjamin following. Edmund started the engine and said, "Benny-boy, tree-hugging has made us famous already. Mom and Dad were totally right," He pulled the truck onto the road laughing. "This is a fabulous idea."

Benjamin said, "To go to the city and get famous. Oh wait, where's the city? How'd we end up in these woods?" They laughed even more. "This is a fabulous idea to..."

Edmund said, "Drive five days straight to go surfing!"

"In a truck that runs on french fry oil, yet my big brother won't let me eat french fries."

Edmund said, "Because it's bad for you, but it just might save the earth!"

Benjamin curled up practically convulsing with laughter. "Now there's a hilarious dichotomy. This is a fabulous idea... to lock myself in a sand-colored truck with a health-food-nut for five days." He wiped his eyes. "Whooo, that game does not get old."

"Maybe if the whole male model thing doesn't work out, you can try standup."

"What were they even talking about? Our parents are so weird." Benjamin settled back into his seat, sobered after the big laugh.

Edmund said, "They are, and they've sent us on a fool's errand 'to get famous.' What exactly am I going to be famous for? At least you have applicable famous-making skills: guitar playing, posing like a tanned sun god in bathing suits. You'll be fine. I'm trained to be the heir to an estate, which means I... what?"

"You excelled at tree-hugging."

"My one true skill." Edmund joked. "Maybe I should start an environmental foundation."

Benjamin sat up. "Hey, you could, that's a good idea. You and I could start a foundation and run it. See, five days in and we have a plan already. Now we can go back and tell Mom and Dad."

"Benny don't get ahead of yourself. There's an idea, but how is that a fortune? And we haven't even started our seeking yet, not really. We've only been driving through." He gazed back up at the treetops, slowing to a crawl. "No, we haven't even begun our story yet. And I didn't want to mention this before, but I don't plan to take Mom and Dad's money. Not anymore."

"What? Are you crazy?"

"If I am, I got it from them. I want to cut my ties."

Benjamin opened and closed his mouth three times before he said, "How about we go without their money while we seek our fortune. I understand that. We do this on our own. You have money in your bank account, right? So we use that and no help, but we keep your inheritance as a possibility. You don't even get it for over a year, a lot can change."

"Our parents won't change. I don't want their money."

"It's not their money, it's your money. You can do something good with it, or just do good. I'm saying let's keep the possibilities open. Until then, we don't ask them for money.

I agree. Though frankly, the money has never been mine anyway, so I'm not giving up much."

"You know I planned that you would always have whatever you needed. Always."

"I know, but still the fortune isn't mine. It's yours. You'd be giving up a lot."

"Well, I just made a deal with my little brother that I wouldn't give it up, until I had some time to think it through."

"You owe me. I planned to have you take care of me my whole life, now come to find out I'm on my own."

Edmund smiled at Benjamin. "Dude, we're seeking our fortune, not crying over our almost-lost inheritance." He rolled down the window. "Future here we come!"

Benjamin climbed his top half out of the passenger window and yelled, "There are so many trees yet to hug!"

An irritated honking came from behind. The minivan-family from before needed Edmund to pull to the side so they could pass.

Edmund and Benjamin sheepishly waved and continued driving north.

CHAPTER FOUR
You have me

Lala asked, "Violet? What ya thinking about?"

"Huh, wha—" Violet's spoon balanced on her fork and they clanked to the table. "Oh, sorry Lala. I had trouble last night balancing my new sculpture. I built the spinning part, then mounted it, happily, perfectly balanced, but the wing arm lolled sadly, hanging and blah and so forlorn. I never figured it out though I climbed and fiddled for hours. I finally had to go to bed."

"It's big?"

"Very. My biggest yet. And heavy. When the spin happens the movement will seem unbelievable, spectacular, that it's somehow up and moving in the wind, dancing on a breeze. The size will blow you away. Yet the parts won't behave how they ought—maybe it needs another spinner for counter balance—see this is why I hate interrupting in the middle, I'll be stuck on the problem all day."

"The good news is most of the day is gone, you slept until one o'clock. That's p.m."

"Early as far as I'm concerned. But it's probably hot as the blue tip on a torch today."

"Oh wait!" Lala ran off, reappearing a few minutes later with a lacy head-covering and a fan. She fanned herself and said, "Why yes, it's hot as a pig's bottom in the noonday sun. Perhaps we might pour some iced tea and set for a spell."

Violet laughed. "Where did you find that?"

"Level 4, eastern storeroom, Aunt Clara's old things."

"Well, she's moved beyond needing them anymore."

"I found you this." Lala pushed an old black and white photo across the table. "It's your mom, about your age."

Violet picked the photograph up and inspected it closely. Lala said, "I know the anniversary is in a few days and..."

"Yeah, it is. Thank you." She paused her fingers, stroking the air, just above the surface. "Do you think I look like her? I don't see it."

"My parents say you look just like her."

Violet nodded. "Have you seen my dad today?"

"We had breakfast together. He's worried about you, thinks you're lonely."

"I have you."

"He's also worried about me, thinks I'm lonely."

"You have me."

"True that. It's basically what I said just before he went alone back to his room."

Violet smiled and said, "I'm worried about him, he seems lonely."

Lala raised the fan to her face and batted her eyes. "How a man can be lonely with so many gorgeous vivacious women around I'll never know. And to change the subject—today we have some old pinball machines from Cousin Kyle to move."

"I'll grab my hardhat, we better get busy while the sun still shines."

CHAPTER FIVE
She's a loner

After the road meandered through the woods for a while, the roadside foliage dropped away and the overhead canopy of trees disappeared. The road left the woods, and the sky opened —a wide blue expanse from horizon to horizon. Edmund and Benjamin headed due north, skirting the western edge of the high desert, an area known for its small sparse scattered shrubs and rock formations. The road, after an hour, would curve coastal and wind through sand dunes before ending in a beach town called, Sandy Shores, and the point break, Tunnels. It would take a couple of hours to get there, another boring couple of hours, even more boring since they had seen the glory of the forests.

Benjamin asked, "Are there any grocery stores between here and there? I'm famished and all we have is peanut butter. And some pretzels."

"You forgot the yogurt. I'm willing to share."

"Plain, Greek?"

"It's delicious."

"Maybe to you, I'm *not* a fan. What's that ahead?"

"Nothing. Not a thing between us and the coastline. Surfing, finally."

"True, for a surf trip this is totally lame. It'll be nice to get wet." Benjamin dipped a pretzel in peanut butter. "What do you think the town will be like?"

"I'm guessing it's a blip. There's a hotel, called the Surf and Stay and a pub and a restaurant. Classic surf town. The cool part is the campground sits right at the end of Main Street at the beach. Ocean-view camping, I appreciate a town with priorities."

"Hope they sell surf wax, I forgot mine." Benjamin put the lid on the peanut butter jar and curled up in the passenger seat for a nap.

* * *

He woke to Edmund whispering, "Ben. Benny, wake up. Check that out."

Benjamin opened one eye. "I've been telling you my whole life, I hate when you call me Benny. Call me Benjamin. I'm out in the world, an independent traveler. I want a three syllable name. Ben-ja-min, What is that?" He sat up straighter.

A mountain appeared on the horizon. A giant mountain. A looming over everything mountain. Edmund scanned the rest of the landscape, the same low shrubs and rocks spread away from the road on every side. Sand lay all around and far ahead. Low and flat, some dunes, rolling. And right in the middle, a lone mountain.

The road followed northwest, the ocean appeared on the left, but straight ahead something was really really big. A lone dune without the sandy roll? A mountain without the pointed top? A mesa, or tableland, completely by itself? Out here right on the coast? It didn't make visual sense and wasn't logical. But contrary to what seemed right and normal, jutting up out of the ground—huge, towering, a plateau, a mountain. With a circumference of a half mile or so. Seagulls fluttered and flew a circuitous, spinning, spiral above it.

Benjamin said, "That's what I was telling you about, the thing I saw."

"I saw clouds, and then I saw a dark shape on the horizon. I assumed it was a weather pattern something or other, but it's indisputable, that's a mountain."

"The color is weird. It's not sand or rock."

"I know, and the birds flying around—and check out the top, see those things? They're almost like windmills. Possibly a wind farm?"

"I don't think so. It doesn't seem organized. Was anything on the map?"

"Nope, it must be manmade."

They continued driving, getting so close the top could only be seen if Benjamin craned his head out the window and exerted himself. The sun settled low and their road turned west, causing them to lower their visors. Edmund's driving slowed as they peered out the passenger window at the sun-reflecting mountain and tried to understand what they were seeing. They drew closer and closer.

Eventually Benjamin said, "Those aren't rocks."

It freaked Edmund out a little to keep driving closer to such a mysterious landform, so he pulled the truck off the shoulder on the opposite side of the road, kicking up a cloud of sand and gravel. He stepped out and stared.

Benjamin remained in his seat and searched his phone's map, but there was no mention of the formation. "It lists all the stores in Sandy Shores and doesn't mention this giant mountain?"

It wasn't rocks. And Edmund had been correct, the mountain was manmade, a towering mountainous pile of things. From their vantage, a quarter mile away, the sun glinted off the points and edges of tons and tons of manmade items.

A pile of trash. A big hulking pile of trash. Way bigger than it ought to be.

Benjamin stepped out and joined his brother in staring. "Nice surf break. Man, that's a pile of trash. Right out front."

Edmund shook his head.

Benjamin, who talked when he was upset, asked, "How can this be, right here by the coastline, what is it?"

Edmund who quieted when he was upset, paused, then said, "I'm glad our camping reservation is only for two nights. I'm going to have words with the park ranger for not mentioning the campground is situated next to the town dump."

"That's not a town dump, that's a city's dump."

"But where's the city?"

They climbed back into the truck and headed west, following the road that curved around the heap.

Benjamin said, "You know what's weird? The trash is uniform. It's not a dump, but more like a *place*, and—" He stretched his head out the window. "I can't see them anymore but those windmills—it seems planned and methodical."

Edmund ducked to see out and up from the front window and then turned back to the road. "Yeah, it's bizarre."

The road curved along the mountain's eastern edge and midway came to an intersection—turn left or continue straight. The directional sign pointed north:

Coastline Highway

The highway continued around the mountain. The directional sign pointed due west to the coast:

Main Beach Road
Sandy Shores 2 miles

Edmund turned the truck and his attention to the left, to the coast, and the beach town nestled in the dunes, but

Benjamin still gawked at the pile. "This section is full of kitchen appliances. That's like fifty washing machines stacked and then all those hubcaps. What is this thing?"

"It's a hulking behemoth of trash. I'll be glad to get it behind us."

"More like it will shadow over us," said Benjamin. He pulled out his phone and searched for mention of the hill on Wikipedia. Edmund scowled, this wasn't the exciting end to their trip that he had wanted. The horizon glowed pink and striped as the sun neared the edge of the sea to take a dip.

* * *

A half mile closer to the coast, having the mountain far enough behind, Edmund felt relief and pulled the truck to the side and stepped out to gaze back.

He could see the mountain well from this distance and direction, and the stark light of sunset threw the details into high-relief. The pile of things had a distinct systemization. It was less pile and more stacks, ordered, almost decorative. There were sections with same things, or same colors. Quilt-like, it made sense, or seemed to, but, yet, was so senseless. Was the mountain the town's hoard? And for what could they possibly be preparing?

The mountain stretched in both directions for a quarter mile at least. The edges slanted at 30 degrees and the top was table-like, or a plateau. Spinning windmills jutted, circled, spun, and pointed at the sky. The mountain glowed red, reflecting the setting sun, as birds circled and swirled creating a wind.

Edmund said, "The thing is so big it has its own weather pattern."

Benjamin shielded his eyes and scanned the top. "Those whirling sculptures and spires are amazing. It's like a church up there. Wait what is that?"

"Where?"

Benjamin pointed at the tip top of the mountain near one of the spinning whirligigs. "There, see that? Somebody's there."

The figure faced the setting sun, staring out over Benjamin and Edmund's tiny, far away heads, toward the bright red glow.

"Who is that?" Benjamin asked no one in particular.

Edmund stepped closer as though it would bring the person in focus. He tried to make out who it might be, though it would be a stranger, of course, and strange in every way. The person—a woman, or girl—had a firm stance that made her seem a part of the mountain, only her blonde hair streamed back from her head in the mountain-bird-created breeze. Her body was rock, her hair wind. Mysterious. Edmund and Benjamin watched spell-struck as the setting sun's light rose along her body, glimmered on her hair and then caught on the wind and flew away.

"There it goes," said Edmund. He checked the west—a paper thin sliver of pink was all that remained at the horizon. He turned back, the sky behind the mountain was a deep, dark, black-blue. The daylight was extinguished, yet the figure still stood.

A flame ignited from the figure's left hand, shooting away from her body.

"She's welding," Benjamin said, as the figure crossed the plateau and dropped out of sight.

"In the dark. That was—unexpected."

The boys got in the truck and drove to the campground in town.

The sign on the campground station read:

After hours: Please set up camp and register in the morning

They chose the site closest to the dunes. It contained a low scrub pine, bent and gnarled from the wind, a picnic table, a cement slab for surf truck parking, and a fire pit. "Everything we need," said Benjamin as he arranged chairs around the pit. "And your truck right there keeping you company at night."

Edmund threw a sleeping bag at Benjamin in response. They both donned headlamps to somehow raise the tent in the dark. It wasn't easy, and they grumbled a lot, well past hungry.

* * *

The brothers walked up Main Beach Road to the Dunes Diner. Edmund slid into the bench seat, absentmindedly opened a menu, glanced, and tossed it to the table. "I mean, what is she doing up there alone at night? You know? It's incredible, who is she?"

The waitress walked up, "Can I take your order?"

Benjamin had been reading the menu and said, "Coke, meatloaf, potatoes, broccoli, rolls, side of pasta, how about some fries, too, and pie for dessert."

"Do you want it all at once, sweetie?"

"Yeah, spread the food out around me so I have choices. It's been a few days with only peanut butter."

"Really, where are you from?"

"East, on the coast, near Kingsbridge."

Through their conversation Edmund stared out the window and tapped his thumb on the table. He leaned forward to Benjamin and said, "Welding? She was young, too."

Offhanded the waitress said, "Are you talking about Violet?"

Edmund hadn't noticed the waitress who stood waiting at the table for his order. He asked down his nose, "Violet?"

"Yes, the girl who welds up there on the mountain."

"Yes, then, who is she?" Edmund's irritation heightened because she gave him explanations that still required explanations.

"That's Princess Violet, daughter of the Chair King. The closest thing we have to royalty in these parts, and that up there is her castle. She's a loner, you won't see much of her. What can I get you?"

Edmund looked at the menu as if it sullied his reputation to need its advice. "A chicken wrap, hold the cheese, more bean sprouts." He stared back out the window in the direction of Sandy Shore's "castle."

CHAPTER SIX
This place is my home

The next morning Edmund and Benjamin jumped out of their bedrolls, gobbled down a protein bar each, and jogged with their boards to the beach. The waves were glassy and well-formed, exactly what they had been hoping for.

Edmund liked to watch for a few minutes, to study the beach, and pick his route to the peaks. Benjamin liked to race into the water and begin paddling. He figured he'd get out into the surf and then paddle where he needed to be. And if there were others out, he'd ask where the best spots were, start a conversation, get to know the locals.

Edmund didn't like to talk when he surfed. He liked to sit and think and be independent and competent. Benjamin had already paddled into the lineup when Edmund had his first foot in the water. There were eight other surfers out. The conditions were good, the swell medium to overhead. Edmund got a few superb rides. Benjamin caught everything he could drop into and laughed most of the time.

Paddling by he said, "Best wave ever!"

Edmund smiled. "You always say that."

"Well, every surf session there's always one best, and each day I get better at surfing, so each session there's a best ever. It's a fact." He splashed water squarely in Edmund's face.

After a few hours the brothers paddled to shore and collapsed onto towels. Benjamin said, "I'm exhausted. Let's go get lunch at that diner."

Edmund leaned up on an elbow. "I'll buy you lunch if you'll go to that mountain with me afterwards."

Benjamin squinted his eyes. "Why?"

"Curious."

"Okay, but we come back for a sunset surf. I didn't drive for days and days to surf for three hours and spend the rest of the day at the local trash heap."

"Sunset surf it is."

* * *

After lunch they drove up Main Beach Road toward the mountain. The sun was high; the top of the mountain gleamed and glinted. It looked hot up there, a giant pile of metal and plastic hot. Don't-touch-anything hot. Sizzling hot. Nothing moved anywhere except the cawing swirling cloud of seagulls.

When the road met Coastline Highway near the base of the mountain, Edmund turned north. They passed piles of mattresses, towers of books, a column of plastic containers, and further on, the lids, and stacks and stacks of tires. Everything ordered and situated just so.

At the northern edge of the mountain Coastline Highway turned east and then after a few hundred feet turned north again continuing on to other towns and cities. Edmund didn't want to go north though, he wanted to go east and solve the mystery of this mountain, but the paved road ended at a small fence, a gate, and a hand-painted sign: **Keep Out.**

Edmund idled for a second and took stock. "The fence has no sides, want to go around?"

"I don't know, the sign looks kind of menacing."

"It's hand-painted," said Edmund as he reversed the truck. He drove through the sand around the fence and onto a dusty dirt, gravel road. The truck kicked up a plume of dust announcing their arrival.

This section of the mountain was composed of stacked televisions and radios, all different sizes and shapes, hundreds, antennae poking up like weeds. Balanced on the top edge of the pile was an assortment of satellite dishes interspersed with a few of the sculptural windmills. The sculptures spun and flashed and twinkled in all directions.

"You want to go all the way around?" asked Edmund.

Benjamin said, "Absolutely, this shit is fascinating, have you ever seen so many televisions?"

The dirt road turned south and ended in a parking lot full of trucks, cranes, bulldozers, forklifts and cherry pickers parked in ordered rows. A crane reached out over the parking lot to an area below the upper plateau. At the point where the crane met the hill, a tiny hardhat-wearing figure pushed and pulled at a load on the crane's sling, the only activity anywhere on the entire mountain.

Edmund pulled his truck into a marked space and stepped out and shielded his eyes. The figure was very high up and far away, but Edmund could see that whoever it was had hair that cascaded down under a glinting shiny hardhat. It was either a woman or a very flamboyant male construction worker.

Benjamin said, "It's that girl from last night."

"I'm thinking so too."

The woman yelled something, and another head appeared over the faraway edge and turned away and then reappeared wearing a hardhat coming to help the first woman. It looked like another female, a smaller female, helping heave a ginormous load.

Benjamin and Edmund watched them with interest—the way someone might stop at a construction site and watch the machinery move. Except watching a worksite involved a sense of normal actions and reactions. Most construction made sense, even to novices. The mechanized movements would seem reasonable, the routine, the end result—it would make sense. This scene didn't make any sense. Two women used a crane to load more things on top of an enormous mound of collected things. No matter how long Edmund looked he couldn't make any sense of it.

Spellbound Benjamin asked, "What are they doing?"

Edmund shook his head as the main woman sensed their gaze. She turned with her hands on her hips and looked down at them hundreds of feet below. Then she hollered through her cupped hands, "This is private property! No trespassing!"

Without knowing why, or even realizing he would, Edmund called, "Do you need any help?"

The woman looked over her shoulder at her partner and made what looked like a smart ass remark. She called down, "Does it look like we need help?"

"Yeah, kind of," Edmund yelled back.

"Well, we don't, thank you. Move along."

She plopped the hardhat back on her head and turned back to her task.

Edmund and Benjamin didn't move and continued staring. The women appeared to be moving a box with an appliance of some kind in it. Using straps they lifted it and stepped sideways in unison. Then they shoved, rocked and shifted the box into place, alongside twenty other boxes the same size and shape.

Benjamin asked Edmund, "Should we go?"

"In a minute."

The second smaller woman ducked away from the edge and disappeared inside. The whole mountainside was such a cacophony of sights and shapes and colors that seeing where she went was difficult. There were many ledges and in some places darkened openings, and now and then, partially obscured from the ground level, doors.

The first woman turned and watched Edmund and Benjamin as they stood looking up at her. Even from the great distance she intimidated them with her stare. Topped with the hardhat, her blonde hair waved and poked at angles all around; she resembled the mound she stood upon, a daunting prospect. She stepped into the basket of a condor and activated it with a shudder—the arm stretched, scissored, and turned with mechanical clanks and grinds—and descended about eight floors. She screeched the basket to a stop, dangling above their heads. "I thought you were leaving?"

She looked young, about their age, but imperious as she leaned over the edge of the basket. She wore a dark gray t-shirt and well-used work gloves. The purple hardhat that perched on her pile of blonde hair sparkled like a disco-ball.

Benjamin looked down at his flip-flops and said, "We should go."

Edmund said, "Sure, I'm thinking the same thing." But louder he asked, "My apologies, but what is this place?"

"This place is my home," she said and with a clank and screech the condor basket ascended away. Reaching the upper level, the girl stepped onto the mountain and into a darkened recess and disappeared.

"Okay," said Edmund. He got in the truck, started it, and drove them back to the campground and the promised sunset surf.

* * *

That night while sitting around the fire, Benjamin pulled out his guitar and played.

"That's really great Benny-boy."

"Thank you, and here's one of your old favorites—" Benjamin played a folksy rendition of Green Day's, "American Idiot."

"Goes great with the acoustic guitar." Edmund sang along until he remembered his parents' plan for him to become a rock star. He scowled and tossed a stick into the fire. His eyes were dark and brooding, his mood turned stormy.

Benjamin remained under a cloudless sky. He strummed a quieter song and said, "I noticed Alicia didn't call you tonight."

"She finally got it that I'm gone for good. I kept telling her, but she didn't believe me."

"That's kind of harsh."

"Well, she's the daughter of friends of Mom and Dad. I only dated her because they pressured me. Her parents pressured her too. She'll get over me, probably already. I'm sure that's why she didn't call."

Benjamin sang a chorus of an unfamiliar song.

"That's good, did you write it?"

"A few months ago."

"I like it. See, you have so much talent. Mom was totally wrong that I needed to be the one to start a band."

"Has she even heard you sing?"

"Well, she does like scream metal, she doesn't really know."

Benjamin said, "It's strange that a week ago we slept in our own beds unaware we were about to be kicked out onto the streets, huh?"

Edmund didn't seem to hear him. He asked, "What do you think her deal is?"

"Whose, Mom's, or Alicia?"

"That girl today at the mountain."

"Oh, wow, what a beauty. Did you see how pretty she was? I wonder if she comes to town very often." Benjamin began a folksong about beautiful girls and moonlit rivers.

* * *

The next morning the waves were smaller, the brothers surfed for a short time and then met up on the beach.

"Well, this is going to be a boring day," said Benjamin.

"A swell is arriving tomorrow, but yeah, this is going to be..." Edmund's mind seemed to have drifted. "Do you have any boots with you?"

"Yes, fancy a hike or something?"

"Or something. I thought we could offer to help the girl on the mountain for a few hours."

"I like the way you think."

CHAPTER SEVEN
They're a little attractive

Violet woke up and stretched. She always slept in, but this was very late. She rolled off her bed, taking all her covers along, and then wrapped up and laid on the floor hoping to go back to sleep. The only problem was that for months she had been paying her cousin Lala to wake her up. Lala listened for noises—like Violet rolling off the bed—to signal that it was time to use force, and Lala liked the steady stream of income.

"Violet, time to get up!"

Violet regretted ever making the deal. "I'm coming," she said, more a whimper than a reply.

Lala banged open the door to Violet's room. "Wake up, it's past noon." Violet huffed to standing and shuffled by, depositing a dollar into Lala's upturned palm. Lala said, "Best business relationship I ever had."

Violet stuck out her tongue and headed to the shower.

Violet dressed in her work clothes, and when she arrived in the kitchen, laid her hardhat on the table and asked, "What's on the docket?" just like she did every day, and like everyday Lala handed her a cup of coffee. "And what is this ensemble, expecting a queen? Because if so, I'm not dressed appropriately." Lala wore a frilly full-length apron over her jeans. It was bright yellow and orange tulle, with puffs over the shoulders, and a flouncy tie in the back.

Lala slid a plate of scrambled eggs with a couple of pieces of toast in front of Violet. "I explored on level three last night and found crates and crates of vintage aprons. This is the Good-Morning-Would-You-Like-Scrambled-Eggs apron." Lala was shorter than Violet and built like an athlete. Strong. Boyish. She had brown hair chopped in uneven chunky layers that flipped and rolled in loose waves and if it wasn't for her gray eyes she wouldn't have looked like she was part of long-lean-blonde-Violet's family at all.

"You about put my eye out with your flounce. Is my Dad up yet?"

"Up, but said he would putter around in his rooms for a while. He wanted to know if we could have dinner together tonight. I said, 'sure.'"

"Sure, I suppose, but I still have those appliances from Uncle Todd to get loaded and then—have you got the list?"

"I do." Lala pulled up a chair beside Violet and read from a well-worn and overused notebook that had every page covered in her handwritten scrawl. "There's a truck full of Cousin Thomas' collectibles, you can put them over by the clocks, there's some cover there. His paperwork said they're in plastic boxes, so that's easy enough."

Violet said, "There's still the appliances to load and shuffle and pile and move. Ever since Uncle Todd discovered that he can rent those cheap containers in Southeast Asia, it's been an endless stream. A veritable river of washers, dryers and refrigerators. I figure we have one and a half containers left."

"Oy."

"I know, and then Aunt Miriam sent some boxes of ridiculously expensive cosmetics. They're light, but we have to move them into the fourth quadrant storage, out of the sun and on the very top of the overflow bins. I hate doing that. We really need a pulley system or dumbwaiter. I mean to build one, but who has the time—six boxes of shoes from Aunt Louise. Oh, and get this, a taxidermy collection from Uncle John, he wants 'them' back soon, so we need to store them in the top layer. And he specifically said, 'them.' Are we talking woodland animals? Or jungle beasts? The whole thing gives me the creeps." Violet wrapped her hair, over and around, creating a loose bun with no pins or bands. It stayed up because she wanted it to.

"Ugh," agreed Lala. "Oh, Uncle Jacques was wondering if you can store a couple containers of chocolate?"

"Refrigerated?"

"Yes, but you better charge him for the use of power, the bills are piling up."

Violet laughed, "That's not the only thing piling up around here. Have you heard from your parents lately?"

"They're in Papua New Guinea, they found a mask collection they plan to send next month."

Violet nodded and asked, "How are they doing?"

"I didn't really get to it. They just talked about the mask collection and its antiqueness. They were pretty excited about it." She banged a spoon on the table to a beat that only she heard.

"We best get started."

They departed their dining room and stepped out of Violet's front door onto a large level patio. It had been built with piles and layers of plywood, old pallets and the lids of boxes, and spread from the front door of the family's quarters to the edge of the mountain where it looked out over the parking lot. The condor basket waited there, pressed into use as an up or down elevator—climbing long ago becoming impractical.

Violet took another sip of coffee and blinked at the bright light. "How does the day, the sun, the cloudless sky, arrange itself so effortlessly?" She yelled up at the sun, "You're a big show off!" And then quickly said, "Forgive me, Sun, I know not what I say, I haven't had enough coffee."

Once her eyes adjusted she crossed the expanse of patio to the low wall of boxes and glanced over. The same truck from the day before was parked in her lot about twelve stories below.

Violet said, "It's those boys again, the hotties from yesterday."

"Hotties? You mean *surfer* boys. The same as every other surfer boy around here. Gawking in their flip-flops." Lala peered over the side, untied the apron, pulled it over her head, and tossed it to the side. One of the gawking boys waved. Lala ducked back below the edge.

Violet said, "They were too, totally hot. Hot as a washing machine stacked in the sun, and you should absolutely find out what they're doing here." Far away down below the surfer boys climbed out of the truck.

"For you maybe."

"Not for me, for you dearest Lala. It's high time you met some hotties, fell in and out of love, had your heart broken by a flip-flop wearing man. You're almost eighteen and haven't done any of that yet," said Violet.

"You too."

"Not me too. First of all, I'm nineteen and I'm too busy for distracting hotties and their sandy toes. I have my sculptures and the docket and my Dad and..."

Lala rolled her eyes as they stepped into the condor's basket and closed its door with a clank. "You are a pathetic old lady." Lala looked down at the young men as the basket swayed and screeched and lowered. "They're in boots today. Maybe, just maybe, they're a little attractive."

"You live in a beach town, surrounded by beach bums, and yet you like...?"

"Punk rockers—boots, pasty white skin, black hair."

Violet rolled her eyes in return. "So we're decided, these boys should hit the road."

"Absolutely. We're both not interested."

CHAPTER EIGHT
I'd be happy to

Violet lowered the condor basket past three towering stacks of antique mail-order catalogs, and five big boxes labeled, "Outgrown clothes." The arm of the condor scissored, the basket arced and swung, and Violet dropped their lift into the exact position she wanted—directly in front of the doors of a shipping container. It would have been graceful except for the condor's awful racket. The condor was old, the reaching arm banged and bent and shook and looked well past its prime lifting age. Aware that they were being watched, Violet stifled a laugh and said quietly to Lala, "Remind me please to oil our conveyance."

Lala said, "You say that every single day." Lala ignored the "hotties" and pulled a large ring of keys from her pocket and flipped through them.

Edmund stepped up and cleared his throat. "Excuse me, we're the fellows who happened upon you yesterday?"

Lala didn't turn or look up. She said, "I remember. I also remember Violet asking you "fellows" to leave." Her voice dripped with sarcasm. She fiddled with a lock until it dropped open and the doors swung wide with a clanging metallic screech. Inside about a dozen large appliance boxes stood waiting in the dark.

"My brother, Ben, and I are visiting Sandy Shores. We're staying at the campground and surfing mostly."

Lala continued to ignore him. She climbed into the back of the container and disappeared into the darkness between the big hulking boxes. Benjamin sat to the side and scuffed his boot in the dirt, eyes shielded from the noonday sun, offering his brother no help at all. Violet stood stoic and still in the condor basket. Her expression impenetrable. Her eyes squinted at Edmund's back sizing him up. His shoulders were wide, his hair a cocoa brown with honey tips on the wavy ends. When he leaned, the muscles along his back strained against his cotton t-shirt. Violet averted her eyes to Ben. He was taller, his smile wider, his eyes blue; she decided that he was the better looking one and then decided that she needed to stop being a silly silly girl. She blew air up at her forehead in an attempt to cool off.

Edmund spoke louder so that Lala could hear him. "There aren't any waves today so my brother and I came to offer you some help. We're wearing our work clothes."

Lala came out with an incredulous look, "Do we look like we need rescuing?"

"Not what I'm saying at all, but those are a lot of appliances, and I'm guessing you could use some more back."

Violet chewed her bottom lip mulling it over. She then startled Edmund by speaking; she had been so quiet and still he had forgotten she might. "We can't pay you."

"We don't need pay. We're just bored. There's nothing to do in this town if the waves aren't ridable."

"Okay, we can use the help, but I'm in charge. Don't start bossing me and my cousin around." She narrowed her eyes.

Edmund said, "Yes, definitely, of course," causing Benjamin to give him a look of confusion, having never heard his brother so deferential.

Edmund said under his breath, "Jeez, she's intimidating."

Violet pretended not to have heard and asked, "What are your names?"

"I'm Edmund, and this is Benny-boy, my little brother." Benjamin gave his brother an I-am-going-to-kill-you look.

"Nice to meet you Eddie, Benjamin. I'm Violet, and this is my cousin, Lala. According to our morning docket these excessively large appliance boxes need to be hoisted to that quadrant over there." She pointed where they had been working yesterday—the southeast top section of the hill. "They're full, so not only are they large, but also heavy. It's nothing my cousin and I can't handle ourselves, but if we could have two backs down here and two up there, it might proceed at a faster clip."

Lala said, "I'll stay down here."

Benjamin said, "I'll go up to the top," and clamored into the condor's basket with Violet.

* * *

Edmund and Lala loaded a refrigerator-sized box onto a dolly and rolled it toward the crane's arm. They lashed it in a sling attached to the crane's hook, and then Lala used a remote control to raise it up to Benjamin and Violet.

While Edmund and Lala waited for the crane to return empty they barely spoke. Instead they adjusted and ordered the next boxes. Lala giving the orders, Edmund taking them, which he rarely did, especially from strangers, but this situation was different. Lala was different. She was a cute, perky, cheerleader-girl, the kind that would take your order at a chain restaurant with a chipper smile and a wink, but then again she was tough, she crouched and lifted and lashed with biceps burgeoning. Compact and strong. Edmund guessed she'd be good at surfing, and wanted to ask if she did, but wasn't one to speak up out of the blue.

Lala wiped the short bangs off her wet face, causing them to stick up in the front. "It's hot. I tell her to start in the morning, but she can't get up until noon most days, so we end up working in the noonday sun. Can't wait for winter." She mopped her brow with a pink-swirled silk scarf she kept in her back jeans pocket.

"And what are we doing exactly?"

Lala looked incredulous. "Moving appliances. Man, you're a brainiac, huh? All that saltwater pickled your brain?" Her smile was wide and playful, she had a way of meeting his gaze that was endearing.

Edmund didn't mind a good ribbing. "Well, my brain might be pickled, but I'm not a—how old are you?"

"Almost eighteen."

"—Seventeen-year-old girl whose work is moving appliances to the side of a mountain in the noonday sun."

"Oh that's right, it's my work. You on the other hand *volunteered*," she said as the crane sling lowered for the next refrigerator.

After five loads Lala called up on her walkie-talkie, "We should grab a drink." Squawk.

Violet's voice returned through the walkie-talkie, "I'm sending the condor down to you." Squawk.

The condor basket had flaked paint and rusted corners, and the safety instructions were almost completely scraped off. Edmund considered refusing to climb in, but decided that would be embarrassing, especially with Benjamin already up on the hill. He gripped the railing with white knuckles as it swung like it wanted to leap off the arm.

Lala pulled the basket beside Benjamin with a screeching sound saying, "We made it alive. This time." She smirked at Edmund and he laughed, though his happiness was mostly due to being out of the machine.

They stood on the patio. Its back walls consisted of stacks of boxes and all different shapes and sizes of leaning empty picture frames and thankfully some shade. Violet emerged from a doorway with a cooler full of sodas and plopped it down in the middle of their circle.

Lala said, "Oh wait!" She ducked into another doorway and came out a minute later wearing a half-apron made of sky-blue tulle layered over fabric printed with images of vintage coke bottles. "My soda drinking apron!"

Violet laughed, but quickly quieted again. She flicked her work gloves and arched up to look at the overhead spinning sculptures. Her irises were pale gray, fringed by black lashes and set off by light expression-filled brows, surrounded by pale alabaster skin and paler still hair. Her dark lashes framed her eyes and set them off, sparkling.

Edmund dragged his eyes away and followed her gaze. "What are those?"

She didn't appear to have heard him so Lala said, "Those are whirligigs. Violet builds them."

Benjamin said, "Aren't they amazing Eddie?"

Edmund shot him a look for shortening his name and said, "They are. Amazing and impressive and beautiful. How many are there?

Violet answered, still gazing upward, "Oh, I don't know, twenty or so. I believe I've been building them ever since I can remember. Since I learned to weld, whichever came first. I have plans for many more, but I don't have a lot of time for creation with my workload. Speaking of—" She looked at her left wrist that didn't have a watch on it. "We should get back to it."

"How about you go down with Lala, Benny?" said Edmund with a smirk.

Benjamin and Lala rode the condor down and away. Violet asked, "Can you help me shove these boxes into that area over there? If I can get them centered I'll be able to fit another row, it's all about how we stack."

"Why so many appliances? Do you sell them?"

Violet looked at him with deep disbelief. "No, I wouldn't sell appliances. I'm not a salesperson by nature. I believe salespeople are incapable of empathizing. They must be if they can force their will on people."

"Oh," he said as if that explained it, though he still couldn't imagine why this girl would have so many refrigerators. Trouble was her demeanor, her very core, repelled his questions. She made him feel like asking questions would admit that he didn't have answers, which equalled being dumb, and he totally didn't want to seem dumb in front of this regal creature.

She asked, "So what do you do when you're not paddling after the pent-up energy of ocean waves?"

"I'm a salesman," He said shoving a box into place.

She arched her left brow. "Well, I guess that will teach me to pontificate on my theories in front of strangers."

Edmund chuckled and said, "I'm only kidding. I'm not a salesman."

She laughed. "So you're a smart ass, remains to be seen whether you're a better kind of person though."

"Hey, I volunteered."

"True, raises you in my estimation by degrees." She pushed at another box, then took off her hardhat to wipe her brow with a black bandana. She blew some spiraling strands of hair off her forehead and put the hardhat back on.

While they worked she shoved and pushed and lifted with what could best be described as gracefulness. Almost effortlessness. Edmund on the other hand grunted and groaned under the strain. His incompetence caused him to be even quieter than usual, figuring he should shut up and follow directions. Together they lifted the next appliance box with the straps. Violet coached, "Step to the left, left, left, okay, drop it slowly."

To take a moment to rest Edmund tried another question. "So this is where you live?"

"Yes, well not on this level, up and to the side and down towards the middle." She shoved the box into its planned spot and turned to push with her back while he stood awkwardly wishing he had helped with that last bit.

"I'm sorry," he said, "I thought it was already in place."

"It's okay. I've learned through the years the fit has to be perfect to make more room. It's all about making room."

"I guess you need a lot of room for a big family?" he asked.

"No, its just me and my Dad and my cousin. That's it. We're all that remains."

* * *

By the time shade covered the East side of the mountain they had emptied the rest of the container. The wind picked up, and the temperature cooled. Lala said, by way of walkie-talkie, "Um, Benjamin asked if they could stay for dinner." Squawk.

Edmund chuckled. *Way to go Benny-boy.*

Violet said, "I don't know, we weren't going to do..."

Lala's voice said, "Yes we were, Violet, we were going to have dinner with your Dad, remember, I told you this morning?" Violet turned her back to Edmund. Lala finished, "I think we should invite them to join us." Squawk.

Violet cast a look over her shoulder and realized Edmund could hear everything. "Okay, sounds good." Squawk.

She turned and said, "You're welcome to stay—"

"I'd be happy to," said Edmund.

CHAPTER NINE
I think I'm in love

Lala led the brothers through a doorway, down a tight hallway made of doors, and into a cave-style interior room. Stacks of boxes made up the walls, and the ceiling had timber supports with more boxes stacked on top.

Edmund glanced up and ducked at the same time. "Will these supports hold?"

"Probably," said Lala more vaguely than Edmund appreciated. Their short tour ended in a room containing a long wooden table surrounded by a bunch of mismatched chairs. Breakfast dishes were still all over the table and possibly the dishes from the night before. Lala tied a new apron around her waist—white cotton, long, the front edges embroidered with bouquets of flowers—and cleared dishes.

Violet disappeared down another hallway leaving Edmund and Benjamin to stand in the middle of the odd room wondering what they should do.

A minute later their awkwardness was compounded when, from a door in the back wall, a hulking older man emerged. He had long gray hair, a full gray beard, and a mustache waxed into swirls. He wore a t-shirt that said, "No Peace, No Justice" and a fanciful colored sarong wrapped around his bottom half. "Visitors! Welcome!"

Lala said, "Uncle Bruce, this is Edmund and Benjamin, they helped with the loads today." As she spoke she loaded dishes into a dishwasher that Edmund hadn't noticed because it was surrounded by four others, in a wall full of appliances, some modern, some vintage.

"Good good," Bruce said, as if that explained everything he needed to know about the arrival of these strangers. "Did you get to Todd's boxes?"

"The entire container."

"Well done!" Uncle Bruce stepped back and sized up the brothers. "Don't sit yet, wait just a minute."

He ducked down his hallway and emerged a few minutes later with a tape measure. He dropped to a knee in front of Benjamin and measured him from the hip to the ankle. Then he raised Benjamin's arm and measured from his waist to his shoulder and then from his shoulder to his wrist.

He said loudly, "Violet this one needs the—wait where's Violet? Wasn't she right here?" He dropped to a knee and measured Edmund's inseam and then his elbow to fingertips and said, "Wasn't she standing right here a second ago? Violet!"

Lala didn't answer and after a minute Violet emerged. "Dad, I was cleaning up for dinner." Edmund looked her up and down. She was exactly the same, except her eyes were reddened like she had been crying and her face shined as if she had splashed water to cover the fact. Edmund wanted to ask if she was okay, but didn't believe he knew her well enough.

"You look lovely daughter. Ravishing. These boys need chairs." Edmund and Benjamin looked around. There were no less than seven chairs, pushed under the table and scattered all through the room.

"Sure Dad, what do they need?"

Benjamin said, "Oh no sir, we'll be fine. We can sit anywhere—"

"Nonsense, I'm the Chair King, famous in these parts for finding the perfect chair for every person and every situation. I used to run commercials on every channel." He twirled the end of his mustache. "Recognize me?"

"No," said Benjamin, "but we aren't from around here."

"Where are you from exactly?"

"We're from the Southeast. Near Kingsbridge."

"Oh. I didn't run commercials there. I've found that Easterners don't respect a chair the way they ought. Do you boys respect a chair?"

Edmund and Benjamin looked at each other. "I suppose we do," said Benjamin.

Bruce laughed, "Look at them, I scared them. Of course you respect a chair." He tapped the side of his head. "That's why you're in the West because you're smart."

He pointed at Edmund. "This one wants a deep chair for brooding. I can see it in his eyes. He wants an arm that stretches so he can gaze at his fingertips as he considers his lot. Retrieve the Armed Nelson for him, Violet. It's in the gallery on the fourth level. It's forest green velvet and will match his eyes."

He thumbed toward Benjamin. "This one needs the Queen Anne. He will perch and talk and lean in incessantly. It will be satin, of a light stripe, to match his wit and charm. He likes to move and flirt. It's on the top-level atrium. With a cloth over it."

Violet said, "Of course, Dad," and ducked out of the room as Edmund called to her departing back, "Do you need any help?"

"She doesn't need help," assured her father. "She loves to move things around from place to place, doesn't she Magdala?"

Lala said, "Yes, Uncle Bruce," though Edmund could see that she wasn't really listening.

Edmund and Benjamin stacked a few of the dining chairs into a corner to make room for the chairs that the Chair King had chosen and Violet carried without complaint. Then they sat while Lala cooked.

"So you boys come from Kingsbridge?" asked Bruce, settling onto a rough-carved low stool. "Seems like a big journey."

Benjamin said, "We're seeking our fortune."

"Ah, a noble quest! Like knights!"

Violet asked, "Are you just passing through then? Surely your fortune isn't on our lowly shore of sand?"

Edmund said, "We don't really know."

Bruce said, "Well, what kind of quest is it then? But I must add that's the perfect answer from a young man with his rear in a brooding chair."

Edmund replied, "What I'm brooding over, sir, is how come I'm in a comfortable chair, and you've chosen to sit cross-legged on top of a stool?"

Bruce looked below him as if just noticing and boomed a big laugh. "Too much comfort ruins a spine. Everyone knows that."

Lala delivered big porcelain bowls full of what appeared to be steaming ramen noodle soup with sliced chicken floating in it with a few peas swimming around. Then she tossed down a bag of white bread, a stick of butter still in its wrapper, and piled in the middle of the table a fistful of silver knives, forks and spoons.

Violet asked, "Why are we using Aunt Edna's china? We should be using Mom's."

Lala tied a brown apron sporting an appliqué of a roasted turkey around her waist. She sat down and pointed with a butter knife at the boys, "Company."

"Mom's is prettier. It's good for company."

"I don't want to break any of it. Aunt Edna has three different patterns in settings of twelve. She won't miss it if one goes chipped."

Everyone tucked into their dinner. Edmund told Lala it was delicious, to which she replied, "I just open the packages. I might do all the cooking, but that doesn't make me a good cook." She grinned widely and then reeled back to the other subject, "They're going on a quest Violet, do you hear this?"

"I do, it sounds like a fine adventure." Violet dipped white bread in her soup.

"We should go on a quest too. We could go to the city and I could sing on a stage and we could have adventures and seek our fortune. It would be grand!"

"It certainly would, but seriously Lala, you forget, I've been telling you to go to the city for months now. You're the age to explore, you should go on a grand trip."

"I can't go without you."

Violet shook her head.

Lala said, "You would have to come too, you know that."

"I can't leave, Lala, my work and—everything."

Lala looked petulant. "Oh, pooh."

Benjamin said, "We wouldn't have left unless we had been forced to. What my brother is too polite to mention is that our parents told us to take a hike and so we have. We're headed to the city, to become rock stars or some such, by way of the beach. We're in Sandy Shores to surf."

Lala said, "Rock stars! Are you musicians?"

Edmund said, "I'm not, my parents are heavily delusional in regard to my charms. Benjamin though is an excellent songwriter and guitarist."

Lala clapped her hands excitedly.

Violet laughed and said, "My cousin has the voice of an angel and sings all the time. She should really go out and sing for other people."

Lala said, "My cousin won't attend me out into the world. She is an immovable force."

"Absolutely, yet my forceful immobility is not blocking your way, dear cousin Lala. I would miss you, but—oh, what time is it? I have to go." Violet shoved her chair away from the table causing Edmund and Benjamin to jump from their seats.

Edmund said, "Can we help—" as she disappeared through a door.

"It's sunset," said Bruce as if that explained it all.

Benjamin said, "We have to be going. Can we help you clean up?" He carried a stack of plates to the dishwasher wall.

"Sure, pile everything here, then I'll load the dishwashers." Lala dropped her brown apron inside a cardboard box that had the words 'Marjorie's vintage aprons' hand-scrawled on the side, and then pawed through it looking for another apron to wear. She pulled out a plain one that read, "Dishes, like revenge, are best served cold."

She grinned and said, "The perfect dishwashing apron! Looks like we'll have three going tonight. That will be a racket, huh, Uncle Bruce?"

He didn't appear to hear her instead humming to himself and staring up at the rafters.

"Uncle Bruce?"

"Yes, dear Lala? My thoughts were on a poem I read tonight, 'The sun glows on the hillside... '"

"We may come back and help tomorrow," said Benjamin. "Do you think Violet will mind?"

"She may mind," Lala said, "but you should come anyway, she really needs the help. Just don't tell her I said so." She added plates to the dishwasher without rinsing. "Do you know how to work the condor to get down to the ground?

Edmund said, "We can figure it out."

"Good. It was super fun. I'm really glad to have met you."

When the boys walked across the patio to the condor basket the sun had settled down. The east side of the mountain was dark and cold. In the minutes it took their conveyance to screech, scissor, sway and shudder lower, they huddled because the air was cool and they were still damp and sweaty from the day.

Edmund asked, "What do you make of all this?"

"I think I'm in love," said Benjamin, "Wow, she's cool."

"Love huh? Well, Lala is—"

"Not Lala, Violet, isn't she amazing?"

Edmund squinted his eyes. "Seriously Benny? She's a total and complete nutter, and we helped all day and I still have no idea what any of this is about."

"Me neither, but does it matter?" They got in the truck and backed out of their space, the lights of the truck splaying across the base of the mountainous pile of stuff.

"It matters, and look at the size of it, matter everywhere. It matters a lot."

Edmund drove slowly on the dirt road, bumping and bouncing and kicking up dust and then continued around the west side of the mountain and turned onto Main Beach Road. Then he pulled the truck over and stepped out to stare back at teeny tiny Violet, who stood at the very tiptop of the pile. She welded with a sparking flame at the base of a whirligig. Stars shone behind her, and spinning, reflective, shiny, metallic, whirling assemblages danced all around, as she concentrated on building her mysterious creations. Edmund seemed incapable of looking away, but finally Benjamin said, "We should get back to the tents, I'm wiped from all that heavy lifting."

· · ·

The next morning Edmund and Benjamin went surfing again. The waves were even better, nearing the size that gave this spot its reputation. Benjamin asked everyone he met about the mountain and Violet, trying to get a handle on her peculiar personality. He learned that Violet was well-liked, but no one seemed to know her presently because she had become so reclusive. The locals wondered what she was doing up there mostly alone. He also learned that Violet had lived in Sandy Shores, or rather the outskirts, her whole life, and the mountain had been made by her family, her very large extended family. Now she and her cousin were the only ones left still working on it.

As Benjamin and Edmund walked back to the campground with boards under their arms, Benjamin said, "Guy named Ted called her a hoarder, but I don't think that quite fits, do you? I mean, that is a big, big hoard, but it's not really hers, right?"

"Best I can tell she's the family dock worker. Or better description, the storage unit supervisor."

"I mean she didn't seem like the little old ladies with the cats all over their apartments crawling in their tuna salad, or the crazy old guys with the stacks of newspapers lining their rooms."

"Oh, she's much more sensible with twenty refrigerators that she doesn't even plan to unbox. But, speaking of the sensible one, what did you think of Lala?"

"Lala? She seems cool, but she's not really my type. Are we going to go help today?"

"Let's have lunch first and then check in with the dock supervisor."

CHAPTER TEN
She created that

Violet woke up at eleven and wondered why she was awake so early. She pulled the covers over her head for a few minutes. "I need to get up, I ought to get up. I really should." But then she rolled over onto the floor anyway with a thump that roused Lala down the hall.

"Violet, time to get up!"

Violet wrapped her comforter even tighter and yelled, "I need sleep!"

The door to her bedroom opened and Lala's palm appeared. "Yes, you need sleep. It's also time to get up. I suspect the boys are coming back today."

Violet threw off her covers. "Why on earth? What? Don't they know they're not wanted?" She jumped to her feet, and when she passed Lala deposited two dollars into her palm instead of the usual one. Lala noticed that Violet had more energy than usual. Violet noticed that Lala had on what appeared to be a Viking helmet.

"You found Cousin Rick's gear?"

"So much cool stuff! This is my hardhat for the day."

"Not sure it's up to code, but then again, what is around here?"

When the girls emerged after their breakfast of hardboiled eggs and toast with jam, the boys stood in the parking lot, waiting.

"Hello!" called Benjamin with an energetic wave. Edmund raised his hand in greeting.

Lala called down, "The condor basket is down there, can you bring it up to get us? I have coffee!"

Benjamin called up "No thank you, we've been up for six hours already!" As they ascended in the condor basket the arm scissored out and arced them away from the mountain, so Benjamin overcompensated by swooping it down to the left, and then Edmund took over the controls, twisted the arm around and almost rammed it into the middle of the pile.

Violet called down, "Up, up! No, not out, up!" After a few terrifying minutes they arrived with a shudder, a jolt, and a deafening screech.

Lala giggled and said, "That was so graceful!"

Violet arched her left eyebrow and said, "Hello Ed, Benjamin. I didn't expect you today?"

Benjamin said, "We came to help again. At your service." He bowed slightly, then asked, "It appears the Vikings invaded while we were away?"

Lala giggled some more.

Violet said, "We read over the docket this morning. I'm not really sure there's enough to do to warrant—"

Lala interrupted, "There's plenty to be done." She held the notebook to her chest wrapped in her arms. "We have the half container of appliances to unload, then the toy collection needs to be cataloged."

"Yes, but we're capable of emptying a container, we've never needed help before."

Edmund looked at Benjamin with his eyes wide.

"You've wanted to move around the third level—Cousin Isabelle's boots for months. If we got through the appliances you might be able to get those other things accomplished."

"Okay, okay. I get your point. Who wants to accompany Lala to the container?"

Benjamin said, "Edmund will," grinning cheekily at his big brother.

The arrangement was fine with Edmund. He had a million questions, and Violet had proven herself incapable of replying with a straight answer. It seemed like Lala was more likely to explain what was happening on the insane mountain.

First chance, Edmund asked, "So these appliances all belong to one of your uncles?"

"Uncle Todd. He thinks if he buys in bulk then later he can resell with a profit. Trouble is he never resells." She hefted up the side of a box with a grunt while Edmund passed a strap around it.

"And so all of this stuff belongs to your family?"

"Well, of course, or else why would it be here?"

They shifted the base of the box onto a dolly and pulled it to the waiting crane while Edmund considered, *why indeed?*

They rode up in the condor's basket after about seven appliances had been loaded and the entire container emptied. Two empty containers, Edmund was pretty happy about that. They met Benjamin and Violet on an upper level and Edmund said, "Well, that's done. Your Uncle can rest assured, it's all stored."

Violet laughed, "Rest? He doesn't rest. The Winslow family never rests, on principle. He needs the empty container shipped back so he can fill it again."

Lala asked, "What this time?"

"Bamboo furniture. He's in Asia. He says the future will be big, giant bamboo furniture. Our trick will be unloading it without letting Dad see the chairs. He'll be furious if they're not ergonomic. Which I doubt."

"I guess we'll store it on level A near the mattresses then?" asked Lala.

"That would be good. We'll distract Dad by uncovering a box of books that he's forgotten about, something with poetry, and we can give him a dictionary to look up the enigmatic lines. He'll be busy for hours."

Edmund and Benjamin still had so many questions as they listened to Violet and Lala chat about their family and their work. What was happening on this mountain?

Edmund asked, "So everyone in your family stores their things here?"

Violet arched a brow. "They're family, I have room. It's simple."

Edmund looked at the stacked art, the door-lined hallways, the shelves and shelves jam-packed with knickknacks, the wooden ceiling supports holding precarious piles of boxes directly over their heads. Did she have room? He supposed so, but not in the normal sense of the word.

They took a ten minute break that lasted longer because they were enjoying the laughs and camaraderie of people who have sweated and built things together. Finally, Violet said, "The day is zooming by, if we're to catalog the boots we ought to begin."

As they all climbed into the condor basket, Edmund wondered about its weight-carrying capacity. He was calculating everyone's general weight, when Benjamin asked, "So, this is okay, right? It can carry us all?"

Violet said, "As long as no one ate a big meal last night." A smile tugged at the corner of her mouth as she swept the basket in a noisy arc to the south end of the mountain and performed a smooth landing in front of a deck about three stories off the ground.

Benjamin said, "Phew."

Lala said, "Don't be worried about the condor, you should see how much we load onto it sometimes."

Violet led them to a grouping of doors at the back of the deck. For a few minutes she couldn't seem to remember which closet she needed and opened and closed a few of the doors before finding the boots.

Benjamin appraised the shelves inside one of the closets, "Who built all of this?"

"My uncles and cousins, the whole family, young and old. For a few years everyone worked together, like a barn-raising, but just like that they all had to leave, places to go. I think it might be genetic, the desire to wander."

Lala said, "Like my parents, they're in Papua New Guinea right now, luckies." She grasped the edge of a box and forced it out, dropping the box above it with a loud crash. Edmund ducked in case the ceiling fell.

Violet instructed Benjamin how to count the boots, fill out a packing list, and tape it on the box, but was interrupted when a bright purple lizard dropped to the ground between them and scurried through their feet into the space behind the shelves.

Benjamin said, "What the hell was that?"

"Some kind of lizard," said Lala. "Violet loves them, but don't believe her, they're totally freaky. Though I guess they're useful—they eat cockroaches. Roaches freak me out even more." She opened a box marked, "Crayons," and peered inside. "Violet painted her hardhat the color of them."

Benjamin said, "I thought your hardhat was purple because of your name."

Violet smiled and slowly shook her head. "Oh, Benjamin, purple and violet are two totally different colors. Have you had any art training at all? Violet appears in the rainbow and has the highest vibration in the visible spectrum. Purple is simply a mix of red and blue." She pointed at the hardhat. "This, my friend, is purple, lizard purple."

Benjamin banged the heel of his hand on his forehead. "I totally should have taken art classes so I could impress the girls with my knowledge of rainbows." Everyone laughed.

Violet began to direct the work again. "If we carry these boxes to that area, we'll make more room here—because more shoes are coming. My Dad's sister-in-law doesn't have enough closet space and is putting her shoe collection in crates according to season. She wants us to ship them back to her every few months, so we'll want to have them in front."

Lala carried a box past Edmund and said, "These shoes have been here for years." She blew dust off the top, coughed, and then skipped-sashayed as another lizard ran between her feet.

After Edmund and Lala had moved all the boxes, they stood together to catch their breath. He asked, "So why don't you go?"

"Where?" she asked.

"To Papua New Guinea, or New York, or Los Angeles, or any place you want—why don't you?"

"Because who would take care of Violet? Violet and Uncle Bruce might have been my legal guardians, sure, legally, but if I don't feed her she doesn't eat, she forgets. She gets too busy, too arty. She ceases to function. I can't leave unless she comes with me."

"Will she?"

"Never. She won't ever leave."

Benjamin and Violet returned and Violet asked, "What are you talking about?"

"Nothing," said Lala, "or rather, the merits of collecting boots—I thought we could invite Benjamin and Edmund to dinner again."

Violet smiled and blew a strand of hair out of her face. "I suppose we ought."

Benjamin said, "Since we've been slogging your things for hours, I figure dinner is the least you can do."

Violet teased, "Benjamin, dear, they aren't my things."

Edmund felt a little stab of jealousy, not because he liked Violet or anything, but because Benjamin always made friends. It was effortless for him. He was sociable. He laughed and joked in the midst of the pile, while Edmund walked around fretting and asking, *Why?*

* * *

As the group ascended in the screeching and whining basket to the top-level living quarters, Benjamin asked, "Do you have a master-list of everything that's here?"

Violet slowed the basket to look at a box marked "Christmas decorations" and four green-camouflaged bins marked "survival prep" and didn't seem to hear his question.

* * *

Violet's father joined them again for dinner, wearing a too-small t-shirt—tie-dyed yellow about fifty years prior—above a pair of gray sweatpants. His beard had been freshly dyed a rainbow of colors. Violet ignored his vibrant facial hair and asked, "Dad, what did you do today?"

"I read a bit more about the original founders of the Aztec empire, *fascinating*. Then, becoming bored, perused the dictionary for a bit. I reminded myself the proper meaning of obstreperous. I had been using it without it's 'B', funny what age does to the mind, my dear. I have also heard on the news about a new app called Where Are Things? It helps one to map and catalog everything you own. I thought you might be able to design something like that."

Violet had been smiling endearingly at her father until the last bit, and then she narrowed her eyes. "Like what exactly?"

"Like that app, there's really good money in apps these days. It seemed like just the thing for you."

Violet rolled her eyes.

Lala said, "Uncle Bruce, Violet doesn't even own a computer!"

"Well, I know Violet, and if she sets her mind to something she can accomplish it. I'm just telling her to look into it."

Edmund said, "Your sculptures are definitely beautiful."

"Thank you," she said simply.

Uncle Bruce continued, "You boys should come down to my library after dinner and see the place."

"Dad, your library isn't really ready for company. Have you straightened a walkway like we talked about?"

"Who needs walkways when you have chairs, my dear, and a good book. But your point is made. I'll invite them another day, after I organize better, soon."

Lala placed china plates in front of Edmund and Benjamin topped with formerly boxed macaroni and cheese and tuna plopped on the side. The tuna held its can shape. She sat down and laid the Viking helmet beside her plate. "Man, this is some seriously ancient helmet head!" She looked around, "Get it?"

Violet said, "I get it, I just can't believe it."

Bruce asked "How did we get so lucky, Lala, that my daughter Violet is sitting down to two meals in a row with us?"

"It's kind of a miracle," Lala said, taking a big scoop-bite of mac and cheese. Chewing, she added, "She laughed a lot today too."

"Her laugh is a wondrous thing we don't get to hear enough of."

Violet blushed. "I'm sitting right here. And you shouldn't tattle on me, Lala."

"Telling Uncle Bruce that you laughed today is not tattling. Okay maybe it is, but not in the way you mean."

Violet huffed at Lala and said, "Having Eddie and Benjamin here has really helped me conquer some of my pressing demands. And to change the subject," she jokingly turned her back on her family and addressed Edmund and Benjamin with a smile, "Ignore them, please. I suppose you're leaving soon to begin your adventure?"

Benjamin said, "No I think we'll stay for a bit longer, right Edmund?"

"Sure," he picked through the noodles on his plate. "Are these your mother's plates, Violet?"

She nodded, and he watched as she ran her finger along the raised pattern on the edge.

Benjamin asked, "So how big a family do you have?"

Violet said, "Dad has six siblings. On my mother's side of the family there are twelve children. All of them married at least once, with at least one child, sometimes more. Then there's the cousins, spanning generations, and yes, it's a big big family. I haven't counted in a while—do you know Dad?"

"Know what? I was thinking about my latest poem. Do you know a rhyme for spectacular that's not perpendicular? I already used that."

Violet sighed and asked, "Is it shape related, Dad? Because rectangular or triangular could work."

"It's a bit more metaphorical."

"Lavender."

"Thank you, that might do very well. You have a way with words, my dear, I've always believed you would become a writer."

"I do write poems, in steel and flame. I inscribe them across the sky."

Her father said, "Precisely."

Violet smiled at Edmund and shrugged her shoulders.

Edmund asked, "How many of your family members store things here?"

"Pretty much everybody, right Lala?"

Lala nodded.

The eldest member of the party entered into the conversation again. "Except my Sister-in-law Eustacia, she keeps to herself and doesn't own anything much. She's an odd bird, that one. You know she came once and asked for a recliner? She's rail thin, wiry, and wanted to recline! I told her she needed to wind up in a deep club chair, it would be easier on her hips, but did she listen? She did not." He added, "Pthbthhhhbt."

Benjamin asked, "What's the weirdest thing your relatives collect?" He had forgotten in the comfortable conversation that Violet addressed most questions with non-answers and misdirects. And he hadn't clued in to the minefield of questions that Violet had to traverse.

"Weird? I don't think collections are weird. Belongings define us, make us who we are. Like my grandmother collecting a china pattern that has green edges and gold filigrees—my mother collected china with matte-black rims and silver accents. What we choose to buy, what we believe is important to hold onto, says as much about us as what we say and do. Possibly more because ultimately it's what we leave behind. Don't you think?"

Benjamin nodded though he looked like he would agree to anything Violet said.

She continued, "That being said, I think shoe collections are weird as hell. I wear one pair of boots. Why on earth would you need any more?" Violet smiled around at them all.

"Hear, hear!" said Lala putting the Viking helmet on her head and crossing her eyes.

Benjamin asked, "But can you be defined by other people's collections?"

Violet squinted her eyes and opened her mouth about to say something, but slid her chair away from the table instead.

Benjamin said, "I mean, I'm just wondering."

Violet said, "I didn't realize it was so late, I need to get going."

She disappeared down the hallway as Benjamin banged his fist on his head. "Stupid, stupid, me."

Lala cleared dirty dishes into the only empty dishwasher. She asked, "Will we see you tomorrow?"

Edmund said, "The swell is rising, the waves are going to be good, really good." He stared at the hallway where Violet had recently walked through and away.

Benjamin said, "Yes, definitely, tomorrow, same time."

* * *

The sun was setting as the brothers drove away. Edmund turned onto the Main Beach Road and drove past where he usually stopped to look. Benjamin asked, "Aren't we going to stop?"

"Why? We've seen her," said Edmund sullenly.

"Oh, okay, yeah, you're right," said Benjamin, arm hanging out the window, wind blowing through his hair, smile on his face.

Then, with a groan, Edmund lost his struggle. He pulled to the side of the road and stepped out to look back. The mountain glowed red like the first night. The whirligigs shimmered and spun and twisted and spiraled around, and the dancing lights of the sunset ricocheted off the edges and shapes. The magical mountain had a giant disco-ball exuberance, random and wild in its movements, and Violet stood at the top accentuated with glowing shades of pink against a blackening blue night sky. She was tiny from the distance, but monumental in her stillness and power.

Edmund said, "She created that. All of that."

Benjamin grinned and said, "Man, she's pretty." He yelled to the hill, "Tomorrow, we'll see you tomorrow!"

She couldn't see or hear them—the wind whipped their words around in every direction and away. The brothers stood in the deep shadows of the base around the mountain, hundreds and hundreds of feet away, grounded, whereas she stood aloft.

CHAPTER ELEVEN
No worries

Edmund had predicted correctly: the following morning the waves were really good, the best all week and crowded. There were more surfers in the water than they had seen since they arrived. Edmund had to compete for every wave, had to paddle far and wide, and then the waves kept getting bigger and bigger, so every half hour he said, *one more wave.*

He finally paddled ashore where Benjamin waited with a towel wrapped around his shoulders, wind whipping his sandy hair. "That was epic, huh, big brother? What waves. Should we go help the girls on the mountain?"

Edmund stood, dripping, holding his board, unable to take his eyes off the ocean. "Maybe—it looks like it's going to be really good this evening."

"Aw, come on, let's go up. Let's carry heavy boxes around and be manly-men with burgeoning muscles."

"You really like her, huh?"

"What's not to like? She's a princess in a tower, and I'm her knight in shiny armor.

"Sand possibly. And sea snot. Let's grab lunch first."

* * *

At lunch Edmund's phone rang. "It's Alicia."

"Probably-already-forgotten-about-you Alicia? Uh oh."

"I better take it. Here's money for the bill. I'll meet you back at the campsite."

Edmund stalked back an hour and a half later and collapsed into a folding camp chair across from Benjamin facing a nonexistent fire. "First Alicia called. She wanted to see how I was faring and had collected a list of reasons why I should come home and be her boyfriend again." He rubbed his hands down his face. "None of the reasons were particularly romantic. She thinks I'm the best match for her life path. And she thinks I should just agree.

"I listened to her reason her way through it, and all I could think was, 'Really? The best argument is that I'm the best of available options?'"

"What did you tell her?"

"That I'm not available. That I wasn't coming back."

"I'm really sorry."

"Yeah, and then, get this, Mom called."

"What did she say?"

"She asked how we were and how we were enjoying the city. I told her it was great. She said the Bed and Breakfast would open soon, the decorator is still ordering pillows, but then she said she needed me to come home at the end of the month because she and Dad want to go on vacation and they need me to run the place."

"Don't they have people to do that?"

"That's what I asked. I also said it would be hard to seek my fortune if she made me leave before I found it. She suggested that I go faster." Edmund leaned his head back and said, "My head aches."

"I guess it's late for going up the hill."

"I think a surf would be better. Do you mind if we take the day? I'll go with you tomorrow. Promise."

"No worries."

They went for a long afternoon surf. The waves were well-formed but smaller. The brothers floated and relaxed on their boards in between their rides, lying on their backs watching white cloud puffs meander through their field of vision. They started another round of "This is a fabulous idea to..." adding, "Break up with your impossibly perfect girlfriend by phone, so she can't punch you for it," and, "Ride in a condor basket with questionable safety without telling our next of kin where we really are."

At one point Edmund sat up and faced shore, looking past the sand dunes and over the rooftops of the small collection of main street shops, to Violet's mountain hulking in the background. It was grayed and flat, a backdrop, and except for the spinning cloud of seagulls, motionless. He asked, "What do you really think about that mountain?"

Benjamin remained looking up at the sky and lazily said, "The mountain? I don't think anything. It just is."

"You make it sound benign."

"Because it is. What are you saying, that it's not?"

Edmund watched the seagulls swoop down to the left and then rise back and around. They were so far away they were glittery pieces, not birds, only birds because Edmund knew they were birds. Birds following the gusts of wind created by the artificial mountain.

"It mars the landscape, that's all."

"You are such a hippie." Benjamin splashed water at his brother. "Just because it was built by man, doesn't make it wrong."

"I know that." Edmund dropped to his stomach and began paddling. "Ready for dinner? Last one to the beach has to buy dinner at The Crabby Shore."

* * *

Edmund and Benjamin dressed to go to the restaurant and were gathering their jackets as a bulldozer pulled, rumbling and roaring, onto the campsite's small road.

Violet drove. Lala rode in the passenger seat waving enthusiastically. "Hi guys!"

Benjamin rushed over as they pulled into a space behind Edmund's truck. "I didn't think you left the mountain?"

Violet said, "I don't on principle, but Lala worried about you and needed to see if you were okay. I offered to drive because she's not good at it at all."

"That's because we never leave the mountain, where do I practice? Sheesh."

Violet asked, "So how are you today? We half-expected you to come and help again."

Benjamin said, "We meant to, but Edmund had business calls, and by the time he was done, the day was almost gone. So we went surfing."

All this time Edmund stood searching through his jacket's pockets as if they were incredibly interesting.

Violet said to Lala, "So they're fine, we can return home reassured."

Benjamin said, "Or you could come to dinner with us. Edmund and I will treat."

Lala clasped her hands. "Yes, Violet, *please,* we'll go back just after."

"We might enjoy some time around the fire pit, too," said Benjamin. "We make world class banana boats."

Violet said, "I can stay for dinner."

Lala jumped out of her seat and danced around. "Goodie, goodie, goodie!"

Violet said, "They'll believe you never get to go out to dinner if you keep acting this excited."

"And Lala," asked Benjamin, "what are you wearing?"

"Oh this? I found all these old baby blankets last night, and I've been wearing them like superhero capes all day." She added petulantly, "Which you would know if you had come to help. This is the Go-Check-On-The-Boys cape, in case you were in need of superhero assistance."

Benjamin said, "Well, we aren't, but a cape like that go perfectly with banana boats later."

The Crabby Shore was a pub, not in the big city ironically-hip way, but in the small beach town way—smelled of smoke, lax housekeeping, and decades of fish, breaded and fried. Violet slid into a booth and Benjamin sat beside, Edmund across. He had a view of Violet's eyes, her rhythm.

Lala giggled and talked the whole time. Lala was on. Violet was up and down and in and around, a pendulum that Edmund watched for the meditative effect. He cycled between entranced and reluctantly pulling away, but unable to leave her face for long, so that when the menus were delivered he forgot to open his because he found himself trapped in the corner of her smile. He shook his head and tried to focus on the menu, but she pulled him back by speaking. "Lala will you be getting the chowder?"

"Of course, my favorite."

"Will you have them bring you bread, too? I love their bread. What about you Benjamin, what are you having?"

"I think the steak and potatoes."

"Ask her for an extra helping of gravy, I want bites." She read her menu again. Then with the low-hanging light caught on her eyelashes causing them to glitter at the edges, she asked, "Eddie, what are you having?"

"I think the fish."

She watched him for a second and then asked, "Grilled?"

"Sure."

"Sounds good to me." She closed her menu.

Lala laughed, "What are you having?"

"I don't know. I'll decide when she takes my order."

The waitress arrived, and they all ordered as instructed, and then Violet said, "I'll have a small salad." She looked around the group, "What? I'm not very hungry." She looked back at the waitress, "And your chocolate cake sounds delicious. I'll have a slice. Thank you."

The food came and Violet ate from everyone's plates, reaching and grabbing and laughing while she tasted the delicacies she made them order. Benjamin slid his plate closer to her, offering to share, but she said, "I only want taste-bites." Then she finished the last of his potatoes.

To get to Edmund's plate she locked eyes first, then reached. He pulled his plate in, making her lean farther, and farther. Then, jokingly he wrapped an arm around the front attempting to block her fork, but she managed to get the best bite of fish anyway. Edmund laughed and started a fork duel. She was good, and the glint in her eye distracted him enough that she grabbed another bite. He asked, "Do you always battle over dinner?"

"Do you always refuse to share with your friends?"

Suddenly she noticed the lateness of the day. "Oh! Oh no! I won't make it to the mountain. You promised," she said to Lala. "You *promised* I would make it back."

"I'm sorry Violet, I didn't realize, and then dinner was so good."

Violet put her napkin on the table. Benjamin jumped from his seat as she pushed her way out of the booth. "I'll go to the beach. I can get there in time. I'm so sorry to leave during dinner, Eddie, Benjamin, you can have some of my cake. Do you need money for the bill?"

Edmund said, "No definitely not, my pleasure," but she was already running out the door and down the sidewalk in the direction of the beach.

"Oh, I feel so bad," said Lala dropping her head into her hands.

"What is it?"

"She watches the sunset from the mountain every night. Has never missed it since, since—her mother died. I don't know if she can ever forgive me."

Edmund tossed his napkin on the table and said, "Come back to the campsite. You can wait for her there and drive her home after."

"Sure," Lala said despondently.

"It will be fine, no worries," said Benjamin wrapping his arm around her shoulder. "I'll make you a banana boat. When Violet gets done she can have one too, and we'll tell her not to be mad. No one can stay angry when they're digesting marshmallows."

Edmund and Benjamin led her down the small main street of shops to their campsite. Once there Edmund busily built the campfire. He waited until Benjamin was distracted, showing Lala where the chocolate and bananas and marshmallows were and how to wrap them in foil for maximum melt, then excused himself saying, "I have to go to the bathroom. I'll be back."

And he walked out to the beach.

CHAPTER TWELVE
You must have been young

The pink had disappeared from the sky leaving behind a deep dark night. It took a minute for Edmund to notice Violet silhouetted against the darkened sea. She stood still and silent, though her whipping hair mimicked the splashing, crashing waves. The sounds and the sea spray caused her to seem even more solitary. So alone. Edmund worried he might be intruding and that he might startle her with his approach, but as he drew closer he realized she stood with her back to the sea.

He glanced over his shoulder in the direction of her gaze. She was gazing over the dunes, past the town of Sandy Shores, to her mountain. Because of its height, the top still reflected hot sunset pink. The whirligigs flashed and sparkled, though from this distance you couldn't see what they were exactly. Merry lights dancing on the top of a darkened mountain.

Edmund walked backwards as he approached her side, unable to look away, as slowly-slower-slow, the last light moved past the final tiptop of the tallest whirligig and disappeared completely. All that remained was the black night sky. The stars.

"You created magic," said Edmund.

"I'm actually glad I came out here tonight, I never saw the sunset reflected on it before. I suspected, but seeing it is something else entirely."

"A new perspective, huh?"

She looked at him surprised. "Yes, I suppose it is."

They watched for a few minutes more, before Edmund turned back to the sea and watched the waves break—noting the size, the pattern, the wind.

"So the sunset was important to your mother?" Edmund risked a lot by asking: it might upset her, she might flounce away angrily, and he wanted to understand. He wanted to know everything about her, what thoughts were happening down deep, but he didn't have the skills to start big conversations. He couldn't ask like a normal person, in delicate ways, so he tried Benjamin's method—jumping in first try without really considering if it would be okay or not.

Violet made it okay by answering with only a brief hesitation, "It was important to my grandmother. She built this house and wanted it to have a view of the ocean. She said that you have to say good night to the sun every night as it tucks itself in the sea or the whole world won't get up happily in the morning. She died when my mother was young, and mom carried on the tradition, and now me.

Edmund's hands were stuffed in his pockets, body clenched against the cool breeze coming off the water. "It's a good tradition," he said. "I should thank you for all the awesome waves."

Violet laughed and wiggled her toes in the sand. "You're welcome. It's my duty, to make sure it's all okay."

Edmund watched the side of her face as she looked out over the ocean. She had the profile of a statue he had seen at an art museum in Kingsbridge. He remembered the face because his tour guide had focused on it, telling a room full of twelve-year-old boys that it was idealized perfection, fictional, unnatural. Yet, here it stood, that face, not stone but living breathing within Edmund's reach.

"You must have been young when your mother died."

"I was twelve. I had a good dozen years with her." Her voice caught in her throat. Edmund nodded and went back to watching the ocean.

"I build the sculptures for her. She made me pinwheels of reflective paper and we put them in the garden all around the house. The day she died, after she had gone, I watched the sunset and those pinwheels reflecting the light. I thought I heard her laugh; she sparkled when she laughed. So I suppose I build them to keep her laugh here."

Edmund said, "I think you've captured it."

She shook her head. "I'm sorry, I'm probably boring you with all this talk about myself."

He laughed and said, "Violet, there's nothing about you that's boring. And Benny thinks you're wonderful."

She looked at Edmund with his angular face, his strong neck and shoulders, rounded because of the wind. He wasn't much older, yet he seemed impenetrable, the kind of strong that could take the bad and shush it and kiss it and make it all better. But he could also laugh, and smile and...Violet was offtrack. She pushed the thought away and said, "I like him too."

Edmund nodded. "He's making banana boats for us."

"And Lala is probably worried about me. We should go back," but she remained still, immobile.

He said, "You know I just met you, but I think changes in perspective are good for everybody."

"Yes, probably. Of course you would say that, you're the kind of guy who goes out seeking his fortune."

"I'm the kind of guy who gets forced to seek and then totally sidetracked by surf-breaks and other things."

"Sidetracked is good. There are no rules last I checked."

They exchanged a smile and turned and walked toward the campground. She asked, "Will you come and help tomorrow?"

"I promised Benny. So even if the waves are great, I'll cut my surfing short, and yes, we're coming to help.

"The waves will be good," she smiled at him, "because I said good night to the sun."

* * *

Benjamin and Lala were talking at the campfire. A look of irritation crossed Benjamin's face when he saw them walk up from the beach together, but Edmund excused himself for a few minutes so that Benjamin could sit beside Violet. Edmund wanted to help his brother out, but without even realizing it, found himself staring at Violet, watching her every move across the flames.

After the warm banana boats, Lala begged Benjamin to play guitar. He began Oasis's song, *Wonderwall*, and she joined in, lending a gorgeous soprano to his folksy voice. He smiled and rocked as he played and though Violet and Edmund joined for a little while, by the last note everyone else just listened appreciatively to Lala's beautiful voice. She stood and took a bow and said, "Now play me one of *your* songs."

Benjamin played one of his best, a twangy love song. After a chorus Lala sang along, and then when it ended she said, "I loved that song! Your mom was right you should go become a rock star."

"Funny thing though, she wanted me to be a male model. She wanted Ed to be the rock star."

"Humph," Edmund said, "I have no musical ability beyond an appreciation of good musicians." He raised his cup to Benjamin and Lala. "Can I get famous from being your fans?"

"Moms suck sometimes," said Benjamin,

Edmund glanced at Violet to see her blink a few times at Benjamin's comment.

Lala said, "A male model? Hmmm, I mean I gu-e-ssssss. You're handsome, but how many models does one need for surf shorts?"

Benjamin said, "Don't forget surf tees, look," he bent his arms, bulged his biceps, leaned awkwardly, and posed full-lipped, eyebrows cocked.

Lala said, "*Puh-lease*, check out mine." She leaned forward and bulged both of her biceps and put on a cocky half-smile. "Body by refrigerator moving. That's right."

"The safety-pinned super-hero cape is a nice touch," teased Benjamin.

Violet stood and stretched, "I need to go home, I have whirly doohickeys to create." Her hair was akimbo, loose, wild, and as she stretched her shirt raised over the top of her jeans by degrees, exposing her tummy to the fire.

Heat crawled up Edmund's cheeks. He'd been around so many girls in bikinis, how come a sculptor in work jeans flustered him with a centimeter of skin? He was off his game.

Benjamin jumped up. "Let me help you gather your things." He fussed around and accompanied them to the bulldozer.

He returned a few minutes later and asked, "What were you and Violet talking about on the beach?"

"Nothing, I went and checked on her after I used the bathroom. That was all."

"I really like her, you know. Really."

"Are you sure? I mean you hardly know her..."

"I'm sure. She's beautiful and—"

"You don't really have anything in common. Are you sure you're not attracted to her mess?"

"What do you mean, her mess?"

"Are you sure you're not trying to save her like some knight in shining armor?"

"Definitely not."

"Then I guess I don't get it."

"Fine, you don't have to. Just don't get in my way."

"Fine."

"I'm going to bed."

"Fine."

Edmund sat by the fire wondering what had happened. And why did he feel so firmly in his brother's way.

CHAPTER THIRTEEN
Change can be good

Violet was quiet as she drove away from the campsite.

Lala said, "I'm really sorry about missing the sunset on the mountain."

Violet looked at her over her arm. "It's okay, I had a good time tonight."

"Yeah, me too. I like them, they're so—"

"Lala don't get too used to them being around. They're going to take off. They're headed to the city. You know that."

"I know. I mean, I get that they can't just surf and help us move boxes forever, but I don't know, having them around makes things different, better. It's fun."

Violet concentrated on the hum and rumble of the bulldozer as it crept slowly up Main Beach Road. "I don't want things to be different," she said quietly. "I really don't want them to change anything."

Lala looked at her cousin. "Change can be good sometimes. Even most times."

"Not for me. Things need to remain."

"Well, they're coming to help again tomorrow. They said they would, so don't run them off. I like having cute boys around."

"I thought they weren't your type. What—it took all of three days and now they're cute?"

"You think so too."

"No, I don't. I think they're nothing but trouble."

Lala noticed that though Violet looked straight ahead at the road, a smile tugged at the corner of her mouth.

CHAPTER FOURTEEN
She can be my girl

The next morning, while eating their breakfast in the campsite, Benjamin said, "I'm sorry I snapped. I got, I don't know."

"I understand, I get it. I won't get in your way, and I won't try to talk you out of it, but be careful, ask questions. Try to figure out what she's like. I wonder if the whirligigs are stirring up dust clouds, obscuring your judgment."

Benjamin chuckled. "Okay, I'll ask questions, but I promise she's the girl for me."

They surfed for three hours. They caught a lot of good waves. Other local surfers said hello and began conversations. One even asked, "Word is out that you two were dining last night with Princess Violet. How'd you get her out of her hoard?"

Edmund's jaw clenched and his anger rose, but Benjamin took it in stride. "I asked, she came to dinner."

The surfer paddled on by and Edmund noticed a few of them whispering. He had wondered how the surrounding community felt about the mountain, but now he understood— Violet and her mountain were an oddity, a spectacle, a place that whispers were passed about and rumors. He would have kept surfing but that seemed like a good time to stop. He paddled to shore with his next wave.

Benjamin paddled behind, met him on the beach, and said, "Let's change and go work."

"Sure."

* * *

An hour later they rode the condor basket up the side of the hill where Violet and Lala waited. Lala wore pigtails that stuck out from her head and a multicolored puffy skirt that flounced out in all directions above her boots.

Violet said, "We are so relieved to see you. My third cousin sent a shipment of thirty pianos, we have to hoist them to the top-level."

Edmund said, "No way."

Benjamin's expression was panicked. "Pianos!"

The girls broke into boisterous laughter. Lala said, "They believed us! Oh, you should see your faces!"

Violet said, "Lala has been planning that all morning." They both laughed again.

Benjamin said, "We did move refrigerators the first day. Pianos really wouldn't be that surprising."

Lala said, "I know, that's what's so funny!"

"Speaking of funny," said Benjamin, "I want to hear about this skirt Lala is wearing."

She said with a twanged accent, "This is not funny, dear, dear, Surfer Boy, this is fashion. I found a box in lower level H labeled, 'Square Dancing.' Inside was this beautiful puff of an awesome skirt. Have you ever seen so many colors on one piece of clothing? And watch this," she spun and twirled and the dress stood out from her body in a right angle.

"I tell my cousin that the boxes are here for storage, not to be pilfered and ransacked by the residents."

"I like to explore. All this stuff and no one uses it? And you're busy sculpting most of the time. I have to have something to do."

Lala twirled again, and Violet laughed, "You somehow gravitate to things that accentuate your lovely quirks, and I'm uncertain who that even belongs to, cousin Jeremy?"

It was Lala's turn to laugh. "Oh sure, this is cousin Jeremy's square dancing skirt, *right*. If he needs it he can come and arm wrestle me for it."

Violet filled them in on the day's chores, "Two new containers were delivered today. There," she pointed at the front of the parking lot near Edmund's truck. "It's my second cousin's vinyl collection. He rescued it from an estate sale and needs me to store it until he finds a museum willing to house it. We're going to put them over there," she pointed at the northeast quadrant, "and stack them and cover them. The good news, it's in the shade."

"Thankfully," said Edmund.

The new containers were tightly packed with boxes and boxes of albums. They moved them with the condor and dollies and it went quicker than when they moved the appliances, but they walked more and lifted lots of smaller loads. By the end of it they were tired and sore in all new places.

At one point Edmund adjusted a box and three tiny lizards squirmed out. Lala said, "Ewwww!" and shivered all over, hopping on one leg.

Edmund got down on his knees and watched them as they flipped and flopped before scurrying away. "I see it now, those aren't violet at all, they're definitely purple."

Violet said, "See, one color theory lesson, and you surfer boys are almost interesting."

Every few boxes they tore open a lid, randomly pulled out a record, and announced its title. Then they speculated about the obscure, old music, making up lyrics and guessing at its sound.

They finished after four o'clock. Edmund pulled open the last box and pulled out a record. "Neil Diamond. I've heard of him. We should listen while we have a drink and take a rest."

He looked at Violet quizzically and then after a beat asked, "Where's your record player?"

"Um, I don't..." She turned to Lala. "Do you know?"

"I don't—possibly in Uncle Morris' radios?"

"No, I loaded the magazines in there recently, I would have seen it. Let me check the third level near the televisions. I'll be back in a minute." She returned fifteen minutes later, upset. "I thought there might be one by the—can you think of anyplace?" She adjusted boxes at the back wall and then walked out a door and back in the door and asked, "What about the upper hallway? Would Dad know?"

Edmund said, "It's not that important, Violet."

She ignored him. "Think, Lala. Where's a record player?" She turned in place.

Lala opened her notebook and ran her finger down the list, flustered by the request. Violet pulled the notebook out of her hand and flipped through the pages. "There's no record player. How is there no record player?"

Benjamin said, "Calm down, it's okay—"

"Calm down? I just want to know where something is when I need it. I don't think that's asking too much." She stormed off the deck they were on and rode the condor basket away.

Edmund asked, "If someone storms off in the condor, how do we get down?"

Lala pulled the walkie-talkie from her pocket, and spoke furtively with her back turned, "Violet, its okay. Send the condor basket back."

Violet cried through the speaker saying something unintelligible.

Lala said, "I know, I know. Look, send the condor basket back and I'll meet you in the kitchen. I'll make you something to eat. I know. Okay."

"She's really tired." She put the walkie-talkie back in her pocket as the condor basket pulled up empty in front of them. "I'll give you a ride back to the ground so you can go."

"Okay," said Benjamin. "Will you tell her we're sorry?"

"She's very tired and probably already calmed down." They rode in silence for the few minutes that it took the condor basket to descend to ground level. It landed with a soft thud and Lala pushed the button to open the gate.

Edmund stepped out with his keys in his hand though he stopped to stare up the hill toward the living area. "Will she be okay?"

Lala said, "She'll be fine." Her hands shook as she closed the gate of the basket and ascended away.

Edmund and Benjamin rode quietly back to the campground.

"Well, Eddie, look on the bright side, we get to surf this afternoon."

* * *

That evening as they walked to the Dunes Diner Edmund asked, "Do you think she's on top of the hill?"

"Probably," said Benjamin, "let's go and see."

So they walked out of town, up Main Beach Road about a half mile. As they approached they could see Violet a million miles away, in the reflection of the setting sun, saying good night, again.

"Good, she's okay," said Benjamin.

Edmund didn't say a word.

＊ ＊ ＊

The following day the brothers were quiet, sullen, and barely spoke until they were paddling in their morning surf and Benjamin said, "I know you think that Violet's behavior yesterday was a sign of her crazy but—"

"I don't think that at all."

"Oh."

"Violet's behavior yesterday was one of the first things she's done that made perfect sense. It's fucking bonkers that there's no record player in that hoard. It's crazy that she can't find what she needs because there's so much stuff, and it's insane that her family makes her into their dock worker. No, I think her reaction was absolutely sane."

"Now I don't know what to say, I had a whole argument." Benjamin smiled.

"I still don't know if she's right for you. What are you going to do, become a dockworker too? Move boxes your whole life?"

"I thought she might come with me to the city," said Benjamin.

Edmund sat up on his board. "Come with you to the city? We're talking about Violet right, not Lala? Come with you to the city? You want the girl on the mountain to leave the mountain for you?"

"Yes, to the city. I'll become a rock star, and she can be my girl."

"All this is making you delusional. Has she given you any reason to believe she will leave the mountain for you?"

"She left it the other night."

Edmund puffed out a burst of air and said, "Well brother, I suppose that's true."

"And she only knew me for a couple of days. When I ask her to come with me she'll come. I'm pretty persuasive."

"That you are."

* * *

They only surfed for a short while that morning because they were still tired from the day before. It was very early when they walked back to the campsite, yet Violet had come and gone, leaving them a note on the picnic table:

Dear Eddie and Benjamin,
I'm sorry about yesterday. We don't have much to do today, but we'd still like you to come.
Your friend,
Violet

Benjamin asked, "How fast can you change?"

CHAPTER FIFTEEN
I'll handle that too

Benjamin and Edmund rode up the condor to the upper level deck and were met by the girls yelling together, "Surprise!" They gestured to a table between them that held a record player.

Benjamin said, "You found it!"

Violet put the album on the turning felt and said, "I imagined where I might be if I were a record player—third level of course. I discovered it in no time at all.

Lala mouthed, "Three hours," to Edmund. She wore a red, velvet-trimmed smoking jacket over her jeans.

Violet asked, "Should we sit?" The chairs Bruce had chosen for them had been brought to the deck for the occasion. Lala pushed a cooler of drinks into the middle of the circle, pulled a large curved pipe from her pocket, and placed it on her bottom lip. Everyone chuckled at her new find.

"Are you planning to smoke that?" asked Benjamin.

Violet answered for Lala, "Dear sir, there's no tobacco here, my family is very selective about what they choose to think is important."

Lala pretend-puffed on the enormous pipe. Then said, "This is definitely important. I should put bubbles in it."

They listened for a few minutes. Violet read the name of the song on the album cover. "'*I Am... I Said*'. I like this song—Benjamin, it's about the city, a good omen for your adventure."

"Not to go maybe. Listen, it's about loneliness," said Edmund.

"There's no way Benjamin will be lonely in the city," said Violet.

Benjamin pulled to attention. "I won't?"

"Of course not, you make friends everywhere you go. You'll be surrounded by people who love you within days." Violet took a drink of her soda.

Benjamin leaned forward, "I thought you would come with me to the city."

Violet .jerked back, "Me? What do you mean, me? I don't..." She looked wildly around for help. Edmund and Lala offered none and stared down at their bottles instead.

Benjamin said, "I didn't mean to say it so abruptly. I want you to come with me to the city."

Violet peered at him intently, brow furrowed. "I'm not leaving my home."

"Will you consider it first—"

"I don't need to. I'm not leaving my home."

Everyone sat quietly listening to Neil Diamond croon.

Lala said, "I like him. It's a good album." She stood and started twirling, waving her arms, occasionally posing with the pipe to the music.

"We have lots more," said Violet darkly.

Edmund said, "You know what I'd like to do? I'd love to see your sculptures, up close."

"You would?"

Benjamin and Edmund both nodded.

Violet looked at them for a long pause. "I don't usually show them, I prefer them to be my solitary endeavor..."

Edmund said, "You do know they can be seen for miles around, right?"

Violet smiled. "True. Okay, we can take the condor up. I usually travel up a tunnel, but we'd have to go through the back rooms, and they're a complete mess."

They clamored aboard and Violet drove the condor basket to a flat area on the top east side. Violet had covered the mountain with wooden decking, metal sheets and plastic tarps nailed down, roofing tiles, a big expanse of linoleum, and a few hundred square feet of carpeting, flat and spreading in all directions.

"My plateau," Violet said pointing to the plastic tarps on the ground. "I attempt to keep the leaks to a minimum by forever adding layers and layers to the ground."

Benjamin asked, "How high up are we?"

"A couple hundred feet or so, but I hardly think it matters when one can touch the sky. Don't go to the edges, I don't trust them generally."

She crossed to the middle and held her arms out. "My sculptures."

Whirligigs surrounded her, tall, some over twenty feet—welded gates and stacks and poles and ladders stretching to the sky, and at the top, spinning pinwheels and mobiles, jutting, turning, spiraling.

"Takes my breath away," said Edmund.

"That's just the wind," said Violet with a smile.

Lala walked near the edge and watched the ever-present cloud of seagulls spin above the whirligigs. Occasionally she yelled, "Scree, Scree!" causing them to spin in another direction.

Benjamin asked Violet, "Are the whirligigs made of street signs?"

"One of my cousins collected old license plates and street signs. He died a few months after my mother. I knew no one else would want them, so I appropriated them. Street signs are reflective that's what creates their spectacular sparkle at sunset."

Benjamin asked, "That one has a—what is it?" He pointed to the top of a sculpture.

"That's a rider on a bicycle, it follows that circular track when the wind blows from the East.

"This one is my favorite," she led them to a tall whirligig. It had three legs and rose to a shockingly high point. A big wheel spun, and small wheels spiraled out rising even higher. The slightest wind and the whole contraption swirled and fluttered. Two cutout characters—a man and a woman—danced in a twirl together and then spun out alone along a bar and turned back and met each other again to spin. There were dozens of intricate moving parts. It astounded Edmund that it functioned so gracefully.

Benjamin asked, "It doesn't need any electricity?"

"No, it's all wind-powered. And balance. I hold a piece of metal and find the place where its energy is stored. Sometimes it's the center, but not always. Once I understand that place, I can stack and pile and build, and the balance remains true. The wind dances across it, and it reacts."

Edmund looked at her spellbound. "You made this. I never met anyone who made things. Not like this." He said it like a statement, so no one said anything in reply.

A sculpture clanked and screeched. Violet walked toward it and looked up with hands on her hips. "And then sometimes the wind creates disharmony. I should oil that one tonight."

"Do you have oil? I'll do it for you," offered Benjamin. "I'd love to climb it."

She pointed, "The squeak is right about there."

He grabbed a small can and scaled up the rungs of the stand and squeaked oil on the joint.

Violet called up, "Better!"

"What? I can't hear you!" said Benjamin. "I'm on top of the world!"

Edmund asked, "Can you see the point break from there?"

"Sure. You aren't missing anything, the waves are super teeny tiny!" Benjamin climbed down, "All those sea gulls—I thought they might land in my hair.

"They won't land, the whirligigs keep them away—sort of a happy coincidence. Though sometimes when I imagine the fortune I might make from their guano I wonder if I should dismantle the sculptures and let the birds land."

"Never, I hope these sculptures always stay," said Edmund. "But I've come to help. What can we do for you? We still have most of the day."

Violet looked at him and smiled. "I need to arrange for the trucking company to pick up these containers, to make room for the next ones, but Lala can do that."

Lala said, "We ought to go down and help Uncle Bruce in the library?"

Violet said, "No, it's too—too—I don't..."

Edmund said, "What if we helped you get rid of some of the newspapers. Helped you make room for other things?"

Lala said, "That is true, there are piles and piles of newspapers over on the north side." She added for the boys, "Great Aunt Millie thinks they're good for something, but Great Aunt Millie needs a computer."

Violet chewed her bottom lip. "Cousin James called and said that Aunt Millie is losing her memory anyway."

"Oh." Lala took the pipe out of her mouth and yelled to the sky, "I'm sorry Great Aunt Millie!"

Benjamin asked, "How many newspapers are there?"

"At least a truck's worth."

"Whoa."

"Look," said Edmund, "can we get rid of them? I mean, is it okay with you?"

Violet blinked a few times. "Get rid of them?"

"Yes, take them to the trash." He stared at her in earnest. Benjamin and Lala stayed out of the conversation, pretending to look at other things.

"I haven't ever done that before. It probably needs permits."

"I'll handle it, but is it okay with you?"

Violet blinked again. "Yes, we can put the newspapers in the trash, or recycle them, that would be better. But shouldn't I go through them first, see if there's anything to save? Maybe Aunt Millie is right—"

Edmund asked, "When did most of them arrive?"

"It's been a couple of years."

"Let's take a moment and try to imagine what could be there that any of us might need."

They stood for a moment and then Violet asked, "What about the crossword puzzles?"

Benjamin said, "You can buy a book of crosswords on nicer paper. I'd like to mention that the city has lots of bookstores with game sections—" He grinned when she smiled in response.

Edmund asked, "Did anyone else come up with anything that we might need a few-years-old newspaper for?"

Lala said, "Recipes?"

"Ditto the bookstore," said Benjamin

Lala said, "See Violet, we need to go to the city." Violet gave her a look.

"Okay, so I'll arrange things, while you guys...?"

"Call about the containers?" asked Lala.

"No, I'll handle that too."

"Okay," said Violet, "we'll go restore the television area back to rights. I made a terrific mess while I looked for that blasted record player."

"Sounds good," said Edmund. "Do you have a trucking company phone number?"

As they walked away, Lala said to Edmund, "You ought to go ask Uncle Bruce if he needs them for anything too."

* * *

Edmund walked into the familiar living quarters, the large living room with the table and the big kitchen. He called, "Bruce?"

He walked down one of the most traveled hallways. Frames and doors packed the corridor. He passed the bathroom he had used a few times and discovered farther down, a closed door. He peeked in, sure that Bruce wasn't there, but curious all the same.

He had discovered Violet's room. Tiny, it contained a wooden twin bed, covered in pillows and wild handmade quilts. A quilt was scrunched beside it on the floor. Brightly colored doors comprised the walls—pink, green, purple, yellow. One small antique table stood beside the bed, and on it an ornate frame with a picture of a young girl and a woman with their arms wrapped around each other. The smile on the woman's face resembled Violet's own. Violet's mother, definitely. Beside the photo two metallic pinwheels leaned inside a beautiful vase. The vase had a painting of a farmhouse in a field.

Violet's welding hat, her gloves, her apron and a pile of work clothes were shoved against the wall, but other than that the room was clean and spare and uncluttered.

He backed out and closed the door and returned to the main quarters. He called "Bruce!" again and followed a different door in a way he had never gone. It opened at the top of a long staircase heading down. Piled objects lined the edges of the steps so that the stairs were tight and barely maneuverable. Edmund whacked his head on the low ceiling at the bottom and rubbed it while he looked around. He could barely discern the door from the pile of things leaned against it.

He called, "Bruce?" and knocked once.

A small faraway voice answered, "Yes?"

"Bruce, it's me, Edmund."

After some shuffling Bruce cracked the door and squeeze-leaned out awkwardly. "Hello Edmund! I'd invite you in but I'm cleaning right now."

Piles and piles of books and bags and stacks of mess and things and piles covered every square inch behind him. Askew pictures covered the walls. Edmund quickly averted his eyes.

"Bruce, I talked to Violet about removing her Aunt Millie's newspaper collection. I wanted to check with you to make sure that would be okay."

"Removing it? Whatever for?"

"We think it might be a fire hazard."

"A fire! Well, of course. Have you read about the great London Fire? Terrible terrible consequences. Yes, you ought to remove it to a safer location."

"We were planning to send it to a recycling facility."

"Does Violet know this?"

"Yes, sir, she said it would be okay."

"Has it been discussed with Millie? I'm not sure she would approve. She definitely brought it here for our safekeeping because it's important. Or she wouldn't have." He squinted at Edmund.

"It's been discussed with Millie," said Edmund, resorting to a lie.

"Okay, but I recommend looking through it first to see if there's anything important." The door closed and Edmund ascended the stairs and went back out to the family's deck.

He started making calls.

CHAPTER SIXTEEN
It's been a long day

An hour later Edmund had arranged everything. By the end of the day a truck would come pick up the containers— one would be empty, the other would be full of newspapers. The trucking company only needed a bit more cash to take the newspapers to the recycling center, so Edmund put it on his card. He definitely didn't want to ask Violet for money to take the newspapers away and cause her to hesitate even more.

He joined the others where they were working on the television stacks. They were laughing and goofing off, and even Violet was so hysterical tears ran down her face.

"What's funny?"

"We were laughing about how the only TV that anyone watches in this place is the one in Bruce's room and it's about twenty years old."

"But, some of these TVs are brand new!"

"That's why we're laughing!"

Lala said, "We loaded these all here and didn't even consider it."

"Here, let's take one and give it to him tonight at dinner." Edmund pointed at a big boxed flatscreen. "But really, when you give it to him, make sure he gives you the old one in exchange."

Lala said, "Definitely, or he'd probably use it as a stand for the old one."

Violet laughed, "He would wouldn't he?"

* * *

The group rode the condor basket to the newspaper area and took stock. There were piles and piles and piles. Benjamin said, "You weren't kidding, those are a bunch of newspapers."

"We'll fill a container, possibly both," said Edmund, "and we better get started, the trucking company comes in three hours."

They divided in two again, passing boxes with the condor basket until they realized they needed more power. They hung a large basket from the crane and filled it with newspapers, so there were two machines working simultaneously, but it was still loads of work. Piles of schlepping and twisting and bending and turning, and when the truck arrived to load the containers they were still bringing down the last newspapers in a hurry. And because the driver had to wait, Edmund tipped him slyly, and then paid extra for the second container of newspapers, too.

"Dinner?" asked Lala.

Edmund offered to take them to the pub or the diner, but Violet balked. "It's been a long day and..."

"Can I bring food here? I'll order and pick up."

Violet looked grateful, "That would be really perfect."

Edmund said, "Ask Bruce what he'd like to eat."

When the food had been ordered, Lala offered to go with Edmund to the restaurant to pick it up. Violet said, "While you're gone Benjamin and I will give Dad his new TV and wrestle the old one away."

Benjamin laughed, stretched out his arms, and popped his neck. "He's a pacifist, I think I can take him."

CHAPTER SEVENTEEN
Nothing but junk and trash

Edmund and Lala left the mountain and were driving down Main Beach Road when she said, "It's been a really long time since I left Violet alone."

He said, "She's not alone."

"True Benjamin is there. Does he like her or something?"

"Probably."

"He won't get anywhere with Violet, she doesn't have plans to be with anyone ever."

"She's with you, her father."

"I mean fall in love. She won't or can't or is scared or something."

"Well, the best part of love is we don't plan it, we fall, and falling hard I suspect is scary."

They pulled up in front of the restaurant and Edmund turned off the truck. "Did you know her mother?"

"Yes, she was wonderful, so sweet and caring. She wanted to teach everyone everything about the world. She loved learning things, traveling places, meeting people. She would have been sad that Violet is so alone most of the time."

"She has you."

"True, but she still spends most of her days and nights alone. I'm alone most of the time. I guess that's why we're so glad you two started coming around."

They walked into the restaurant and picked up the bags and bags of food. Edmund had ordered more than necessary, because they had worked so hard, and because he felt magnanimous.

Back at the mountain Bruce joined them for dinner, and they sat talking and laughing around the table. The camaraderie level was high, the mood jovial.

Violet said, "Lets play a game—when you were seven what was your dream? You first, Dad."

"Seven, that was a long long time ago, but probably a sea captain."

Lala was next. "A veterinarian, or singer on a grand stage. I don't really like animals very much though, so I suppose singer it is."

Bruce said, "It's lovely that you're young enough that your seven-year-old-dreams are still hopes instead of regrets."

Violet said, "Dad, you're bringing the mood down, and it's my turn. I won't say like my mom because we're trying to keep this all lively. So, I'm pretty sure I wanted to own a hotdog stand."

Benjamin was incredulous. "A hotdog stand?"

She laughed and said, "So what's yours?"

"I wanted to be a surfer and a rockstar and a superhero as well. I wanted my superpower to be rock-starring and carving terrific backsides on the biggest waves ever surfed. In Fiji. He grinned around at the group. I figure I'm right on target, living my dreams!"

Edmund laughed. "You are, Brother, you are."

Benjamin asked, "What about you, Eddie?"

"You guys will poke fun at me."

"No, we won't."

"You will, my seven-year-old self was lame."

Violet said, "The dreams of seven year olds are never lame. They're always illogical and grounded in magical theory."

"Mine were, I wanted to run my Dad's company." He smiled around the group and they all laughed.

Benjamin said, "That is totally lame."

"I thought the family business was interesting, like it was doing something, but come to find out by the time I was part of the lineage there was nothing interesting about it. Now it's money signs on a computer being passed back and forth with questionable integrity."

Violet said, "So if you think about it, your seven-year-old dream was just as hokey as all of ours, because it wasn't grounded in reality, it was based on your need to be in charge, in control, you know, a boss."

"Who said I want to be a boss?"

Benjamin dropped his fork and looked dumbfounded. Violet laughed a high twinkling laugh. Lala giggled and said, "You totally want to be in charge of everything."

"Really?"

"Yes," Violet said. "What was the one condition I gave you if you were going to work here? You had to let me be in charge, and what did you do all day today?"

"Told you what to do."

"Yes, you told me what to do. You're bossy, no point in arguing against it. I'll win."

Edmund chuckled at the insight. "Okay, okay, you pegged me. Sorry about that."

Benjamin said, "He's lucky to have such an easygoing brother to boss around."

Bruce said, "Sorry kids, I need to go to my rooms—all this rich food. I need to do yoga. Anyone want to join me?"

"Yoga, Dad? Where?"

"I have a place. I cleaned today."

"I didn't see anything leave your room at all. Not a thing."

"I organized. If everything has a place, you don't have to get rid of it."

Violet rolled her eyes. "I'm going to go see the sunset. Can I leave you this mess, Lala?"

"Definitely, we'll clean up, won't we boys?"

Edmund and Benjamin nodded.

Benjamin asked, "Will you come back, or work late?"

Violet looked around the group. "Will you still be here?"

Benjamin said, "Absolutely. I've got nowhere to be, right big Brother?"

Edmund nodded looking down at the table.

"Okay, I hate to leave a nice party like this. I'll return in about a half hour so we can visit more. I can work later." She left through a back door.

Benjamin and Edmund cleared the table into the trashcans, and then Benjamin offered to take the trash down in the condor basket to the ground floor.

When he left Lala said, "I haven't seen Violet this happy in a long time."

Edmund wiped a counter clean and said, "Yep, Benjamin is pretty great."

Lala screwed her lips to the side. "I told you that I wouldn't count on Benjamin being Violet's thing."

"Sure, but he has charm." They wiped the rest of the counters and then carried the easy chairs out to the deck just as Benjamin returned.

"Hullo!" he called. "I got to say, riding a condor like an elevator is kind of the coolest thing in the world. Living on a mountain is kind of amazing. Up high like this, able to see the whole wide world."

Edmund said, "Too bad this deck looks out over the land. I wish it faced the ocean." The three of them settled into the semicircle of chairs and bundled their jackets around their arms.

Benjamin said, "See that glow, way over there?" He pointed to the Northeast. "That's a city, right, *the* city?"

"Could be."

Benjamin said, "How about these stars? It's so dark."

"Violet will be back soon," said Lala.

Stars sprinkled the sky. Benjamin pointed, "There, Orion's Belt. This is such an amazing house."

Lala said, "Yes, it is—"

Edmund scowled. "It's not a house, it's a freaking mountain of stuff. There isn't even a visible house here at all."

Lala said, "There's the rooms. Because you can't see it from the outside doesn't make them nonexistent, doesn't make it less a home."

"They're caves to hide in, away from the world, carved into a mountain of nothing but junk and trash." As soon as he said it he regretted it.

Lala's eyes opened wide.

Violet appeared in the doorway. She said, her voice raised, projecting, "It's not junk, Edmund, these are my things. They belong to me and my family. How dare you?"

Edmund jumped from his seat. "I didn't mean—" He held onto the side of his chair.

Her hair whipped around her face as she stalked across the deck, her face flushed, red splotches appearing on her cheeks, her eyes furious. "The original house, here in this spot belonged to my grandmother. She and my grandfather built it together and when he died she kept adding to it. They built it with beautiful dark wood and amazing craftsmanship and filled it with antiques and curiosities and wonderful art pieces. It was absolutely not junk."

Violet glared at Edmund, her fists clenched. She circled the group of chairs.

"When my grandmother died she gave the house to my mother because she loved it best. My mother filled it with things she loved, and things she wanted to show me. My mother made it a magical place, every corner had a beloved memento in it. Does that sound like junk?"

"No, it—"

"When my mother died, when she died, she—"

"Violet, I wasn't—"

"She collected memories. So many memories. Everything important and things that might seem inconsequential. Memories. She *died* because of them. She died under the weight of them. Carrying all those memories, all that weight, wanting to share it with me... that's what killed her."

Lala stood, shushing, and bundled a blanket and her arms around Violet. "It's okay he didn't realize."

"She died under the weight. It crushed her. It's not junk. It's her, it's me, it's not—" Violet sobbed and buried her head in Lala's shoulder.

Lala comforted, "I know Violet, I know. Do you want to go inside?"

Violet nodded, and the girls shuffled together through the door to the interior of the mountain.

Edmund looked at Benjamin for help, but Benjamin asked, "What were you thinking?"

"I don't know I..."

"Why would you say that?"

"I thought it needed to be said." Edmund stood with his hands in his pockets braced against the chill. He couldn't sit down, didn't feel he deserved to be comfortable. How could he cause someone so sad, so much more sadness? Only fucking jerks said things like that.

Lala came back to the patio. Edmund turned and said, "Lala I didn't—"

"I know Edmund, you didn't mean it, and you didn't realize."

"Her mother died here? Here?"

Lala sobbed. She dropped her face into her hands and cried for a moment before she continued, barely able to say the words, "Yes, here. The house fell. Everything was destroyed. The family begged the authorities not to excavate."

Benjamin asked, "You mean her mother's body is still here? In this mountain?"

Lala nodded, tears streamed down her face, but she attempted to collect herself. "Our extended family helped build platforms and decks and floors so that Violet and Bruce would have somewhere to live, but Bruce couldn't bring himself to finish anything. He left the whole house unbuilt and then our family began to store things here. The pile started years ago and grew and grew. First around the collapsed house and then over and everywhere." She wiped her eyes with her sleeve.

Edmund stepped closer and put his hand on her shoulder. "I'm so sorry."

"I know you are, and you should tell Violet, but probably tomorrow."

"I'm not really okay with leaving without saying it."

She sized him up. Then led him to the interior rooms and pointed down the hallway to Violet's door.

CHAPTER EIGHTEEN
You want to save me

Edmund knocked quietly. "Violet?"

"Go away."

"I can't. I'm just so sorry. I had no idea. Everything was a mystery and had I known I would never have...Violet, please."

Silence.

He put his hands up on the sides of the doorframe.

"Please tell me you're okay." He leaned his forehead on the door and listened with all his heart.

Silence again.

Edmund's voice broke, and he begged, "Please."

The door opened and a red-eyed Violet stood in the crack of the doorway. She didn't look at him, wouldn't meet his eyes.

"Violet," he begged.

She turned her face to his. Her eyes were so full of pain that he said, "I didn't mean to—I wouldn't."

She leaned against the doorframe and with her bottom lip in her teeth said, "Mhmm," and nodded.

"You know that right? You know me, right?"

She pushed forward and kissed him.

He pulled away for a moment and then leaned forward and kissed her back. Her eyes were gray clouds, her face pale and shimmering, rained on. Forlorn. He said again, his mouth, his breath, at her ear. "I'm so sorry." She nodded, her hands clutching the front of his shirt, his arms around, holding her close. Their kisses deepening, their hands grasping. He propelled her back through her doorway and pressed her up against a wall. Her arms went up around the back of his head, pulling him in, they kissed, deeply, desperately, the pain of the last conversation dissolving away as a breath of shared air entered their lungs. They kissed and kissed and kissed.

He reached out and closed her bedroom door with a click.

Violet took him by the hand and led him to her bed. She pulled his jacket down his arms to the ground and then pulled his shirt off over his head. She kissed his collar bone. His shoulder. He closed his eyes with a moan.

He unbuttoned the front of her shirt, slowly pulled it off, and then fumbling, figured out how to open her bra. He kissed the heartbeat at the edge of her throat.

They kissed for a few minutes chest to chest, her hands caressing along his shoulders and his back, and his fingers trailing along her curves. He said, "Let me help you with your boots." She dropped to the bed, leaned back on her arms, and watched as he attempted to untie, kneeling in front of her, lost in his mind. He reeled if he looked up at her, beautiful, in her splotchy-skin paleness and flinging blonde hair, breasts exposed, and botched the shoe laces and pulled at them madly.

She leaned forward, kissed him on the corner of the mouth, and said, "I'll take mine off, if you'll take off yours." And so they took off their shoes and their pants and then Edmund wrapped his arms around and pulled her down to the bed.

He kissed her face, her cheeks, the side of her neck and her shoulders and down the length of an arm and then her breast, and she rose up to meet his kiss.

They made love on her tiny twin bed in the mountain that was her home, her mother's burial place, her grandmother's house, and it wasn't junk anymore. To Edmund it was a magical place, a brilliant place, but a place he thought would eventually destroy this girl that he loved. And he did love her, it had crashed into him with the shut of her bedroom door, but it had been there all along. He loved her, and her home would eventually destroy her, and the trouble was he didn't have any idea how to rescue her from it.

At the end, still laying on her body, his lips kissing her neck, just at the point of her heartbeat, he felt her take in an uneven breath, a sob. "Wha—?" He pulled up to look down at her face in time to see a tear roll down her cheek. "Violet?" She shook her head and buried her face in his shoulder. "Violet, talk to me."

"It's just—all so hard. And it's the anniversary this week and—I'm just so overwhelmed by it all. And you're here...and I want..." She cried inconsolably leaving her want unsaid.

Edmund held on, unable to find the words he needed to console her, but nodding into her hair, and kissing her cheek, and hoping that was enough, until finally her tears subsided and she returned a slow sweet kiss on his cheek and whispered a breathy "Thank you" into his ear.

He pulled up and looked down at her, a thumb at each of her temples, caressing the edge of her cheeks. "I'm so sorry I made you cry."

Violet stared into his eyes. "Edmund, you also made me laugh."

He nodded and then with an unbelievable amount of stoicism, said, "We need to get back to Ben and Lala." He rolled off and over onto his back.

She said, "Yes we do," but remained sprawled on the bed.

He asked, "Do you feel better?"

"Yes, by degrees. I just have a lot..." Her voice trailed off.

He asked, "What are you thinking about?"

"You." She rolled to her side and studied the angle of his jaw, the way it crossed in planes to meet his chiseled nose and then climbed up to his dark brows that overhung his deep eyes reflecting nothing but her own face. She reached out and ran her fingers down his stubbly cheek. "About how you want to save me."

"I do, I want to." His voice was so low it vibrated in her core.

She said, "I know."

She sat up and then stood and pulled her pants up to her hips in a graceful move that showed off every curve and angle and fastened them. She stood for a half-beat half-naked, eyes red, nose shiny, hair a mess.

He said, "God, you're beautiful." He shook his head to bring himself back to the present and pulled his own pants up with jerks and failed attempts. Then he swept his fingers through his hair and looked for his shirt.

While he turned away he built up his nerve. "Can we not let the others know? Hide it? I really need to talk to Benjamin. He really likes you."

"Yes, until it's okay, it's our secret." She finished dressing. "I'm going to go up. I'll tell them you're in the bathroom." She gave him a last long lingering kiss and then left to go back to her strange version of reality.

CHAPTER NINETEEN
She makes the stars shine

Benjamin saw Violet emerge from the door at the back of the patio. "There you are. How are you doing?"

"I'm better, we talked it out, and..." Edmund emerged from the doorway as she said, "I apologize for my scene."

She dropped into her easy chair and wrapped a blanket around her body. She had Benjamin to her right and Lala to her left. Edmund's chair had been placed beside Lala, but he moved between their chairs so that he could brush his hand along Violet's back as he passed.

He sat in the chair that Bruce had picked out for him. It was a perfect chair for brooding, but not as good for tonight when Edmund wanted to sit attentive, yet pretend-relaxed, two chairs away from the girl he secret-loved.

Lala said, "So it's all good? Between you?" Edmund's eyes met Violet's and his heart leapt. They both nodded.

Lala said, "Wait, I have—back in a second!" She disappeared through a door and returned in a few minutes lugging a big box. She dropped it on the edge of the deck and rifled through it. She put on a furry winter hat with teddy bear ears, then grabbed a small armful of hats and brought them to the chairs. She handed a stuffed hat that looked like a giant king's crown to Violet. "For the Princess." She pretended to size up Benjamin and then handed him a pink hat with floppy bunny ears.

He said, "Perfect, I wondered if there would be a pink one."

Edmund picked a red and white striped top hat from the leftovers. It towered about two feet above his head.

Lala said, "The Cat in the Hat! I'm so glad you picked that one, it's my favorite Dr. Seuss."

"I wasn't a big fan of it, much preferred *The Lorax*, but this hat looked warmest." He pulled it down as far as he could and grinned and crossed his eyes with the hat towering above his head.

Lala took off her own hat, hit him with it playfully, and then returned to her seat and segued the conversation. Benjamin and I were having a fascinating conversation about the lizards."

Violet said, "Our purple lizards?"

Lala said, "Your purple lizards. They totally gross me out. Benjamin looked them up."

Violet turned to Benjamin "What did you discover?"

They used to live all along the coast, but now they're endangered almost to the point of extinction."

"Except here," said Edmund.

Benjamin continued, "They usually live in rock formations, in caves and outcroppings. I guess they don't care about the substrate. They think this mountain is as good as any.

"They eat bugs—mosquitos, cockroaches, ants, really anything that we humans don't want—they eat. Actually having them in your house is excellent bug control." At the word house Edmund's eyes flickered to Violet's face. She met his eyes with a soft smile.

Lala shivered. "Ew, that's gross, but also the only reason I put up with them."

"They aren't 'ew,' they're beautiful," said Violet. "And useful. Why are they extinct?"

"Their home has been built over mostly, and they have a tricky infancy. They hatch and most of them are eaten by seagulls, attracted to their bright purple skin and delicious gooey interiors."

"Oh—my whirligigs are saving the lizards?"

Benjamin said, "Your whirligigs. Isn't that cool?"

"Yes, yes it is," said Violet.

Everyone enjoyed a moment of silence in the cool air of the evening under the shining array of stars.

Then Benjamin said, "So, I want to tell you again, Violet, I would love for you to come to the city when Edmund and I go. You should come. It doesn't have to be for long. Just come with us and see what happens."

Violet wrapped her blanket closer and said, I'm not really a See-What-Happens kind of girl. I have a docket." She smiled jovially, but Benjamin wasn't in the mood to find her refusal amusing, or to think it was her final word.

He turned to Lala. "You'd like to go, right? We could all pile in the truck and have an adventure together."

Lala put her hand on Violet's arm. "It would be super fun, Violet. We could go for a short time. Let's go see the world."

"You know I can't leave, Lala. What would happen with Dad? Who would take care of him?"

Benjamin said, "I could arrange for someone to come and cook and clean for Bruce. I would do that."

Benjamin twisted his chair, leaned forward, and put his hands on Violet's knees causing Edmund to inhale sharply.

Benjamin pleaded, "Come, with me."

Without looking at Edmund, without taking his eyes from Violet's face, Benjamin asked, "Eddie, don't you agree she should come with us to the city?"

Edmund was leaned back in his chair unable to take his eyes off his brother pleading with Violet, the woman Edmund loved. The two people he cared most about and Benjamin wanted his help. With *Violet*. What could he say?

Violet needed to leave the mountain, but—please, oh please—she had to leave with Edmund.

Benny-boy wanted her to runaway with him. He was asking her to come. Pleading with her, persuading, using all his charm, and Edmund couldn't say a thing, not with honesty. Not without giving Benjamin a brutal blow. And maybe, perhaps, the best way to get her to leave would be with Benjamin's charm. So Edmund—though inside his heart yelled no—agreed. "Yes, you should come with us to the city." His eyes looked down at his fingertips stretched along the chair that he had been measured for.

Violet watched him quietly. Hair blowing toward Benjamin. A subliminal question on the tips of the strands. She searched Edmund's face and then turned to Benjamin and asked, "What would I do in this city?"

Benjamin smiled and looked into her eyes and said, "You could have a hot dog stand like in your dreams."

She looked at him for a minute, deciphering, but unable to grasp the meaning. She was code-breaking their words, the letters of their words, the in-between spaces.

She answered quietly, "Those were the dreams of my seven-year-old self."

Benjamin leaned back in his chair defeated.

Edmund continued to look at his hand and said, "You could find a gallery to show your sculptures. You could rent a studio on a street that faces west and open the garage doors every day and say good night to the sun every evening. You could go to art shows and gallery openings and watch Benny-boy here when his band plays on the weekends. Lala could be your roommate, and she could become a singer, and Bruce could live in the upstairs apartment, and he could open a street level shop that sells chairs, special order, perfectly-sized.

"You could do that because I believe you can do anything, but that's what I thought contemplating for only a few minutes. I bet there's lots of other things you can do or be and maybe you don't even know what they are yet."

They sat silently and Benjamin said, "Hear, hear to that."

"You planned what I can do and what Benjamin and Lala and Bruce are doing, what about you?"

Edmund shrugged, and didn't answer, but his eyes met hers.

She said, "I can't leave, I have things. I have responsibilities. I have to be here to keep it all together."

Benjamin said, "Eddie's got some great ideas, so what I'm saying is don't decide now, just think about it."

Violet said, "I can't leave, Benjamin."

She leaned forward and said, "This mountain is a part of me. How would I go to the city with this baggage? Where would it all fit? Imagine me dragging it behind me, the saddest girl in the city.

"My heart belongs here. Would you have me cut my heart out and leave it behind, with my eyes on the mountain top to watch the sunset? I could go to the city like that, an empty shell of a girl, not whole, the saddest girl in the city? Benjamin, you don't want to go to the city with the saddest girl."

Edmund gulped. *Violet wasn't ever leaving.* He had known it, deep down, she wasn't ever going to leave, but hadn't considered how he could possibly stay.

Benjamin repeated, "Just think about it, Violet."

She nodded. "Speaking of which, and I hate to leave you all, but I have a sculpture without a whirl. I should get to work."

"Aw don't leave yet," said Benjamin, "stay and talk a little more." He clasped his hands and batted his eyes and said, "*Please.*"

She laughed, "But only because you look so cute in the pink bunny hat, and I appreciate that you still want to talk to me after my depressing turn. What should we talk about?"

Benjamin said, "I need a band name. Something cool, so I can put up signs in the city advertising for band mates, and people will want to join. And I'm feeling sentimental so make it something about this week together. Okay, starting with you, Eddie."

Edmund had struggled the entire conversation to act normal, but with every move he failed and felt sure they could see. He laughed more than he ought. He sat quietly when he should have been engaged. Yet somehow he made it through the whole awkward and messy evening. He answered, "The Hot Sculpted Whirligigs," and everyone laughed.

Violet said, "Lovely imagery. I see the design of the t-shirts now."

Benjamin asked, "Lala?"

"The Royal Purple Lizards? Or better yet, the Royal Purple Lizard Princes."

Benjamin said, "I could wear Violet's crown on stage. Definitely a contender. Violet?"

"It would have to be Sweet Stolen Mountain Moments." Edmund locked eyes with Violet.

Benjamin looked at his drink and said, "That's really nice."

She continued, "Or what about Benjamin and the Refrigerator Boxes. Because that's how we met."

Edmund watched his brother's face light up. Benjamin was clutching ahold of every smile or look as proof that Violet returned his adoration. It made Edmund want to stand up, stalk over, pick her up, and carry her off like King Kong.

Luckily Violet saved herself from being carried up the building by Edmund's inner beast by saying, after looking at her bare wrist, "But look at the time, I really have to go. Will you come tomorrow?" She placed her crown in her chair and disappeared through a door headed to the tiptop of the building on her own accord.

Edmund stared in the direction Violet had gone. He wondered if he could follow her and not come back. He could drop the keys to the truck by Benjamin's chair and say, "I'm staying," and go inside. Let Benjamin and Lala figure it out and then deal with that later. But he looked over at Benjamin deflated after Violet left. Going through the motions with Lala.

Edmund couldn't figure out why Benjamin wasn't interested in Lala who bubbled over with cuteness. She loved music. She wanted to go to the city with him. They were talking animatedly right now: Lala said she loved the band, Smudge the Universe, and asked if Benjamin had heard them. Benjamin answered that he had their debut album and had she seen the video of their live concert at Bonnaroo? Lala called it her favorite and said she listened to it over and over.

Benjamin was a fool, but also, Edmund had to admit, Lala had been eclipsed. She was the sidekick to Violet—the star— the heated glow and sparkle bursting from a star. Violet was the kind of girl who created mountains on top of her sadness and lived there with grace and generosity and decorated the top with welded steel and collected gusts of wind. She was the kind of girl whose hardhat was painted the color of an endangered creature's skin. She was weird, and beautiful, and maddening, and possibly, probably fatally flawed. He felt like he might suffocate just thinking about kissing her.

He came back to, as Lala said, "What do you think Edmund?"

"Me? Oh, um, I'm sorry, my mind wandered." Without waiting for a response he asked Benjamin, "Are you ready to go? The surf this morning, the piles and piles of newspapers... and this wind is lulling me to sleep." So he and Benjamin took leave of Lala and headed down in the condor basket.

Edmund had trouble looking Benjamin in the face. He needed to talk to him, to tell him, to explain to him, but where to start? What to say? They drove north out of the parking lot, through the gate and around the northwest curve of the mountain on Coastal Highway. At the intersection with Main Beach Road, Edmund turned and drove for a few minutes, and like every night, pulled the truck to the side and stepped out to look.

Violet stood surrounded by the twenty-some whirligigs, backdropped by the stars and the rising moon, her welder's torch glowing from this distance, sparks rising from the point of her focus.

Edmund said, "It's like she makes the stars shine."

Benjamin said, "True that."

Simultaneously they climbed into the truck. Edmund turned the key, and as the engine rumbled and the wheels kicked up gravel and dirt and sand and pulled onto the pavement, he said, "I love her."

Benjamin turned. "What, who?"

"I love her, Violet."

* * *

Benjamin didn't say a word, he stared out the front window. From Edmund's peripheral vision he saw Benjamin blink repeatedly. The first lights from Sandy Shore's storefronts came into view and slid by as they drew closer to the campground.

Benjamin said, "You don't get to."

"What do you mean?" Edmund was confused by his response.

"You don't get to love her. You don't."

"Look Benny, this isn't a First-One-to-See-Her-Gets-to-Call-Her situation. At all."

"Exactly. You walk through your life entitled to everything. You get all the money. You think you get all the girls. You even think you get to take care of everyone else because it makes you feel powerful. But I'm not yours to take care of. Violet is not yours to take care of."

"I think she might be."

"Might be what?"

"Mine."

"Oh crap. You are so full of yourself. You think you're what she needs? You want to watch her up on her mountain and mold her into what you've decided is good for her. I want to show her the world, to show her there's a future and fun and hopeful things happening."

Edmund pulled up to their campsite's parking space. "I hear you saying this to me, and there might be some truth to it. There is also truth in that I didn't want to fall in love with her, and that I was happy for you that you liked her, but here I am, loving her and I need you to... I don't know, to..."

Edmund paused because he honestly had no idea what he wanted Benjamin to do, but he hoped his brother would step in and help, say something to rest his mind. Instead Benjamin opened the door, stepped out of the truck, and stalked off to the tent.

Edmund rested his head on the steering wheel and then exhausted, lay down across the seats in the cab of the truck and fell asleep.

CHAPTER TWENTY
No plan

The next morning when Edmund awoke, Benjamin was already gone, along with his surfboard. This was a good sign. It would be hard for him to be angry for long if the waves were good, and they would be today. As Edmund ran the path to the beach he chuckled thinking, of course the waves would be good, Violet had said good night to the sun, and wasn't it cool that he, a surfer, had fallen for the girl responsible for the waves?

He felt hopeful and energetic, until he reached the break and Benjamin, still, silent, and sullen.

"Benny, can we talk?"

"No, what are you going to say, that you love her again? I swear if I have to hear that one more time." Benjamin splashed his hand into the water. "What—are you going to ask her to go to the city with *you* now? Are you going to live with her on the mountain? What's your plan, you always have a plan, right?"

"That's what I tried to tell you last night, I have no plan. I love her. And I don't know if I'm the right guy or right friend or even the right brother, but I had to tell you."

"It must be serious if Edmund Hawkes doesn't have a plan. Did you hear that world? Edmund Hawkes, the big brother of Benny, the heir to the Hawkes family fortune, the driver of the truck, the lover of the girl, on this day he doesn't have a plan!" A couple of other surfers paddled in the opposite direction.

Edmund said, "That's starting to sting little Brother."

"Good."

Edmund paddled back to shore. He sat on the beach trying to wrap his head around his problem. He tossed seashells and tried to think it all through, but was absolutely so jangled that he couldn't straighten his mind. He wanted to punch a wall. He threw another shell. It didn't help him get his aggression out. He also felt guilty as hell. If Benjamin was this furious because Edmund loved Violet, imagine his fury if he found out what happened last night.

Another surfer joined him and asked, "Are you sitting this one out?"

How could Edmund sit on the beach chatting while Benjamin suffered and sulked silently? He couldn't. He replied with a half-smile and a grunt. The surfer stood with his shadow blanketing Edmund. A claustrophobic Edmund. "You and your brother are staying at the campground?"

Edmund said, "Yes, we are."

"You guys are hanging around with Princess Violet, huh?"

Edmund wanted to punch the guy for no reason, but instead said, "I ought to tell him it's time to go."

"Sure okay." The surfer walked away.

Edmund paddled back out, and, because he didn't want to be a liar, paddled to his brother's position in the lineup. Then he sat. He waited Benjamin out. Benjamin was a talker, he would have to, eventually. And forgiveness would have to come soon after that. He was angry, but if Edmund let him have his say the anger would burn quicker. Edmund sat and counted waves while Benjamin paddled and huffed and refused to speak. Benjamin's nonspeaking was noisy and frenetic and obviously difficult. Edmund was better at not speaking because of practice.

Finally Benjamin looked over the beach to the north and asked, "Has anything happened between you two?"

Edmund said, "Yes."

Benjamin stroked away.

CHAPTER TWENTY-ONE
Kind of disconcerting

Violet went to bed exhausted and fell asleep within seconds. The next morning, way earlier than usual, her eyes blinked open and wide awake. "Oh man," she said. "Oh *man*." She flung her covers wide and lay spread-eagled on her bed. "Wow. Edmund huh? Whoa."

She bounded out of bed humming one of the Neil Diamond songs from the day before, and then stopped. *Get a hold of yourself.*

As she placed her hand on the doorknob to her room she remembered Edmund pushing the door closed and kissing her up against the wall. A shiver traveled down her whole body. She put her forehead against the door for balance. *Remain calm, it's only Edmund. He's departing any day now, headed to distant lands, and that will be the end. He was fun. Enjoy that moment and keep it normal.*

She pulled the door open and as she walked down the hall said, "Good morning!" causing a coffee spill and about scaring Lala out of her wits.

Lala had been reading and waiting to hear Violet plop to the floor like she had every morning for like a thousand days. "What are you doing up?"

"Getting a start on my day." Violet said like it was the most normal thing in the world. She was humming.

Lala squinted her eyes. "It's 9 am. You usually sleep until noon, sometimes later. And I get a dollar a morning for waking you up."

Violet filled a coffee cup with half milk, two teaspoons of sugar, one teaspoon of cinnamon, nutmeg, and a dash of coffee. She reached in the drawer, pulled out fifty cents, dropped it in Lala's palm, and sat down. "So what's on the docket today?"

"Um," Lala still looked suspicious as she pulled the notebook open, "it looks like we have a truckload of curriculum coming from Aunt Bethany. She said the school system is changing to a computer storage system and she'll need to eventually scan everything, but until then she wants to store it here. There's tons and tons."

"What time are we expecting the truck to arrive?"

"Probably noon."

"Good the boys will be able to help."

"The boys? You sound almost breathless, the *boys?* Are you okay? You seem really upbeat. It's kind of disconcerting."

"No, it's just good to have them around. They give me a new perspective. It's a welcome change to our normal———"

Part 2
SLiDiNG

CHAPTER TWENTY-TWO
Don't want to leave

Edmund watched from his surfboard as Benjamin stalked up the beach to the campsite. He gave him some time, and then followed and found Benjamin slumped in one of the camp chairs glowering. Edmund leaned his board against the truck.

Benjamin finally said, "Mom called. She said for you to call her. It's an emergency."

"What—an emergency? What did she say?"

"She didn't want to talk to me. She wanted to talk to you."

Edmund walked to the next empty campsite to return their mother's call. She picked up on the first ring and said, "Edmund I'm so glad you're in. How's the city?"

Edmund ran his hand down his face. "Fine."

"We have a problem here and your father and I need you to come home."

"Mom, I can't, I..." He looked over his shoulder at his furious brother and turned back toward the woods.

"We wouldn't ask you to come back unless it was an emergency."

"What happened?"

"Your father's lawyers are up to no good. There's a mess of the accounts, piles of futures are upside down, or something. I don't understand these things, and your father and I can't really deal with this right now—the Bed and Breakfast just opened, and we leave for Fiji tomorrow."

"Mom, how can you open a Bed and Breakfast and then go on vacation? People don't do that."

"Well, first of all, how do you know what people do? Second of all, we deserve a vacation. Your father and I have worked very hard. And third, Bed and Breakfast owners have to go on Spy-cations and see how other B&Bs run. It's good business sense. I fear though, Honey, that all the money is at risk.

"All the money? *All* the money?"

"That's why it's an emergency. I'll have Johnson pick you up at the airport. Just call us once you've bought your ticket."

"Mom, what do you and Dad expect me to do?"

"You need to go through the books with Anderson and Silvers and run the B&B. None of your father's lawyers understand how. They're frankly incompetent about such things."

"Mom, they're lawyers, not hotel managers. No one you employ is a hotel manager, so why on earth did you open a hotel?"

"It was our dream Edmund. You can't argue with a dream. We'll be back in a few weeks, and we can meet and go over everything."

Edmund stood shocked looking at his phone, not really understanding anything but that his livelihood was disappearing, and his parents were insane.

She continued, "I'm sure you'll figure this out, dear. If you want to stay here, call Claudia, she'll put you down for a room. Johnson expects you tomorrow!" The phone clicked from her end.

Edmund held the phone to his side looked up at the sky and yelled, "AAARRRRGGGHHH! This sucks, this fucking sucks! They kick me out, they send me away, and now—how long has it been, two weeks—they call me back and want me to fix things? How the hell did they break everything in two weeks?

"I told them I wanted to work for them, but they wouldn't let me. And now I'm at the beach and I have to get there tomorrow and put it all back together?" He kicked the sand and sent a puff flying. "Dammit. DAMMIT." He crossed his arms and stared at the ground.

"I have to go. I have to go and figure this out. Those people will run the company and the money into the ground, and Benjamin and I will have nothing."

He traced his toe through the sand. "Anderson and Silvers are good men, they'll help me figure it out. I just have to meet with them." He sighed deeply and kicked the dirt again.

He would give them five days and be gone before his parents returned from their stupid vacation. He would fix it and then come right back—would it be okay to leave Benjamin here with Violet? Would he want to come or stay or head on to the city? He looked over at his brother, sitting on a chair, staring at his phone, ignoring Edmund on purpose. Fine, Edmund would go by himself.

He stood at the edge of the trees in a campsite on the edge of a town on the edge of a continent and found and bought an airline ticket online, and then called for a local car service to take him to the airport. Then he went back to the campsite to tell Benjamin he was leaving and ask him what he wanted to do.

* * *

"Ben?"

No answer.

"Ben?"

"Yep?" He looked at Edmund, his eyes brimming with contempt.

Edmund felt his anger rise—there had been an 'emergency,' and Benjamin wasn't even curious, much less alarmed? "I can see you're desperate about what the emergency is with Mom and Dad."

"I'd like to know. I would appreciate Mom and Dad telling me directly though."

He had a point. Edmund took a deep breath. "Mom says the bank accounts are messed up, the money is at risk, there's no one to run the B&B, and she and Dad are leaving for vacation in Fiji tomorrow."

"Mom and Dad are going to Fiji? They hate surfing. Why are they going to one of the best surf spots in the world? Yeesh."

"This is not the vexing point. It's not even the point at all. The point is our money is disappearing and no one is there to run Mom and Dad's stupid B&B. I have to go. Mom said I have to be there tomorrow. I have to meet with the lawyers about the money and run the B&B while they're gone."

"Living the dream, huh?"

"No, not. I don't want to leave. At all, but I have to. It's our money at stake."

"A few days ago you didn't want your money."

"I was angry. It's ours, I can't watch it get squandered. I should do something good with it, like you said. I don't want to leave though."

"You don't want to leave *her.*" Benjamin said it like a statement, a contemptuous angry charge.

"Yes, and you and our adventure—what is that noise?" A low rumble shook the earth where Edmund stood.

Benjamin jumped from his chair. "Whoa."

The rumble continued for a second, rising to a roar, and then the sound of metal screeching and more vibration.

"An earthquake?" asked Benjamin.

"Oh God, the MOUNTAIN!" Edmund ran to the street with Benjamin shadowing a step behind. They sprinted out of the tree-shrouded campground and five strides up the sidewalk before pulling short. People were emerging from the businesses, filling Main Beach Road—stressed, worried, confused—turning toward the mountain.

A quarter of the north side of the mountain was in the process of slicing off, or rather sliding off, and avalanching down and away. It was only possible to see portions of the action because a gigantic cloud of dust obscured the whole.

Edmund yelled, "Violet!" as he and Benjamin raced forward, shoving through the gawkers and halfway up the store-lined street before another rumble, and more of the mountain rushed away from it's normal position. A larger cloud of dust rose to the air. People in the gathering screamed.

Edmund screeched to a stop and for a second stood in indecision—running to the mountain or turning back for the truck?

Benjamin panted, out of breath. "We should get the truck, it's a mile or so." The brothers pushed back through the crowd, shoving and excuse-me-ing to the campground.

"Dammit dammit dammit," said Edmund as he started the truck and reversed it out of the campground and then crept up the street through the gathering crowd. "Get out of the way!" he growled.

Benjamin waved his arm out the window. People were so intent on the disaster they had lost all reason, meandering in the road as they watched the town's mountain fall.

Benjamin said, "They might be in the condor basket planning to meet us in the parking lot."

"They were still asleep, you know it, I know it."

They left the crowd behind and drove up the straightaway. The whole northwest quadrant had fallen off the mountain. The platform that made up the enormous plateaued-roof hung over the shorn side, curving downward, succumbing to the perilous drop. Of the whirligigs, one of the biggest, Violet's favorite, had fallen down with the mountainside, three leaned at perilous angles, and at least two others farther from the landslide were broken and dangling parts.

Benjamin, with a hand on the door and a hand on the glove compartment, craned out the window "Edmund, the sculptures are—"

"I see them." Edmund picked up speed.

Edmund whipped the truck around the corner and two hundred feet further squealed to a stop. The mountain had fallen on top of the road. An impasse of refrigerators and chairs and mattresses lay scattered all across their usual route. Edmund said, "No no no no no oh no oh no."

Benjamin asked, "What about the southern curve?"

"There's no road and a huge sand dune. We have to go around this pile. The sand looks packed enough, right?" He nosed the truck off the pavement into the sand and inched forward. The truck drove and slid until they came to the physical end of the stuff-slide and then Edmund turned the wheel and the truck sank into sand.

Edmund beat the heel of his hands on the steering wheel. It hurt like hell, but brought a modicum of sense back to his swirling panic.

Without saying a word they simultaneously jumped from the truck, and Edmund grabbed their camping shovel. Edmund dug out one wheel and then passed it to Benjamin who dug out the other, and then they sprinted to the front and back into their seats.

They each kept their doors open with an arm, watching the back wheels as Edmund pushed the gas and the truck mermaid-tailed through the sand, back and forth and barely forward, until finally the wheels reached traction.

Benjamin yelled, "Go go go go go go go!" He and Edmund slammed their doors and drove around the farthest point of the slide. Past appliances and televisions and mattresses, half-submerged in sand, and scattered around.

Benjamin craned again. "Almost all of this side is down."

They reached the fence and drove through the surrounding sand and the fence's outer point and sped to Violet's parking lot, screeching to a stop and jumping out of the truck. They both cupped their hands around their mouths and yelled, "Violet! Lala! Violet!"

The condor basket was parked up at the family's level. Edmund rushed to the cab and searched for the keys, looking under the floor mat and between the seats, but they weren't there.

He spun, ran to the dump truck's cab, grabbed a tire-iron out of a toolbox, and whaled and banged on a bulldozer while they both yelled for Violet and Lala at the top of their lungs.

They listened for a moment. "Do you hear anything, see anything?" Benjamin scanned the family's patio level for any sign of life.

"We have to get up there. The only thing I can think of is the condor. That's the only way up."

Benjamin ran to its cab and rechecked the seats and compartments for the keys.

"We could climb, but how safe is any of it now, a sizable portion of it's been dislodged, violently. We could get crushed."

Edmund banged on the bulldozer again, clangcrashbang, clangcrashbang. "Lala!!!!"

They backed up to try for a better view of the highest levels. And then saw a glimpse of a head near where the patio would be. Edmund yelled, "Lala!"

Benjamin joined in, "Lala!"

Lala, tiny tiny far away Lala, looked over the edge and yelled something incomprehensible.

Edmund and Benjamin yelled, "What?!"

Lala yelled something again, but the wind picked up her words and sailed them away.

Benjamin yelled, "What did you say?" While Edmund looked for the keys to the condor for a third time. He returned to Benjamin in time to see Lala climb off the deck into the condor basket. She was coming down, alone.

As she descended Edmund climbed onto the roof of the cab to meet her. Benjamin was climbing the cab to stand beside his brother when Lala pulled the basket's movement to a stop about thirty feet over their heads. "Edmund go away, she doesn't want to see you!"

Edmund arched back and yelled, "What?"

"She doesn't want to see you, go away!"

"Lala come down here. I need the condor so I can—"

"No! You have to go away!"

He said, "What the hell?" and reached for the arm of the condor and tried to find a foothold to climb it.

Lala jerked the basket to the right nearly flinging him off. He stumbled back and Lala said, "Oh my god, Edmund, are you okay? I didn't mean—Violet told me you can't come up—not to let you come up." She started to cry.

Benjamin and Edmund looked at each other. Benjamin finished his climb and asked, "Lala are you all okay, is Bruce okay?"

"We're okay," she sobbed. "We haven't gotten Bruce out yet, but we can hear him, and Violet is digging—"

Edmund panicked, a roar filled his ears, and he couldn't hear her anymore, *Violet was digging out her father?*

Benjamin said, "Lala let us up, we can help."

Edmund yelled, "Let us up NOW!"

She held up a hand and said, "Hold on." She put a walkie-talkie to her ear and listened, and then the basket began it's slow shuddering noisy glide back up the side of the mountain.

Edmund and Benjamin yelled together, "Lala!!!!"

Edmund tried to climb the arm of the condor again, but there were no holds to grab. He moaned, "Arrrgh!" And then, "Dad would totally be able to climb this." He kicked the base of it for good measure.

Benjamin asked, "How do we get up there?"

"We could use the crane. Check its cab for keys."

Benjamin hurried for the keys while Edmund watched Lala step onto the family's patio leaving the basket empty and totally out of reach. Benjamin yelled, "The keys aren't in here!" He ran to the forklift. The keys were gone from it too. Benjamin spun in a circle and realized the crane had the tallest cab, so he climbed it for a better view by degrees.

Edmund said, "Do you see anything?"

"No, no movement at all."

The brothers stood, waiting, too panicked to breath correctly. Staring up at the edge of the patio waiting for a sign that everyone would be okay.

Ten minutes passed. In the distance they heard sirens. Benjamin reported, "A firetruck, coming from the south."

"Is it a ladder truck?"

"Nope, looks small, probably a first responder."

"Ambulances?" asked Edmund, eyes still on the ledge.

"Not yet."

"There's no way they can get here, the road is impassable."

He sat down on the cab turned away from the mountain to rest his neck.

"Anything?"

"No."

They waited another twenty minutes or so, before Benjamin yelled, "I see—I see—Lala!"

Edmund jumped up and yelled, "Lala! Lala! Lala!" She looked over the edge.

Benjamin said, "I see the top of Bruce's head! Bruce is okay!"

"Where's Violet?"

Benjamin stood on tiptoes and stretched as far as he could and said, "I can't see her."

They both yelled, "Lala! Violet! Bruce!"

Lala stepped back into the condor basket.

Edmund said, "Thank God!"

It neared, closer and closer, so infuriating slow.

At about thirty feet again Lala stopped the basket and peered over, "Edmund, Violet doesn't want to see you, ever again. She said for you to go away. Go AWAY!"

"Why? She has to come down. You have to come down. It's not safe. The mountain is falling. Lala, why?"

"Because this is all your fault! You did this! You took things away, you broke everything!"

Edmund started to climb the arm again. "Lala let me come up there. I have to talk to Violet."

"No!" She jerked the basket, dropping him to the ground. "Go away, you've ruined everything!"

Benjamin said, "Lala, let him talk to Violet, *please*. You guys have to come down from the mountain, you have to."

"And come with you to the city? You think we're little girls you need to save? We were fine until you showed up."

While Benjamin distracted Lala, Edmund managed to climb with pure stress and terror up about ten feet.

"Edmund, no! I'll move the basket, I will. Don't make me!"

"Dammit, Lala." Edmund slid to the roof of the cab. "I just want to talk to her!"

Lala talked on the walkie-talkie for a moment—too long, so Edmund said, "Lala! Let me see her, I have to talk her into coming down!"

Lala said, "Edmund, I'm going to lower the basket and give you the walkie-talkie, but you have to promise not to try to board. Okay?"

"Fine."

"Promise?"

"I promise!"

She lowered the basket about fifteen more feet and said, "Will you catch it?"

Edmund stood for a minute trying to figure out what to do. "Lala, please let me come up."

"She doesn't want to see you Edmund, she *doesn't*. Can you catch the walkie-talkie?"

He had his hands on his hips, so frustrated he wondered if he could bend the arm of the condor with his bare hands. Like King Kong again. Of course then he'd have to climb the mountain anyway, so as plans went it was one of the dumbest. "Yes."

She dropped the walkie-talkie and Edmund caught it in a football hold, two hands.

His fingers shook as he pushed the button. "Violet?" The walkie-talkie squawked.

Her voice was so small, so muffled with interference, that she sounded miles away, on another planet away, another lifetime away. She said, "Go *away* Edmund."

"I can't. You have to come down." Squawk.

"You took the newspapers away. You made me do it."

"Violet you have to come down. It's not safe." Squawk. Benjamin climbed down from the crane and walked over to the condor.

"You broke it. You broke everything. My sculptures, my house. Me."

"I was trying to help."

"You were trying to fix me, like I was wrong." Squawk. "And now look what you've done."

"Violet, I don't want you to die, please come down."

"We all die Edmund, every one of us. Go away."

"You can't do this to Lala, to Bruce. Violet, I can't go away, I love you, don't make me." Benjamin climbed up on the condor and put his hand on his brother's shoulder.

"I never want to see you again." Her voice was calm and quiet. "I hate you."

"Don't, please." The walkie-talkie was silent.

"Violet?"

Silence.

"Violet?"

Benjamin took the walkie-talkie from Edmund's shaking hand. "Violet, this is Benjamin." Silence. More silence. Looming silence.

Edmund asked, "What do I do?"

Lala hovering in her basket said, "Go Edmund. I'll talk her down eventually, but it would be better if you weren't here."

He nodded. "Okay. I get it. Benjamin, is there food in the truck for you, water?"

"There's a little and the water jugs."

Lala jerked the condor basket and said, "Can I come get the walkie-talkie?"

Edmund said, "Yeah." He dropped off the cab of the condor to the ground and stood with his back to the mountain.

"Benjamin, you won't try anything?"

"I won't, but Lala, talk her into coming down. You and Bruce need to come down."

Lala lowered the condor basket and reached Benjamin. He handed the walkie-talkie to her. "It's not safe, the whole side of the mountain fell off. The whirligigs are broken and falling off."

"I know, Violet is up there trying to save them."

Edmund sprang. He didn't have any idea he could, but he scaled the cab in two movements and had his hand on the basket before anyone realized what was happening. Lala jerked the basket to the left and right, and Edmund dropped back to the cab where his brother grabbed him and secured him and kept him from falling off.

"Edmund, you've done enough damage," said Lala coldly as her conveyance sputter-shook up and away, back to the tenuous mountain, and its unsettled negotiations with gravity.

Edmund stood in shock watching it go.

Benjamin asked, "What are you going to do?"

Edmund said, "She's up there trying to fix the sculptures."

"I know, but I think you've done all you can."

"No, I haven't. I should have climbed the mountain. I should have leapt up the side of the mountain. I should have gotten to her before she hated me."

"Whether she hates you or not, we have to get her down."

Edmund nodded and stared at the side of the mountain. The piles of clothes and papers and books and mattresses and lumber and piles of hardware and tools. He stepped forward to focus on the handwriting on a box, it said, "Unmatched socks" and then in a scrawl, "important."

"I'm leaving you the food and the water and the truck. Try to talk her down. Talk her into going to the city, okay? Talk her down."

"Okay, I will."

"I'm leaving in the morning for Mom and Dad's mess. I've got a car coming to take me to the airport. Call me, tell me what's going on."

"I will."

"Okay," he dropped off the condor to the ground.

Benjamin said, "Edmund?"

"Yes?"

"I'm really sorry about all of this."

"Just talk her off the mountain," and Edmund walked away to the north.

CHAPTER TWENTY-THREE
Step back to the crowd

Edmund hiked a sandy, untraversed route. The mountain had slid so far and wide that his path was long and circuitous and surreal. He picked his way around a box of spilled toilet paper rolls, hundreds, and a scattering of keys. He stooped to close the lid on a box containing plastic Christmas ribbons and glitter ornaments. He had forgotten water for himself. The mountain gave him the benefit of shade until he rounded the stuff-slide and the full sun beat down. Beat him down. It was about four in the afternoon. He passed two firefighters in full, heavy, hot gear picking a path around the messy spill. Spacemen on a different sort of planet, sandy, dry, hot, peppered with human-made stuff.

"Are you coming from the mountain?"

"The base of it."

"Do you know how many people are on it?"

"Three, and my brother is in the parking lot at the bottom."

"Are there any injuries? It will take a long time to get an ambulance through, and a while to get a helicopter."

"No, everyone seems okay, but they don't want to leave."

The two firefighters in unison arched their backs and looked up at the mountain.

"They have to leave. It's a deathtrap."

Edmund's stomach lurched.

They parted, and the two firefighters continued on to the parking lot. Edmund walked for another ten minutes until he finally reached a large crowd gathered in the intersection of Coastal Highway and Main Beach Road. The crowd gawked in the midst of two firetrucks, an ambulance, and two police cars forming a roadblock. Another roadblock of emergency vehicles was positioned at the southern entrance to the town. There was no one getting through to the mountain now. Edmund was glad he and Benjamin had gone before the roadblock was set up. Relieved that he had gotten through. Lot of good it did him though, banished as he was.

As Edmund approached, a police officer asked for his driver's license and carried it back to his car to do a cursory background check.

The other police officer pulled out a pad and asked questions. "Where are you coming from?"

Edmund turned and looked up the mountain. The northern edge was overhanging. His heart beat faster at the sight of movement at the top, a half-second of Violet's tiny, faraway head.

The police officer tapped his pad of paper.

"The east side of the mountain. It belongs to my friends, so I went to see if they were okay."

"You made contact with them?"

"Yes."

"Were there any injuries?"

"I don't think so."

"Do they have a way to descend from the mountain?"

"Yes, but they won't."

The police officer spoke into his radio using codes and phrases that were mostly unintelligible. Edmund searched the top of the mountain for another visible sign of Violet.

The other police officer brought Edmund back his license and the two officers spoke in hushed tones.

"Am I free to go?"

"Yes," they said as if he were inconsequential. Which he was. He considered the girl on the mountaintop a friend, he loved her, and he couldn't talk her down. Her life was at risk and he couldn't talk her down. She hated him.

The crowd milled about behind the police cars mesmerized by the insane spectacle before them, whispering, wondering, speculating. An avalanche of stuff was sliding down beside their sleepy beach village. The police were gathered, the media descending. They would be on TV.

A few pointed saying, "There's the Princess Violet." Edmund turned and looked. Violet crawl-walked across the surface of her world.

* * *

Edmund walked up Main Beach Road headed to the campsite, when one of the local surfers, a familiar face, pulled over in a truck. "Do you need a lift?"

"To the campground," Edmund said as he climbed in.

"Sure, I'm Kai. I've seen you out surfing, right?" He looked in the rearview mirror and ducked his head a bit. "That's some crazy business back there, huh? Princess Violet is some kind of nut job." Then to himself he asked, "Why won't she come down?"

Edmund answered, "She's not crazy. It's her home."

"Did you know her mother died there? It's almost like she has a death wish staying on—"

"Let me out here, thanks." Kai barely pulled to the edge of the road before Edmund jumped from the moving car.

He walked the rest of the way to the campground and packed up his things into a backpack, retrieving what he needed for his trip home. Then he hoisted the pack and walked up Main Beach Road toward the mountain again.

He reached the police's roadblock at the intersection and joined the audience watching Violet as she shoved and pulled at one of the whirligig's legs. She donned her welding visor and attached a joint so it didn't hang brokenly but leaned awkwardly.

Edmund dropped his bag and watched as the day lengthened and shadows reached toward the mountain. Another slide hadn't happened (because perhaps the north face had stabilized?) But there wasn't any sense to why. The top of the mountain jutted precariously over the avalanche and it was only a matter of time before gravity got hold and pulled. While Violet was on high.

Edmund phoned Benjamin. "Hi, what's happening?"

"Not good. Lala won't come back to the edge now that the firemen talked to her. They demanded she come down, and she refused. They left after an hour or so. They told me they were going to work on clearing the roadblock, but they didn't want to unsettle the mountain."

"Are they bringing the ladder?"

"They said that with the potential for slides and the surrounding sand they couldn't, not until they deemed it safe."

"Damn, this is a big problem."

"A mountain of a problem."

The sun began its set. Violet turned and stood. Her audience pointed and stilled as the red light glowed and reflected off her body and her sculptures on top of the gleaming glinting mountain.

Benjamin asked, "Edmund? Edmund? Where are you?"

"I'm on the other side of the mountain watching Violet say good night to the sun."

"We'll do whatever it takes to get her down, okay? Whatever it takes."

"Yeah. Okay, whatever," said Edmund but he wasn't really listening.

• • •

For a few hours the crowds remained heavy. Once the sun went down the darkness enveloped everyone in the road and accentuated the flashing lights of the police cars and firetrucks and Violet's lone flame burning steel a hundred feet above, and the stars spilled out all across the sky.

A helicopter appeared and circled overhead shining a light on the figure of Violet. After a few moments of circling the pilot transmitted a message: Please leave the mountain. The mountain is unsafe. Exit promptly. Please leave the mountain. The mountain is unsafe.

Edmund phoned Benjamin again, "Violet isn't leaving."

Benjamin said, "I don't see Lala or Bruce either. I think they plan to stay up there all night."

After a dozen or so circles the helicopter swooped back north in the direction it had come. Panic and anger flooded Edmund's body. The helicopter had seemed like a good idea, a plan, a Doing-Something-to-Stop-the-Madness plan. Now it was leaving? He shoved through the crowd to the police cars. "Where's it going? Why did it leave?"

Because of his tone an officer said, "Sir I'm going to have to ask you to calm down and step away from the roadblock."

"I'm friends with the people on the hill. Why did the helicopter leave?"

"The helicopter pilot was concerned the wind from the propellors would destabilize the mountain. You know, if you want to help, you could talk them into coming down. Other than that you need to step back to the crowd, and let us do our jobs."

Edmund stepped back. He and the crowd watched the Princess Violet try to make her castle stand again, but as the night wore on most of the citizens of Sandy Shores wandered home. Late at night Edmund was mostly alone—except for two police cars, a firetruck, and the ambulance, waiting for what might come crashing down.

Edmund slept on the side of the road, head on his backpack, jacket pulled around his body. He woke up to an alarm on his phone and for a minute in the dark, thought that the whole problem had been solved. He jumped up and scanned the top for Violet. She wasn't there. Violet was no longer on the mountain top, yet everything else remained the same, the lights, the dark, the mountain. Oh God, did she go inside? To sleep in her bed?

He willed the mountain to stay standing. He begged the mountain. He wished he had remembered to say good night to the sun so he could make the day be what he needed.

He passed through the emergency vehicles. Using a polite and deferential tone he asked the police, "What will happen to the people on the mountain? What's the plan?"

A police officer said, "They'll be forced from the pile. If they don't die first."

Edmund fought back his desire to grab the officer by his collar and shove him up against the police car. Through a clenched jaw he asked, "*How* will they be forced?"

The State will condemn this trash heap, probably in the next day or so. Then we'll sweep in, and they'll leave, or we'll arrest them. We're waiting for the paperwork and the word."

"After they condemn the hill what happens?"

"Bulldozers."

"Oh, okay. Thank you," he said.

"Where are you going?"

"A driver is picking me up on the southern route at dawn."

They allowed him passage through the roadblock, and he walked around the southeastern bend. He called Benjamin, who sounded like he'd been sleeping, although that wasn't a surprise, it was still pitch-black night.

"Hey, how's it going?"

"Sleeping, in the cab of the truck, not much else."

"I'm walking to meet the driver and head to the airport. The police told me they plan to condemn the mountain, and arrest everyone. Then they'll bulldoze the place."

"Violet won't cooperate."

"I know, and her heart will break."

"Yeah."

"It would be a lot better if they came down on their own before they get arrested. Try to talk to her, okay? Or Lala or Bruce, try to convince them."

"Sure, have a good flight."

They hung up, and he turned south. He paused now and then to look back at the mountain, but under the whirligigs no movement could be seen.

About three miles into his walk the sun began its rise. He paused and dropped his bag to the dirt and said, "Good morning, Sun. May I ask a favor, will you watch over Violet today? Maybe cut back on the gravity in her corner of the world? You might have a lot of people to remember, but she's the one that says good night to you every night. Please keep her safe."

This would be the last thing he would do that day for which Violet would think him kind.

He leaned down and picked up his bag as his limousine drove into view.

CHAPTER TWENTY-FOUR
Other arrangements

Edmund climbed into the car and rode south to the airport without once turning around. Violet on her mountain receded behind him. He was leaving her behind, no sense struggling. If he looked, he might balk and reconsider, run back and stand like an idiot staring at her as she fell to her death. Instead he rode forward in the direction of home and the chance to change everything.

He rode to the airport making phone calls. When you have the command of such a large fortune, even when it's merely by proxy while your parents are on vacation, you get to wake people up at dawn and they get to listen to you. He called Johnson, his parent's driver and all around assistant, and organized his ride from the airport.

Johnson asked, "Will I bring you home to see your parents before they leave on their trip?"

Edmund said, "No, I need you to bring me my dark gray suit, and take me to Anderson's office."

Johnson said, "I'll find it, sir, most of your clothes are packed in boxes in the attic." Edmund hated wearing suits and only owned them because he had to, but he didn't like hearing they were packed away. Were they bundled and wrinkled?

Edmund gulped, pushing his anger down. "Johnson, will you make sure it's pressed?"

"Yes, sir, I'll pick you up at 9:15."

Edmund confirmed his meeting with Anderson and Silvers to meet at their Kingsbridge offices when they arrived in the morning, 10:00 am.

He then researched and planned and then sat back in the limo as it slid into the car queue at the airport.

Edmund paid the driver and walked through the airport to his gate. The television screens in every corner covered a recent bombing in the Middle East, but then suddenly they weren't—the story out of Sandy Shores appeared instead—the mountain and Violet and the whirligigs. Edmund walked up to the screen. The camera angle was shot from the air, from a hovering helicopter. In it's sweep he saw a tiny Benjamin in the parking lot, Lala and Bruce on the patio, the chairs, one of them toppled, and then Violet crouched on the upper top of the mountain shimmying up a whirligig's tower to repair its spin. Going, even now, ever higher.

Edmund muttered, "Oh no no no no no, please come down," but she kept going higher as the camera angle spun in a circle. Edmund felt vertiginous, like he might fall down in a heap watching it.

A man in a nearby chair said, "What a nutter."

Edmund's hackles raised, yet he couldn't say a thing; he had used that phrase only days before, and truthfully, a lot of nutty things were happening on that mountain.

The news coverage pointed out that the inhabitants of the manmade mountain and the authorities were at a standoff; it wasn't violent—the people on top of the mountain simply refused to come down—but it was weird and kind of dangerous, and probably would end in death, or a boring surrender, but either way, enjoy the show. People enjoyed gawking from a safe distance. It satisfied their need for fun, watching standoffs on the news. A commercial came on and Edmund's plane began to board.

On the plane Edmund noticed he had sand all over his shoulders and tried to surreptitiously brush it to the floor, all over his bag and shoes. He wondered if the waves were good that day. Had Violet's magic done the trick?

* * *

In the Kingsbridge airport, as he walked through the gates to the baggage claim he checked the television screens as he passed, no coverage of the mountain. Had they taken her down during his two hour flight, or had Violet's manic welding become so boring the media stopped covering it?

Edmund passed a newsstand and bought the newspaper for Sandy Shore's closest city. The editor had placed the story on the front page below the fold. The photo's composition was glorious, an aerial shot of Violet, stilled, caught in time, mid-walk across the mountainous plateau. He saw it vividly in his imagination, the shimmers, the colors, the sunbeam gleams, all conspiring to create magic and mystery.

The readers though probably couldn't comprehend this bland, sort of blurry, black and white photo. How could you see in your mind a hill that big when you've seen a two dimensional version of it? Edmund guessed that a mind wouldn't grasp it, couldn't grasp the enormity of it all. Violet was a nutter who lived on a trash pile. That's all they would see, could see.

The story was as black and white as the photo. The pile was big and falling. The girl was stubborn and possibly crazy. The authorities were doing what was right, she was wrong, of course.

Edmund folded the newspaper and put it under his arm. Feeling that he, like the photograph, had lost all color, but unlike the story he had retained his shades of gray. Because the hill was big didn't make her wrong. Edmund had proof of that in his heart.

Johnson met him at the airport. When Edmund climbed into the backseat his suit and a briefcase were waiting for him.

Edmund said, "The briefcase is a nice touch."

"Has everything you need for your meeting." Johnson closed the door and walked around to the driver's seat.

Edmund opened the case. It contained a box of crayons, a pad of construction paper, and a pair of safety scissors. He chuckled as he pulled his suit pants on and then his shirt. He fumbled his tie for a second and remembered fumbling with Violet's boot laces. He closed his eyes and took a deep breath trying to collect himself.

"Johnson, can I use the rear view mirror for a minute? My tie isn't cooperating." By the time they pulled in front of the offices of Anderson and Silvers, no one would be able to tell that Edmund had spent the night lying in the sand under the swinging lights of police cars.

Edmund stared out the window at the imposing building. There was an emergency with his family's money, and he had to summon the courage to walk up the stairs. The girl he loved was in danger, and he had the shakes because he needed to ask his Daddy's lawyers for a favor.

He leaned forward and asked, "Johnson? What do you think of this story?" He passed the folded paper to the driver and let him read it for a moment.

Johnson said, "Ah, the poor girl on the trash heap. I saw it on the news last night. It reminded me of my grandfather, he was a hoarder. The trouble is their stuff is their stuff, and they can't let go. Won't let go."

"What did you do with your grandfather?"

"We forced him to let go. He never forgave us."

Edmund nodded and said, "I'm staying at a nearby hotel tonight, so I won't need a ride."

"You're not staying at the B&B?"

"No, I made other arrangements."

CHAPTER TWENTY-FIVE
It's a good deal

Edmund took a deep breath and walked up the steps. He checked in at the security desk and entered the elevator bank. He had been here before with his father on Introduce-the-Heir-to-the-Office day, but it had always been informal visits and never alone, like this.

The doors opened on the steel and glass walls of the law offices, modern, tasteless, imposing. Edmund told the secretary that he had arrived, and she called him "sir" and buzzed him through immediately. He was a buzz through kind of guy. He could get used to that power. Probably. Benjamin and Lala and Violet seemed to think so. They told him he was a control freak, that he wanted to play boss.

He entered the office and shook hands saying, "Hello Anderson, Silvers." Edmund wasn't a hundred percent sure he got to call the lawyers by their last names, but putting a mister in front of them felt too immature.

These two men had been his grandfather's lawyers and then his father's lawyers Edmund's entire life. Tall, balding Anderson wore good suits. Silvers was gray haired, dumpy, shorter, and his suits didn't fit as well, or his body didn't work as well in a suit. The two men were always suited, even for casual events, like holidays, and family-style parties. They always behaved stiffly and steered conversations to money matters or laws.

Because of their awkward excessively civil and pompous manners, and the fact that they never brought wives to the dinners. Or even dates. Just themselves, together, Edmund and Benjamin always assumed they were gay, and *together*. The two boys had spent a lot of time speculating about it while growing up, mostly because the two lawyers were so boring that being homosexual might make them interesting.

Anderson and Silvers offered Edmund a chair and Anderson said, "We're so glad you came Edmund, there's a problem."

Edmund said, "Mom told me something terrible happened with the money."

The two lawyers exchanged a glance and Silvers cleared his throat and folded his hands in front of his mouth. "We have something to tell you, sir."

Anderson mimicked Silvers, folding his hands in front of his mouth, and said, "We told your parents things that weren't entirely true to have a meeting with you today. We were wondering what you thought about your parents getting in the business of B&Bs?"

Edmund hadn't prepared for this kind of conversation, his thoughts? Okay, he had very specific concerned-style thoughts about the B&B. "They made a terrible decision. One of the worst. I'm concerned with the amount of money they spent, especially considering the current downturn in our fortune."

The two men leaned in and whispered for a minute. Edmund worried he may have gone too far. Was it impolitic to insult his parents in front of their lawyers? But just as he opened his mouth to backpedal, Anderson said, "Sir, to continue with this meeting today we need you to have some abilities. We've prepared a formal transfer of emergency powers. Your parents have signed it in light of their impending, um, B&B Spy-cation."

Silvers pushed a piece of paper and a pen in front of Edmund with his short chubby fingers, one brandishing a gold ring. "We need you to read it and sign the bottom. Take your time."

The two men whispered together and shuffled papers while Edmund read through a stack of papers containing so much legalese he couldn't understand most of it. He ran his fingers through his hair dropping a spew of sand on the table and tried to quickly brush it off.

Anderson asked, "Were the waves good today?"

"I didn't surf this morning, I slept in the sand."

"Ah," said Silvers, giving Anderson a knowing smile, "the follies of youth."

"Folly abounded last night, but my share was completely serious." Edmund tried to steel his nerves. He wanted access to his trusts, but considering the downturn in his family's fortune it might be too much to ask. Plus he didn't want to seem greedy and irresponsible, and ultimately what he planned to do with all of his money, wasn't it irresponsible?

"So what this paper says is, while my parents are in Fiji on their Spy-cation, I, with your advisement and guidance, get to make all the decisions?"

"Yes," Anderson leaned forward and pointed at one particular section, "and that if you learn of secrets in these meetings, you won't share them with other members of the board. There are some big ones." Edmund signed the bottom of the form.

Anderson called in his assistant to have the form filed in triplicate. When the assistant left he said, "Let's begin."

"First," said Edmund, "is the money okay?"

The two men looked at each other. Anderson said, "Can we back up a bit? Your grandfather, our former employer was a wise and very very rich man. He prepared your father to become heir to the estate, but from very early on determined he... um—"

Silvers said, "Was *unprepared* for the job. Your grandfather put into place a series of protections on the estate to keep the money from being squandered on B&Bs and Spy-cations to Fiji."

"Like my Trust."

"Yes, your Trust. Your grandfather's intent was for you to receive it when you were eighteen, but your father had the date extended, as you know."

"To when I'm twenty-one. He decided I wasn't ready."

"He was terribly determined, and we ultimately agreed, because—we are about to indulge a secret, one you mustn't share with your parents."

Edmund nodded. He put his elbows on the arms of his chair and tried to appear relaxed, instead of hunched and panicked.

Silvers continued, "Your grandfather also has a type of Trust, an *allowance* for your parents, and convinced them it was the entirety of the estate. We were given strict orders to conduct meetings with your father at yearly intervals and to give him enough information to believe he conducted the business though he is simply a figurehead with an allowance."

The two men leaned back and regarded at him.

Edmund said, "Seriously? My father doesn't run the family business?"

"No, sir, he does not. Your grandfather wanted you to run it when you came of age. Because of this we were understandably concerned when your parents sent you away.

Anderson concocted a story about declining futures so that your mother would call you back and we could discuss this with you."

Edmund leaned back and laughed.

Silvers asked, "You aren't upset about this?"

"No, I'm not. At all. I've worried for a long time that my parents would bankrupt the family, so I'm relieved there are protections. In fact the first thing on my agenda would be to turn the B&B over to a management company. I researched and found three that I would like you to get proposals from. My parents will be vacationing for quite a while, so I'd like to free them from their uh, responsibilities."

"Yes, sir, we will put that at the top of the list. Edmund, um, sir."

"I'd appreciate it if you'd call me Edmund."

"Here's the thing, we told your mother that the accounts were in disarray, but in actuality there's been a windfall."

"A windfall?" Confused, Edmund asked again, "A *windfall?*"

"Yes, Edmund," Silvers said, "we could get in trouble for our um, selective truth telling, so I hope you will protect our secret."

"What kind of windfall?"

Anderson handed a stack of papers across the table for Edmund to see, corresponding to one he himself had. "Here on page one, the bottom number is the amount of your family's operating budget."

Silvers said, "Commonly."

"Flip through to page three. That number at the top is your parent's perception of the company's operating budget."

"The number on page four is the totality of your trust fund. At present, it grows yearly of course." The number was a third larger than Edmund had expected.

"The last page is the Estate's extra."

The number made Edmund fall back in his chair, "Whoa."

"Whoa is right. Congress is very friendly to banking and market interests right now. Your grandfather had many friends in high places. Friends that he gave large sums of money to. It's paying off handsomely."

"The trouble is there aren't any instructions for what we should do with a windfall of this magnitude, so we need a member of the family to decide where the money should go."

"We would like it to be safe, but ultimately the decision is yours." The two men dropped back and folded their hands. Mirroring each other perfectly.

Edmund asked, "What about real estate? Would real estate be safe enough?"

"We prefer a more lucrative market strategy, but real estate is acceptable. Especially in a place that we've made, ahem, governmental investments." The two men whispered to each other. Anderson said, "With development the investment might grow. Do you have a piece in mind?"

"It's coastal property."

"That's generally a good choice. What real estate company is offering the land?"

"It's not for sale." Edmund opened his briefcase and embarrassed by the crayons, visible to everyone at the table, explained, "Johnson, my parent's driver, playing a joke."

He pulled the newspaper out of the briefcase and handed it to the lawyers. "This is the land I want. It's about to be condemned, then I assume it will be auctioned. I want to buy it before that happens."

"How would we?"

"I met the current owners, I suspect I understand their price. I'd like a letter sent making an offer on the property. The money contingent on the current owners vacating the mountain today."

"I'm not sure, Edmund. This doesn't sound very—"

"The land will be a bargain. Look at where it's located." He pointed at the photo, "See that in the top right corner? That's an idyllic beach town. I believe it's a no-brainer."

"Is this like a B&B? Why this land?"

"It's in front of my favorite point break." Edmund blinked. "Call it the folly of youth."

"What if the family doesn't want to sell to you?"

"I want the deal to be anonymous."

"Okay, what if the family doesn't want to sell, period?"

Edmund dropped back in his chair. "I don't know." What if Violet wouldn't sell? What if Violet wouldn't leave? Edmund had planned only one plan, predicated on the girl that wouldn't leave the mountain, taking money and leaving the mountain.

Silvers said, "Well, I suppose it doesn't hurt to make an offer…"

Edmund asked, "Have you been following the story?"

Silvers said, "We saw the headlines when we were on the train this morning, but no, not really."

"The hill is unstable and there are three people on top. I spoke to law enforcement, and they said the government plans to condemn the property. How does that work?"

"It's tricky business, the state is taking private property from a citizen, no one is ever happy with the outcome."

Anderson interrupted, "Except the developer that buys it after it's been condemned, they're happy with the price. Very happy."

Edmund stared at his hands. He leaned forward about to say something, but then reconsidered, and then said it anyway, "If the family doesn't accept the offer, I want to buy it before, or during, or right after the state condemns it. Do you think that's possible? Did Granddad happen to know the Governor?"

"They were friends."

"Good, can you call him? Would you tell him that if the current owner doesn't accept my offer, we'll give the state an offer by sundown? The offer would be contingent on the current owners being off the mountain by tonight."

Anderson asked, "An intention to buy, to the state?" The lawyers whispered to each other. "This sounds risky, Edmund."

Edmund had to clench his entire body to keep his hands steady. To try to appear stable and not about to fall out of his chair into the fetal position on the floor. "Well, as Anderson said, If the current owner doesn't leave the hill, the governor will have to condemn it. Look at its location. The state condemns a mile or so of property *that* close to the ocean, there will be an auction, the price will be crazy low."

"We recommend waiting for an auction, Edmund."

"But I might not win it in an auction, and it's possible I would end up paying more."

"Who will deal with that pile?"

"Us. It will still be a good deal. Just tell the Governor that your buyer wants the people off by tonight."

Anderson buzzed for his assistant to get the Governor on the phone.

I'm the kind of guy that gets to buzz the Governor, thought Edmund. He loosened his tie because he felt a little strangled.

While the Lawyers conferred with the Governor's office, Edmund stared at his hands.

Then he texted Benjamin: **Anything changed?**

Benjamin texted back: **Talked to L. Freaked out they want to condemn the place. She's crying. Said she would talk to V.**

E: **Have you seen Violet?**

B: **No. Working on sculptures again.**

E: **Have to go. Still in meeting.**

Edmund's feet jiggled, like they wanted to jump up and run around the room, dragging him behind. He was trying to be cool, calm, collected, but had instead developed crazy feet. He put his hand on his knees to still his legs and stared at the lawyers through the conference room windows, willing them to work quickly.

Silvers came back a half hour later. "We explained to Governor Wilson that we were making an offer to the family and that if they didn't accept by 6:00 p.m., we would fax an offer directly to his office. Condemning private land and declaring it the property of the State is politically difficult in our conservative towns, so he's grateful for the escape route. His constituents would much prefer that a private property owner be the reason for unpleasantries, such as removals and arrests."

"Here's the trouble though, if I buy the property, I don't want anyone to die. They need to be off the mountain before any kind of slides, or —"

"The governor said that if he accepts the offer he'll have them off the mountain by nightfall.

"Did you tell him I want to remain anonymous?"

"Definitely." Anderson dismissed Edmund for an early lunch and told him to come back in two hours while they prepared the paperwork.

Edmund shook from hunger but also didn't like the idea of leaving. He wondered if the wheels would stop rolling if he turned his gaze from it, like Violet wondering if she forgot to say goodnight to the sun would the world stop working.

He went to a local deli. One with news channels on every television and a television on in every corner.

The spectacle had grown. There were at least two helicopters and when they swept the surrounding area there were more police cars, a larger road block and at least five media vans. Crowds of people stood all around. More people than the town occupied. "They must have bussed in," Edmund said under his breath.

Edmund sat at a table and ate a sandwich by himself. He wasn't used to doing that, almost always eating with friends, or Benjamin. He felt nauseous whenever he watched the televisions, but bored and lonely when he looked at the empty chair across from him. He wiped his mouth with his napkin and tossed it down.

He checked his phone for the tenth time. No calls from Benjamin. He carried his trash to the can and took a last glance at the television. The video swept over Violet wearing her helmet, welding a sculpture. The view angled over her shoulder and took in the scope of the mountain slide and Edmund realized more of the mountain must have descended. It hadn't stabilized, it had worsened. What would happen if another slide occurred while she remained on her mountain?

Edmund walked slowly back to his lawyers' building. He entered Anderson's office and offered to sit alone while they finished the paperwork in another room.

After another hour, Anderson and Silvers hustled in. "Here's the Plan A offer for the family." Silvers dropped it in front of him with a thud.

Edmund broke out into a sweat. There was too much at stake for his shoddy knowledge of legalese to stand in the way of a deal, but he didn't want to sound like his father. He tried to concentrate on the forms, flipping through every page. He stopped and really analyzed the section that said the current owner had until 6:00 p.m. to accept the offer and vacate the premises. It discussed the government's option to condemn the area and arrest the occupants. It sounded threatening if the deadline wasn't met. *Good.* He hoped it would be enough.

Edmund asked, "Do I need to sign?"

"Sign this one instead, for anonymity." Anderson handed him a copy of the documents and he signed it. The other documents were faxed to Sandy Shores' local lawyer.

"All right, this is the Plan B offer for the Governor. It's half of what you offered the family, but it will become the responsibility of the new owner to clean that mess. Are you sure about this?"

"It's a good deal right? That many acres with a view of the ocean?" Edmund fiddled with the pen, checking its shape and length and girth. "I'll practically own the town. It's a good deal."

Silvers said, "So now we wait to see if the family accepts the offer. Plan B will be sent to the Governor if they don't accept."

"It's big enough right?" asked Edmund. "Plan A will work. They'll take the offer, right?"

"Only an insane person would pass it up, but then again, you kind of want them too, you prefer the price of plan B."

Inside his head Edmund yelled, *I don't prefer the price of plan B, I don't!* He shoved his clasped hands against his mouth to keep his calm.

"You sound nervous Edmund," said Silvers, "big deals are like that. It gets easier. You have to just think of the dollar signs and the bottom line."

"I really want this offer to go through."

"Don't let yourself get emotional about any of it. If you win you win, but a loss is only that, you move on. Why don't you go check in at your hotel, and we'll call you when we hear anything."

* * *

Edmund walked to his hotel needing the distance of six city blocks to work off his frenetic energy. He worried about calling Benjamin and acting natural. So much stood in the way of a casual call—their anger, the distance, the stress and fear of the moment, and finally the plan he had contrived without Benny's knowledge.

He couldn't let Violet or Lala find out that he implemented the offer. Ever. Ever ever ever. Would they recognize the offer as coming from him? He didn't think they could. He had mentioned his family's business, but never the scale of its wealth. But possibly Benjamin had in passing at some point? The lawyer was carrying the offer to Violet. He decided to call Benjamin and work an excuse.

Benjamin picked up immediately. "Another slide happened, a few minutes after we texted last."

"Oh God, did anyone get hurt?"

"No, but it was terrifying. I was sure that was the..." Benjamin's voice trailed off, but Edmund couldn't help him finish the sentence. "Lala immediately came to the edge of the patio and called down that they were okay, but in all this time I still haven't had a glimpse of Violet."

"I've seen her on television when I went to lunch for a few minutes. I've been in meetings since I got here dealing with Mom and Dad's mess."

"Pretty bad, huh?"

"With time I can get it under control, but it will consume most of my energy." That should do it, he had an alibi. "Well, since I'm so far removed keep me in touch about what's going on, okay?"

"Wait, a man just walked in. Hold on—" Benjamin spoke to someone else, "Can I help you?"

"I'm a lawyer, David Adams, from the village. I have paperwork for Bruce and Violet Winslow."

Benjamin came back to Edmund's phone call, "I have to go, there's a lawyer here to talk to Violet." He hung up.

Edmund walked around the block to steel his nerves. Then he went around again.

CHAPTER TWENTY-SIX
Waiting like all of us

Edmund waited in his hotel room watching the clock tick. He lay on his bed slumped in an excessively large bank of hotel pillows alternately searching for news and then something to watch besides the news. Nothing else would hold his attention, but the news from Violet's Mountain was too much to take in.

The camera still swept, and occasionally took in Violet's patio as well. He made out a couple of heads, but not Violet's, hers would stand out. And when was it filmed, live, or earlier in the day? If the videos were live, Violet and Lala and Bruce had to be going crazy with the circling helicopters. It must be maddening.

Benjamin didn't call. Nothing must be happening. Did the lawyer ride up in the condor? Or did he make the offer by bullhorn or hands cupped around his yelling voice, traveling up eight stories of mattresses and appliances and shoes and other bits and sundries?

What was Edmund doing spending a fortune on a pile of trash anyway? Junk. He was as crazy as his parents, his lawyers just hadn't figured it out yet.

He fell asleep for a little bit and woke up disoriented and ashamed. He checked his phone for messages, the voice mails, the texts. Nothing. He had slept almost an hour and now it was 4:30. Time infuriated him with its slow crawl. He checked the twenty-four hour news station. He checked the one in Korean, the one in Spanish. There was no news, all weather. Why did the stations all turn to the same thing at the same time?

He brushed his teeth and ran water over his face and through his hair. Someone on the television said "Sandy Shores" so he stepped back to the TV. This time the view swept over a growing crowd in the parking lot of the mountain. They had walked in, or by the looks of it, ridden off-road cycles and four-wheel drive trucks. Still no ladder truck, sadly. The reporter discussed the pile and the odd collections seen from his vantage. Large stacks of old user manuals and phone books were of particular interest, and he smirked the whole time. *Violet, come down. Come down off the mountain.*

He called Anderson and Silvers, but they hadn't heard anything and assured him that this was normal. That if the family accepted the offer, good, but if they didn't, even better. So don't worry. But he did.

Edmund walked back to the offices, ordering pizza and a soda on the way. Why didn't anyone think to build Kingsbridge by a beach of some kind? He could totally use a surf. Of course he couldn't surf, much less take a shower, he didn't want to miss anything. Violet would come off the mountain. She had to.

Edmund walked up the imposing steps of the building. *Please come down. It's not your stuff, you can walk away. Please, take the offer.*

Anderson showed Edmund into the lounge, sparsely decorated with a leather couch flanked by two leather chairs. He wondered what Bruce the Chair King would think about their matching seats. These were lawyers from the East after all. The chairs were low, wide and uncomfortable, and they matched, though Anderson and Silvers didn't match at all.

Anderson's tall frame was stiff and unsettled in his. In the other, Silvers looked sunken and shorter than before.

Anderson gestured for Edmund to take a seat on the couch. He chose the middle for the symmetry and immediately regretted it. There were no arms, and the back was too low. His only focus—the square coffee table in front of his shins and the gigantic screen TV.

"It's five," Silvers said, "it's not looking good for plan A." He rubbed his chubby palms together with an expression of glee.

Edmund sat in a state of heated perspiration that probably had a tinge of desperate edginess to it. He felt a little hysterical but swallowed it down, and tried to appear calmer than he was.

Anderson said, "David Adams, our lawyer in Sandy Shores, told us he delivered the paperwork but had trouble getting an interview with the owners of the hill. They're completely cut off from communication and seem to be ignoring the media circus all around them. He delivered the papers to a young lady named, Magdala Winslow, at 3:30 p.m. and he's waiting for a response in the parking lot."

"Waiting like all of us for something to happen," said Silvers.

"I don't think the family is planning to accept your offer, Edmund. They've had it for over an hour now. Why they would want to stay on a mound of trash instead of taking the money and running, I'll never understand."

"It's her home." Edmund stared at the phone in the middle of the coffee table, willing it to ring with news.

"We have until six, would you like a drink while we wait?" Edmund shook his head.

Anderson picked up the remote control and flicked through the channels searching for news of Sandy Shores. He and Silvers were cool and calm and taking it in stride. Terrified, Edmund sat alone on the couch wondering if he had any idea what he was doing.

. . .

At 5:30 Edmund asked, "How will they arrest them when they do?"

"We aren't law enforcement, I don't know, but it will be messy. They probably have guns, right? The police will have to be very cautious." Anderson had no idea what he was saying. Silvers got up and left the room. There was only the weather on after all, and nothing happening on any other news channel.

Edmund wished he could leap across the square expanse of empty coffee table and wrestle the remote control out of Anderson's hands. He was sure if he were in charge he would find more news out of Sandy Shores. Something, anything. What about a lighthearted, feel-good story, why not one of those?

Hey, Kids, guess how many tchotchkes are contained in the mountain? Nope. *Hundreds of thousands.* The owner of the mountain, a beautiful girl named Violet, told her Uncle that she loved figurines, and now everyone in her family sends her knickknacks for every holiday and all her birthdays, too. Or, sometimes as a thank you for storing all their crap.

And guess what's hilarious? The beautiful girl realized early on that she didn't even *like* knickknacks. Isn't that a laugh riot? And now she might die in an avalanche of them. And now, back to Live in the Sky coverage...

The drama and excitement of this day had him untethered. He desperately needed a break.

Silvers walked in, "No news from our lawyer in Sandy Shores yet?"

"No."

The screen flashed, "BREAKING NEWS," and showed a shaking, ground-level camera-view over the shoulder of a terrified newscaster. "We're here at the Sandy Shores Standoff, where a large section of the trash mountain has swept down the south side—" An enormous and elemental crashing sound caused the newscaster to duck and run off screen. A moment later she returned, collected herself, and said, "Whoa, did you hear that? The whole earth shook."

She gestured toward the mountain. "It seems like the south side has now begun to avalanche. I can't imagine that it's safe for any living being up on top of this." The video switched to helicopter-view. The hill had collapsed at both ends and the top was small and precarious. Violet clutched onto a leg of one of the few remaining whirligigs.

"Dammit," said Edmund under his breath. "Dammit Violet, I'm trying to help."

The newscaster said, "I spoke with one of the police in charge. They're most concerned with this area right at the top." The camera angle swept up. The top layer of the mountain balanced on a small point, while both ends underneath had fallen away. "It doesn't look good for the family inside—"

The newscaster held her ear as she received new information. The video changed again to the overhead view and the helicopter angle swung around to the eastern side and the family's deck. It focused in on two figures, wrapped in blankets, stepping onto the condor's basket.

Lala and Bruce were leaving the mountain.

The newscaster said, "It appears a couple of the family members are leaving the pile of trash. We're not entirely sure, but there may still be one—yes, reports are that there is one more person refusing to leave the gigantic heap. The Sandy Shores Standoff continues." The screen showed a still photo of the pile with Violet on top. A hastily drawn circle around her proved that she did indeed exist. She did indeed refuse to leave. She did indeed balance precariously. She had become a character in a play-by-play.

Edmund's phone rang. He excused himself, "I need to take this," and walked to the back of the room.

Anderson said without turning, "It doesn't seem like the family is going to make the deadline."

Benjamin's voice through the phone said, "Lala and Bruce are coming down."

"I see them on the news."

Suddenly Benjamin said, "Lala! Bruce!"

Edmund heard Lala crying. "She won't come down. She won't. She refuses."

A loud rumble caused Edmund to turn to the television. The crashing collapsing rumble roared in stereo through the phone and the TV at once. Lala's voice screaming through the phone to his ear and on and on and on.

Benjamin came back on the phone. "They're forcing us away from the pile now. I'll call in a few minutes when I know." Click.

"It's 5:55 p.m.," said Edmund standing near the wall.

Anderson glanced over his shoulder. "She doesn't look like she plans to sign, she's going down with the ship."

Anderson's phone rang. He picked it up, telling them, "It's David Adams."

Edmund sat back down on the couch flanked by the two lawyers in their club chairs. Edmund needed his arm rests. He wasn't in a comfortable brooding position. He was in a

Thrown-Back-Off-Your-Feet, Sinking-into-the-Cushions-Behind-You, Wondering-Where-the-Blast-Came-From-That-Turned-You-Upside-Down kind of position.

At 5:59 Anderson hung up the phone and said, "David Adams spoke to the father, a Mr. Bruce Winslow. He said his daughter owns the land, and she won't leave and she won't sign."

Silvers checked his watch, "It's 6:00 p.m. Deadline time. Yes! Let's send your offer to the Governor's office." Anderson and Silvers were giddy. The land, if the price was accepted, would be an incredibly good deal.

CHAPTER TWENTY-SEVEN
The signed papers

Thirty-eight excruciating minutes passed. Edmund kept his eyes on the TV. The breaking news wouldn't even go to commercial. It was too exciting, the possibility that a young woman might die on top of that pile—the horror, the craziness, the stupidity. What a freak show. He pulled forward toward the TV and hunched over his legs, rolling up into a ball, concentrating all his energy on Violet not dying.

The phone rang, Anderson spoke for a few minutes and then told Edmund, "The Governor accepts the offer. The signed papers are being sent now. As the new owner of the land, what is it you'd like him to do?"

"Anyone still on the pile is on my land and trespassing, if they won't leave…" Edmund ran his fingers through his hair. "Um, they'll have to be arrested. I want it cleared within the hour."

Anderson relayed his message, while Edmund stared blankly at his hands.

CHAPTER TWENTY-EIGHT
Fuzzy dark far away

The helicopters came from the North, two, military-looking, black. The news reporters on the ground were breathless with excitement. The gawking crowds were pushed as far away as possible. They had a better view, but couldn't quite make out Violet up so high. The mountain top balanced upon a pinnacle. Violet remained in the middle. The sun began going down.

The sun was going down. Violet wanted to say good night to the sun. Crap. Why hadn't he thought of that? Of course she would want to say good night to the sun. He should have given her the chance. Maybe if the deadline had been later, after the sun went down, she would have accepted the deal. Maybe. Maybe.

The helicopter video showed her with an arm around the tower of a whirligig, the wind of the helicopters whipping her hair, red sunlight glowing on her face, wind threatening to knock her down.

He wanted to call them back.

I forgot about the sun. She wants to say good night. I forgot. I wasn't thinking.

Rope ladders dropped out of both of the helicopters, and the video feed from the helicopter's view turned off. In case of something traumatic. In case it got messy.

The news reporter on the ground speculated what was happening up high, but no video recounted it, only the sound of choppers and Man-On-the-Ground interviews.

Edmund closed his eyes. *I'm sorry I forgot. I'm sorry I'm sorry I'm sorry. Please don't fight, just go, please. PleasepleaseI'msorry.*

At the top of the mountain there was movement, tiny, barely distinguishable—shadows moving, the tops of heads. The sun almost gone for the night. A reporter's voice said, "We hear that the teams have collected the last remaining resident." The camera focused on the top, at the fuzzy dark far away, ladders hanging from the helicopters. The team raised a bundle into one, a shadow, a dark blob. Was that Violet? Raising into the open maw of a helicopter? After a few minutes the helicopters swept in a circle and headed back to the North.

The reporter came on and said, "The Sandy Shores Standoff is over. The family has been evicted from the pile of trash."

The television showed a final sweeping view of the pile, empty now, though massively covered in trash, empty. Violet believed that she kept her mother's heart inside, yet she was the heart. The heart of the mountain, and without her presence it was just a pile of junk, a falling, sliding, collapsing empty pile of trash. And that was all that remained. He had shifted its contents and caused it to break apart. And the fact was, Edmund was the owner of it all.

CHAPTER TWENTY-NINE
Things going on

Benjamin called. Edmund sent it through to voicemail because Anderson was speaking, congratulating him. "Well done, well done, Edmund. You just bought ocean view property at a massively discounted price! I consider your first day at work quite successful!"

He pumped Edmund's arm, and then Silvers pumped his arm, and they clapped him on the back, and Edmund felt green, totally neon green. Like he would throw up on their leather couches if he didn't go home. Or in lieu of home, the hotel. Because he was homeless, the facts were clear on that too.

"I'm speechless, and super tired," he said, making his way out of the room.

He stopped at the doorway. "It dawned on me that when I left Benjamin he didn't have much money in his account."

"Do you have his bank address?"

"Sure I can make deposits. That's what I've always done."

"We'll put a big chunk of the windfall in your account. You can disperse it to him. We'll do it tomorrow early."

"Thank you, Anderson."

He shook their hands again and walked to the elevators.

Once the doors closed he slumped up against the wall. Eyes closed. *I'msorryI'msorryI'msorry.*

Edmund gathered himself to walk across the lobby to the doors just as his brother called. Benjamin began speaking immediately, "They arrested Violet. They're taking her to the city."

Edmund stepped stepped stepped stepped stepped to the hotel. "I saw."

"I have Lala and Bruce. We need to stay at a hotel here tonight, but will go to the city tomorrow."

"Good plan. I'll add money to your account, for hotels and food and you know, things."

"When will you meet us?"

Step step step step. "I don't know." Step step. "I have more meetings scheduled... all the rest of the week and things going on and the B&B and..."

"Okay."

"Just let me know what's happening. If you need any help. Let me know."

"Okay."

"I'll talk to you."

And step by step by step by step Edmund walked to the hotel.

He took a shower, the most grateful relief, the best shower he ever had. He needed to not only wash the sand, the dirt, the day's events, the travel, but also the stink, the filth, the inscrutable motives, and the possibly murky ethics of what he had just done. It was all over him. His lies. He was a leaden, heavy, clean on the outside, asshole. There was no getting around it. What kind of guy does that? What kind of guy?

He stepped into a white robe and rubbed a towel over his head and climbed into bed. Starving, but sleepy. What sucked is like almost everything in his life, what he really wanted was

clean and easy and perfect and not messy at all, but the bed
was covered in sand.

CHAPTER THIRTY
The mess here

The following morning Edmund let the phone go to voicemail and then immediately listened to Benjamin's message: "Lala and Bruce and I are packed and headed north to the city. We should be there by this evening. Talk to you soon, call me when you aren't in meetings anymore."

He met Silvers in Anderson's office. Silvers advised, "Emergency crews have created an access route in and out of town for the residents of Sandy Shores, but the pile has created a massive road block, astonishingly big. Your development company will need to clear the roads, first thing."

He showed Edmund photos of the pile and the spill, from the ground and the air. "Oomph," said Edmund.

"We'll send in bulldozers. The governor has arranged dumping rights for you at the municipal dump, but it's going to be a big effort."

Edmund said, "The most important thing is to secure the hill. I don't want anyone getting too close, climbing on it or around."

"Here's the name of some construction companies. It's a big contract, I'll ask them for bids."

Edmund said, "Sounds good. Thank you. Will you call me once you have them?"

"Where will you be staying, Edmund?"

"At the Grand Suites hotel down the street, while we organize all of this."

"At the hotel? Where's Benjamin?"

"He's in the city, seeking his fortune."

"You don't plan to meet him there?"

"Not anytime soon, I have this to do right now. I want to focus."

And just like that Edmund had a full day free and no one to spend it with. He walked to the park and around and wished for a beach of some kind. Though it wouldn't matter, his surfboards were now on top of his truck headed to the city with his brother and much of his money and yes, his heart as well.

＊ ＊ ＊

Edmund was sitting on a park bench staring at dog-walkers when Benjamin texted:

We're getting close to the city. Bruce spoke with the police. Violet's first day in court is tomorrow at 10.

Edmund found a list of three lawyers and sent it to Benjamin.

Tell Lala to call these and pick a lawyer for Violet. You have money in your account.

Benjamin texted back:

Thanks!

Of course, Benjamin assumed Edmund was in a meeting instead being bored, incredibly bored.

Nothing happened that day. Nothing at all.

Benjamin texted Edmund:

We checked into rooms in the city. Lala has a lawyer on retainer. We're all meeting at the courthouse tomorrow morning.

Edmund texted back:

Sounds good. Gotta go to sleep, been busy today.

He stayed up watching TV for three more hours.

* * *

At Anderson's office the next morning Edmund received three bids for the construction work. Two of them were cheap, one of them offered to get the fences up and the roads cleared in half the time. He chose that one.

The wheels were finally in motion for the second half of his plan. The crew said they would have the fences up by the end of the following week. Edmund wished it would go faster, he worried that Violet was a climb risk when she got out on bail.

Edmund pretended to be interested in choosing the management company for his parent's B&B. He asked Anderson, "Will the money come out of the company's operating budget, or my parent's portion?"

Anderson answered, "Your parent's portion."

Edmund chose the most expensive bid.

* * *

At noon, when he dined at the Deli again, and they greeted him with a familiar hello, Benjamin called. Edmund picked up third ring.

"I saw her," said Benjamin.

"How was she?"

"She's pissed. Some assclown bought it, the land, the pile, everything on it. She's so mad, she would kill him if she was in the same room. We'd have a murder trial instead of a civil trial."

Edmund gulped, wiped his fingers on a napkin, and ran his fingers through his hair. "What are the charges?"

"Public endangerment, a bunch of trumped up fines. The lawyer said the new owner will probably want her family to pay for the clean up. I thought she would leap across the table and strangle him. I swear I thought I might need to ask them to handcuff her."

"When will she get out of jail?"

"Depends on if the new owner presses charges, and how much bail is set for, but I tell you Brother, I worry she'll hitchhike back to the hill. She's just so angry."

"Tell her lawyer if you think she's a flight risk. He ought to know the risks if they ask the judge for bail."

"She'll be so furious at me if I do."

"Yeah, but it's your money. You're paying the lawyer right?"

"Well, technically you."

"It's your account. I'm dealing with the mess here. I have nothing to do with it."

"Sure, well, I made it to the city."

"Yes, you did. Look, I have to go, Anderson wants me in another meeting."

Benjamin hung up and Edmund sat for a while with his head in his hands.

CHAPTER THIRTY-ONE
New circumstances

Edmund spent the afternoon at a department store and bought toiletries, two more dress shirts, and a tie. He bought more underwear, jogging shoes, and a couple of exercise outfits for his new non-surfing regimen. He located a tailor and scheduled a fitting for the next day. He went back to his hotel room, and fully unpacked his backpack, dropping his old clothes to the floor and kicking them under the bed. He carefully folded his new shirts and ties and put them in the hotel room's drawer. It all looked meticulous. Like his idea of a businessman's life, how that would look.

He closed the drawer and called Anderson, and told him he wanted the construction company to start running a security patrol that night. "Looters," was the reason he gave.

• • •

The next day, a tailor fitted Edmund for three new suits, in the latest style. They looked good on him. He also looked older, more important. Kind of boring. Like the kind of guy who worked in an office. He had wanted to be the boss of his company for a long time—but the-surfing-and-appearing-occasionally-at-board-meetings version. Not this man—The Hotel-Sleeping, Office-Meeting, Alone-Eating Man. Sitting-On-A-Park-Bench-Because-He-Had-Nowhere-Else-To-Go-

Man. But he slowly adapted to his new circumstances. Life had pointed in a new direction, and he had stepped onto the path. Edmund couldn't turn back. He could only buy suits, and play the part.

The rest of his day stretched long and boring. The lawyers handled almost everything for him making him Useless-Man too. Edmund met with Anderson and Silvers in the afternoon and then ate dinner and watched TV in his room.

Benjamin called around 8:00 p.m. "She's out! We picked her up. We're eating at a restaurant—the guy who owns the property said he wouldn't press charges, so they let her go, and there's just fines to pay."

Edmund stood and leaned against the room's entry wall. "That's really great. How is she?"

Benjamin said, "She's upset and freaked out. Clouded over. I think sad and angry is understandable though."

"Did she—"

"I have to go Brother. The food is coming to our table now. Do you think you can come soon?"

"I'm not sure. Hey, where are you guys stay—"

The phone connection was already dead, but to be sure Edmund stared at it for a few minutes trying to make sense of the thing.

He could picture Violet in the strangest of places—dressed in her boots at the top of a mountain of stuff, welding whirligigs, purple hardhat gleaming in the light of the moon, red glowing sunlight as she wished the sun good night. He saw her lifting refrigerator boxes, shifting stacks, driving heavy machinery. These were the visuals. He even had a special one of the pub in Sandy Shores, a moment on the beach, a conversation around a fire, and naked on her bed. These things were her places.

Now she had been in a jail, in a city, had eaten in a strange restaurant, checked into a different hotel. He had only known her for a week, but missed her so much he wondered if a part of his self had gone missing.

His normal self was an organized self, highly controlled. But his shelves now had a gaping space where memories of Violet used to reside. He read along the bindings looking for the missing album, barely a week old, a thin book, but it was no longer there, had tumbled out and down, scattering memories in a messy heap on the ground, unorganized and unrecognizable and incomprehensible. He needed to clean up the mess, but all he could manage was to sit and stare at that empty space.

* * *

The following evening Benjamin called and said, "Hey Edmund, I found a second to step away and call you."

"Good," said Edmund, though why did Benjamin step away? Did talking to Edmund constitute a big deal, a thing to hide? "What did you guys do today?"

"We tried to keep Violet's mind off home. We did some sightseeing. Lala and Violet plan to go shopping tomorrow while I search for an apartment, a three bedroom, not permanently, but until we figure out what to do next."

"You'll live with them?"

"I think so, for now."

Edmund closed his eyes, to concentrate on the in-betweens. "Look for an apartment that's west-facing."

"Edmund, I know you have feelings for Violet, and it was rough between us before you left. I feel really bad about it all." Benjamin's voice sounded far away and echoey. An apology from outer space. Not really helpful at all because of its lack of proximity.

"Sometimes things don't work out. She and I weren't meant..." Edmund's voice trailed off. "Can you tell everyone I said hello?"

"Of course, Lala and Bruce ask about you every day. What should I tell them you're doing?"

"Benjamin? Ben—" Edmund pretended that his phone went dead to get out of the conversation. It wasn't very adult-like, but totally necessary at the time.

The next three days Edmund didn't answer his phone.

CHAPTER THIRTY-TWO
Better things to do

The construction company had a full security detail in place. They had erected the fence, or most of it, except for an open area in a big sand dune to the south, and that would be fenced within the week. The bulldozers were clearing debris on the north side, the part covering the road.

Edmund gave them instructions to sweep the debris—the appliances, the televisions, the mattresses, the things big enough to constitute property, and that were a pain in the ass to move—to cordoned off areas on the eastern side of the land. Doors and mattresses and wooden pallets and metal sheeting, tarps and linoleum and rolls of unused carpeting, were given to Habitat for Humanity; one of the biggest scores they had ever received. All the trash—the albums, the books, the things exposed to water and rain and wind and sun, and the paper, the reams and reams of paper, were photographed and sent to a recycling center or dumped in a landfill miles away.

* * *

September 22 was Edmund's birthday. He almost forgot about it, except Anderson and Silvers asked what he would be doing to celebrate, because they had assistants to help them remember those kinds of things. Then Benjamin called and wanted to ship his surfboards to him, saying, "You're the guy who has everything but your *surfboards*. So that's what I want to send you for your birthday."

Edmund gazed around his living quarters—a small room, in a landlocked hotel, in a life that didn't go to the beach. Just because. If he didn't have his boards, he had an excuse not to go surfing. He needed that excuse. If they were leaned in the corner of his room they would beg to be surfed. He'd have to go, and he couldn't. Or wouldn't. It was all the same.

"Benny I need you to hold onto them for a little longer. Things are busy here and I'm not even sure where I'll be—"

"I could send them home, to the B&B, and you'd have them."

"Just hold onto them."

"Okay but that was my best birthday idea. You should hear what Lala wants to get you."

"Coffee of the month club?" asked Edmund.

"She wants to buy you a hat, like the Cat in the Hat, like you wore the last—"

"Glad you talked her out of that one." Edmund forced a laugh.

"Well, I still have a few days, but if it's late don't blame me. What about a plane ticket to come visit?"

"Benny-boy when I get a few days I'll come. You know that."

"Sure sure, okay, talk to you next week."

The day of his birthday came and went. The next day Johnson called and said a box had been delivered to the B&B, and would Edmund like it brought to Kingsbridge?

Edmund took the box to his room to open, using the bed as a work surface, and peeling the tape, because he had no tools or even keys to use. A second box rested inside the first and an envelope. The card's front was a picture of a hippo carrying a surfboard under its arm. Inside it read, "Hippo Birthday!" signed, Benjamin, Bruce, Lala and Violet.

On closer inspection though the signatures were all written in the same hand, a girl's writing. Probably Lala's. He opened the box. They had bought him a mountable, waterproof, adventure camera. For filming his adventures.

Photos of hot young adults adorned the camera's box. They hugged and laughed, filming themselves hang-gliding, creating videos to share, to watch together and laugh about later. Edmund shoved the box under his bed beside his backpack and his surf clothes, the leftover things from his fortune-seeking adventures. Relics from an earlier person. It was thoughtful, but clearly intended for someone else.

* * *

When the construction company started working on the pile they took off layers with the crane and condors. The men had to use harnesses because of the shifting surface, the difficult, dangerous work. Edmund's instructions were simple, throw it away if it's trash, store it if it's not, but the construction company still asked for instructions daily: Paperwork marked super important and dated ten years ago, keep or trash? Should we keep the bags and bags of beaded necklaces? Taxidermied otter?

Some days Edmund made so many small decisions— whether things should be saved or trashed, that for hours afterwards he couldn't do anything besides sit and stare. Keep or throw away these antique birthday cards? What about the film cans marked 1966? Keep or destroy? It exhausted Edmund being the god of all these things.

These arrangements were against the advisement of his lawyers. Anderson and Silvers did not recommend keeping, storing, or sorting any of the things that made up the hill. Edmund though wondered, *What if it's important?*

Whenever Anderson and Silvers questioned his business savvy, he would remind them of the great price he got the land for. He had cut an amazing deal. It won him a lot of leeway making decisions.

* * *

The holiday season arrived. Anderson and Silvers invited Edmund to come to Anderson's house for Thanksgiving, but he claimed to be busy. It had become his default phrase, "I have too much to do," or "I have someone to see that day," or, "I already have plans." He wore the badge of too busy as a deflecting armor, protecting his soft underbelly. The one that wanted to stay in bed under the covers and not talk to anyone, about anything, anymore.

Benjamin called, "I had planned to come home for Christmas, but now—it's not looking like I can get away."

"Oh, yeah, well I'm not sure how much time I would have anyway—and Mom and Dad are in Estonia or someplace." Edmund was relieved he wouldn't have to make too many excuses, but also sullen and pissed that his brother wouldn't even make the time to come. "How's everyone doing?"

"That's just it, they're not doing so well. I mean, I think the holidays are just really hard."

"Yes, I suppose they are."

"I mean when you've lost everything—Lala is bummed, her parents are still traveling around the world. Did you know they only send occasional letters?"

"Kind of like ours."

"Sure, but we don't let it bother us. We have better things to do."

"How's Bruce?" asked Edmund really wondering about Violet.

"He's the same, keeps to himself, unless he's talking about his latest book find. Then he wanders around the house talking to whoever will listen. This is normal for him though, what we're used to dealing with. Violet seems really sad."

Edmund closed his eyes. Benjamin was mentioning Violet for the first time in a long time. His updates had stopped, and instead he said, "We," meaning himself, Lala, Bruce, and Violet, but covering the fact that he meant "Violet." As if "we" translated better than "me and my roommates" or better than "me and the girl that you love and her family." But really "we" wasn't better at all.

Edmund didn't want to spook Benjamin, wanted him to keep talking about Violet, wanted him to think the subject matter safe, so he said, "Um hmm." It was the best he could do.

Benjamin said, "She wishes she had her tree ornaments and stockings and her mother's china. It's all *things*, but she really misses being home. She spends almost all of her time in the studio, barely comes home to eat."

"I'm sure it must be hard."

Edmund throttled his desire to bang the phone against the wall. How unfair that his brother was intimate with Violet's feelings. *She confided in him.* How fucking unfair. Edmund listened and wished and wondered if somehow he could set the past months aside, and just show up in the city. *Okay I'm all done now. Let's Christmas party!* Instead of celebrating by himself in a stupid hotel room in Kingsbridge.

"Yes, it is, that's why I think I better stay and help hold it all together."

"Of course, spread cheer for me."

Edmund spent the evening in the gym. Lifting heavy things required concentration and made him feel a bit better. Lift, pull, punch, run.

For Christmas he told the lawyers that he had plans with Benjamin in the city. The lies flowed easily now.

CHAPTER THIRTY-THREE
I'll come

Over five months had passed since the avalanche. Benjamin called. This was noticeably different—they only ever texted each other now. Cursory texts. Checking in texts. Nothing more, sometimes less.

Now, though, the phone rang, and Edmund, who had worked out at the gym and completed his afternoon run, found himself in the mood to answer. "Hey," he said as if talking to Benjamin was normal, customary.

"Edmund, my birthday is coming up next week and guess what?"

"I know it is. I thought about it yesterday, and what?"

"I got a gig, on my birthday, right down the street, at a little place that me and—that we all go to—and I really want you to come. I know you have a million things to do, and you probably can't come, but it's all that I want for my birthday. You, here, hanging out with me."

"I'm not sure..."

"I get it, it sucked last time we were together, but you have to come. You can stay here. We have plenty of room, and we can have dinner. I'll even cook, so you don't have to eat Lala's concoctions, and we'll go to my show. You have to."

Edmund took a deep breath. "Benjamin I think it's too—"

"Please do it for me. We're brothers. It's not okay to let a girl come between us. I can even tell her not to come, if that makes you feel better."

"No, that wouldn't—"

"She might not anyway. Like I said, she spends most of her time at her studio, but it's not about that at all. It's about you and me, and you have to come.

"Okay."

"Wait, what?"

"I said, okay, I'll come. It's the night of your birthday?"

"Yes, you can bunk here."

"No, that's okay I'll stay at a hotel. I don't get to do that much." Edmund was walking across the lobby headed to the elevator bank of the hotel he had been staying at for so long he had forgotten what a home was like. "I can probably only spare one night."

"Okay, okay. I'll text my address."

Edmund spent the evening analyzing the satellite images of his brother's apartment. The home Benny-boy shared with the girl Edmund loved. He wished he could see what it was like, garner some information about the life they lived, to take away the surprise.

Were they together? He could never tell. But they were all like a family, and he wasn't. He was the guy who had been sent away because he wanted to save her life.

CHAPTER THIRTY-FOUR
Set for four

Ten days later Edmund drove his rental car up to his brother's apartment building even though he had tried to talk himself out of coming every minute for the last week or so. He planned to attend for Benjamin; it would be awkward, but necessary. He couldn't stay away forever.

And he and Benjamin still had parents in common, money in common. They shared accounts, they shared histories, they had to be able to carry on together in some way. He would drop in, be grand and charming and celebratory, and then fly away and go back to his own life. That would be fine.

He peered up at the address, an unimposing brownstone in a hip neighborhood. Little bookstores and pubs and eateries with cheerily striped awnings peppered the block. It was cold out, Edmund's favorite city weather. He had bought a jacket, shirt and slacks for the occasion, a style he thought of as Trust Fund Kid, meets City Hipster. He hoped he appeared moved on, even a little out of their league. Like he ran an empire. He had considered it from every angle, and that was the only way to protect his heart—to aim for cool.

He found a parking space and called Benjamin to meet him downstairs. He didn't think he could walk up the steps by himself. He needed the distraction of conversation, and that's what he received.

Benjamin bounded out of the door, his blonde hair longer, pushed back from his face, he wore a band t-shirt and when he threw his arms out wide there was a new—Edmund couldn't tell what it was of—tattoo on the inside of his bicep. Benjamin hugged him in a giant bear hug. "Eddie!" And hugged him again, hoisting suitcases and carrying them upstairs with Edmund following. Benjamin said, "We were lucky to find this place. There aren't many four bedrooms in this area, and this street is one of the best. We were psyched to get it." Edmund nodded while counting bedrooms and residents in his head.

Benjamin swung the door open and announced, "Everyone, Eddie's here!"

At the word "everyone" Edmund's heart skipped a beat, but as he glanced around Bruce beamed and Lala jumped and clapped excitedly. Bruce and Lala and no Violet at all.

Bruce hugged Edmund and said, "I have the best chair waiting for you."

"Thank you, sir," said Edmund. "I've been sitting though, on the flight, and could use a stand."

Lala hugged him joyously. "You've been away too long. You have to promise not to do that anymore! And look at you, dress pants? Dressy shirt? You look like a stuffy business man!"

He said, "Life has gotten really busy."

She cocked her head to the side and said, "Well, you're always welcome, and let us give you a tour!"

They showed Edmund the living room, furnished in an artsy and bohemian manner, eclectic, but like someone had bought everything all at once, as he supposed they had. He asked, "Who decorated?"

"Me," said Lala. "Isn't it great?"

Edmund nodded as they led him down the hall and gestured to the bathroom door, and opened the door to Benjamin's room.

"Wo ho, there they are!" He walked to a rack of six surfboards, three of them formerly his own. He ran his fingers along their edge. It had been a long time since he had gone surfing. He missed it every morning, but wouldn't be sidetracked, had to retain his focus. Not having a board right now was the only way to keep his sanity.

"You can take them back with you, to Mom and Dad's, when you leave," said Benjamin.

"I could, but I'm too busy to surf, and having them might make me feel worse about it."

Benjamin groaned, "I know, every morning it's like they mock me. I keep telling them there's no ocean here. Why couldn't I live in a city by the beach?" Edmund chuckled because that's what he said to himself, every day, at least once.

Benjamin cracked the door to Bruce's room. Books were piled from floor to ceiling and on every surface. Benjamin smiled and whispered, "He brings home books every single day."

Edmund called to Bruce who had skipped the tour to remain in the living room, "You don't have any chairs in your room, Bruce?"

Bruce's voice traveled down the hall, "All a man needs for support, Edmund the Brooder, is a firm constitution, a yoga mat, and a book."

Benjamin teased, "This is a lot more than one book." He smirked at Edmund.

"I'm not comfortable without a library to peruse, my boy."

Benjamin called back to him, "Speaking of that, don't forget, I'm taking you to the library on Monday to get you a library card."

"I look forward to our visit Benjamin. I read that the city library has one of the best collections of poetry in the state."

Benjamin called back, "I heard." He stepped further down the hall, "And finally Lala's room." Brightly painted, the walls were covered in photos and posters and mirrors and decorations.

Lala stepped in and twirled around. "It's a little boring. There's not as many collections for me to pilfer, but the trade off is everything is mine."

The end of the hall had a closed door that no one even gestured to, Violet's room. Perhaps she was even inside, here in the house, and just wouldn't come out. He thought he sensed an emanating vibration. Was that Violet breathing, or the ripple of her absence? He considered going up and standing with his hand on the door. Maybe it would even accidentally open. He could stumble in, and while he found his way back out take the opportunity to look around Violet's new space. He needed to get a grip. *Calm down.*

They went back to the living room, and sat awkwardly, Lala exuberantly smiling at Edmund and Benjamin in turns. Edmund's chair was comfortable enough, but his knees pressed into the coffee table. To relieve the pressure, he leaned forward and his attention diverted to a book—*Everything That Remains: A Memoir by The Minimalists.* He pried open the front cover, revealing his brother's familiar scrawl on the inside leaf: Dear Violet, I saw this and thought of you. What remains is good too. Maybe better. Love, Benjamin.

Edmund closed the book. Then mindlessly pushed the book across the expanse of the table, not knowing why, just wanting Benjamin's note—far, far away. But his thoughtless shove tipped a knickknack, some kind of Hindu god, rocking the statue back and forth for a moment, before it spin-fell-smashed to the hardwood floor. Edmund leapt to his feet. "Fuck!"

Benjamin ran for a broom, calling back over his shoulder, "No worries, Edmund!"

Lala knelt beside the broken statue, picking up the pieces, cradling them in her palm.

Edmund said, "I'm sorry, Lala, I needed some room. I..."

"It's okay Eddie, it was just a little thing I picked up at Sally Army, a goddess to watch over us, but it was only more clutter anyway—" Benjamin bustled in with the broom and he and Lala worked together sweeping the sculpture up and away, while Edmund sank back into his seat watching the whole scene. The knee-pressing coffee table wasn't a big deal anymore. Actually, the mild pain brought his trip back into focus. He was supposed to be cool and detached, not riding waves of anger and anguish. Shoving books. Flustering. *No worries, Edmund. What remains is good too. Maybe better. No worries.*

When Benjamin and Lala returned to their seats, Benjamin said, "Seriously, don't worry about it."

"Yeah."

"We're all good."

"Sure." Edmund shook his head to clear it. "So, tell me about your show tonight."

Benjamin said, "The band and I have been together for about three months. I sing and play guitar. I think we're good."

Lala said, "Are you kidding me, you guys are great!

"Are you doing anything musical Lala?"

She clasped her hand over her mouth and spoke through her fingers, "It's a surprise, but Benjamin is going to call me up on the stage so I can sing with him tonight!"

Benjamin laughed and said, "That literally took you ten minutes, you're already telling everyone."

Edmund laughed too. "Is there anyone who doesn't know?"

Lala beamed. "No, I'm terrible at secrets!"

"Bruce, what are you up to these days?"

Bruce waved his hand and answered, "I've got all these books to organize. I've been cataloging them and plowing through. It's going to take awhile."

Benjamin raised his eyebrows in Edmund's direction and said, "I should start making dinner."

Lala asked, "Need any help?"

"Nope, we're going a step beyond macaroni and cheese. I'm using a recipe."

"I can follow recipes. I simply choose not to."

Edmund and Lala sat on barstools at a bar on the edge of a grand gourmet kitchen. He said, "So it looks like you're all doing well. This place looks great."

Benjamin said, "Who would have thought when we drove up to that mountain, all those months ago, that I would be living in an apartment with these guys?"

"Not me, I never saw it coming," said Edmund.

Benjamin said, "Well it probably wouldn't have, if the mountain wouldn't have fallen. Here's to gravity!" He raised a glass of water to the ceiling.

"Hear, hear!" said Lala.

It surprised Edmund to hear gravity get the brunt of the blame and credit—he had gotten used to it all being his fault.

Benjamin prepared pasta and sauce and salad and French bread, simple yet delicious looking. "My show starts at nine. I have to get there early, and you and Lala should come with me to get good seats. It's going to be standing room only."

Lala and Edmund set the dinner table for five. Edmund's heart beat faster expecting Violet to walk into the room at any moment. But Benjamin's phone rang and he turned away and said, "I know, sure. I understand. It's just that Eddie is—okay, I'll see you later?"

He came to the table and said, "Only set for four. Violet won't be eating with us tonight." Edmund's stomach lurched uncomfortably. He tried to enjoy the conversation, the camaraderie, but all he really wanted was to see *her*.

"Bruce will you be coming to the club tonight?"

"No, I love a good concert, but my ears aren't what they once were. Besides I'm working on the poetry of T. S. Eliot and don't like to interrupt my process."

"By working you mean—"

Benjamin cut Edmund a look and they moved the conversation along to something else.

After dinner they dressed for the night out and met at the door to walk to the club. Lala scrawled a quick note that said:

We went to Benjamin's show. Better get your ass down there. Love, Lala

They arrived early. Benjamin greeted the bouncer and joked with the club manager and they passed through a dark, poster-adorned entrance hall. The building was laid-out like long hallway, the bar at the front with a few cursory tables scattered around, a few more tables scattered at the edge of the open floor, and a small stage in the way back. The walls were covered in black with splattered blue paint on top, chipping and dirty. The carpet was a disgusting stained mat of spilled drinks and who knows what else. Edmund glanced around and looked forward to the lights dimming for the show.

"It's formerly a punk club," said Benjamin.

"Now it hosts the likes of you?" asked Edmund.

"If I promise to do at least one stage dive."

Lala and Edmund grabbed the closest table to the open floor while Benjamin went back stage to tune up. Lala said, "It's like we're on a date!"

Edmund nodded to be polite.

As it got closer to showtime, more and more people arrived, causing Edmund to turn his head every time. He tried not to care, tried to act like their entrance interrupted him, surprised him, made him have to look. Just because. Not because he waited for anyone in particular or anything.

The place filled up. Every table taken and people lining the walls. A few young girls gathered around the open floor waiting for Benjamin's band to start. Finally, at a respectable 9:53 p.m., Benjamin and the band walked onstage and the crowd clapped and hooted and cheered.

Benjamin said, "We're Ben Hawkes and the Whirlies!" The band launched into the first song, a surf guitar loaded rocker. Benjamin's lyrics were haunting and melodic,

Under the canopy,
Drowning our fears,
Seeking our fortunes,
Dropping in...

Edmund nodded. *Oh that's right, Benjamin is seeking his fortune, the one part of this whole stupid year that made sense. That made sense from the beginning.*

About three quarters of the way through the first song, right as Edmund had almost forgotten he might have a chance to see her, a hand rested on his shoulder. He spun around—eye to eye—with Violet.

He stood up so fast his chair fell behind him.

CHAPTER THIRTY-FIVE
The whole world had shifted

"Violet," he said.

"Hello, Eddie."

Tears welled up. Embarrassed, he fumbled for his dropped chair, offered it to her and grabbed the other one. He sat back down and took stock.

Violet glowed. She had swept up and twisted her blonde hair on top of her head, accentuating her long and regal neck. She emanated beautiful. She wore a V-neck t-shirt in a purple color that reminded him of the lizards.

She wore casual jeans and a big leather belt with a buckle and her black boots. Compared to the rest of the crowd she was underdressed, but somehow looked twice as put-together. Edmund, Lala, and Benjamin wore blacks and darks and hip, straight, pleated conformity. Violet whirled and sparkled.

Lala leaned towards her and asked, "Were you working?"

"Yes, I came as fast as I could."

Edmund watched their exchange and wondered how many times the excuse of "working" was used to avoid painful moments. In his case, all the time. In Violet's case, he supposed, at least as many.

He watched her as he leaned in to take a drink from his glass. She bopped her head to Ben's music. She stared straight ahead and bounced, oblivious to the million different electrical shocks he suffered from her indifference.

She looked at him in a flash through her peripheral vision and just as quickly turned her attention back to the music. Then she leaned in and said, "It's good to see you by the way."

"Yeah me too," he said.

He tried to pay attention to the music and casually take drinks and somehow calm his hyperawareness of her every move, but everything he did felt awkward. She vibrated his skin making him incapable of normal movements. He almost knocked his drink. He clapped before songs were finished. He couldn't concentrate. Her energy was causing a core meltdown.

Yet it was impossible to speak because Benjamin's band played so loud. Good, but loud.

The next song started and Violet and Lala squealed, "Our favorite! Let's dance!"

As they rushed away through the crowd to the front of the stage, Violet called back, "Hold the table!"

Edmund lost sight of them and sat alone nursing his drink. The song was an anthem that Benjamin must have written recently because Edmund had never heard it before. The crowd danced and banged their fists in the air, and Edmund bounced his head along, because he felt out of touch if he didn't. And he wanted to be in touch, desired it more than anything, but couldn't make out any of the words.

Violet and Lala dropped back into their chairs, color raised, cheeks flushed. Violet had a glistening of sweat across her nose. "They sound spectacular tonight!" she said loudly as the song wound down.

Lala said, "He's got birthday mojo or something!"

Edmund spun his drink in his fingers and watched it go.

Benjamin announced, "We're taking a short break, back in twenty," and left the stage, descending toward their table.

He said, "Whoa, we're on fire!"

He walked up to Violet's chair and kissed her on the cheek and close to her ear, whispered, "Glad you made it."

Edmund thought, "Oh." Now he understood, *they were together*. He jumped up and stiffly offered Benjamin his chair, but Benjamin said, "No, you stay there. I have to get a drink and work the room for a few minutes." He wandered off.

The noise level was lower, so they no longer had to yell to be heard. Violet asked, "So you've been busy working? That's why you haven't been around?"

"There's a lot going on with my family's business—"

She said, "Yes, I have the same thing. Have you been able to go surfing?"

"No, Benny-boy has everything. I mean, my boards. What I need."

He changed the subject, "You look really good." A blush rushed up her cheek. He continued, "I don't know if it's the city that agrees with you, or you're happier, or just that I haven't seen you in—"

Benjamin returned with a birthday hat on his head and a cupcake with a lit candle. He placed it on the table and led everyone, "A one, two, three, four!"

The entire bar yelled, "Happy Birthday!"

"Why thank you, thank you!" Benjamin took a bow and blew out the flame. He pulled out the candle, locked eyes with Violet, and said, "Okay, I'm eating my chocolate birthday cupcake. I don't even like them that much. I'm really more about the candle and the wishes, but I plan to eat it now." He lifted it slowly, slowly to his mouth.

Violet batted her eyes dramatically and said, "I'd be happy to eat it for you, as long as you really*, really* don't want it."

"It is my birthday," he teased. "The bar gave me a cupcake, seems like I should be the one to eat it—though I'm not very hungry after that big dinner." He winked at Lala.

"Right! I missed dinner! I might starve without that cupcake." Violet put her hands together and begged with woeful eyes.

"And the Oscar goes to the lady who was going to get it anyway." He passed her the cupcake. She held it in both hands and took a big bite smearing frosting all over her upper lip and chin.

Benjamin gave Lala a thumbs up and went backstage. Edmund took a deep breath. Maybe someday he would get used to Benjamin and Violet being together, but not now. Not yet. He needed Benjamin to be up on the stage, anywhere but here, causing Edmund to be the third wheel. The third, squeaky, deflated wheel. Violet smiled, pretending to be oblivious to the glob of frosting on her face.

Edmund said, "You have a little something right there." He pointed at the corner of her mouth, the same corner where a smile for him had been off-centered so long ago.

"Where?" she asked, taking another big bite of cupcake.

Edmund laughed and said, "I give up, it's pretty much everywhere."

"Just like life," she said, "cupcakes are messy."

"Sweet too," he said.

She smiled.

Edmund said, "I hear you have a studio, are you welding?"

"Yes, and no. I'm sculpting, but little tiny miniature things."

Edmund's heart sank. Everything about her was different. She was completely altered from the girl on the mountain of mess. It was kind of breaking his heart or crushing the last pieces of the broken one. "Oh, that's, um—"

"I had to figure out how to work without the scale. The city is confining you know."

"Yes, I suppose it is."

"I also think that losing big things is so much harder, the hole in my heart bigger. If I lost a tiny whirligig I think I would get over it faster. Maybe. I hope."

"Don't lose one, I think you've had enough heartbreak."

"I'll hold on."

"I'd love to see them. I wondered what you were working on."

"Oh no." She shook her head. "You can't see them, definitely not."

"Oh." Edmund sank back in his chair.

"I didn't mean it like that. I meant, no one has seen them. I don't know why. I can't share them, not yet."

Edmund smiled to cover his disappointment. Had Violet shown them to Benjamin? Did she think Benjamin was an exception, special? Was his smile coming across as a grimace? He couldn't think of a thing to say.

Violet folded the cupcake's wrapper. She said, "I don't know, I guess in my former life I was exposed, too exposed, a spectacle. Now I feel the need to be private."

Edmund nodded. "You still have frosting right here," he pointed at her face.

She grabbed the napkin out from under her drink. "Well, I don't have eyes on my chin." She handed it to him and leaned in.

Edmund wiped the frosting off of her perfectly formed mouth, wishing he could kiss it and make it all better.

Benjamin climbed on stage and began his second set. The loud music made it better to not even try to talk. Sitting beside Violet was still awkward and painful and vibrational. They had gotten past, or over, the How-Do-We-Chat-With-Each-Other phase. They did that. They could do it again. But now a great weird void of physical space gaped between them. And time.

Benjamin rocked the stage and then called Lala up to sing. Edmund and Violet stood and cheered and whistled and helped the crowd get excited to see her. She reappeared a few seconds later having donned a bright blue tutu over her jeans with a long flowing scarf looped over her shoulders. The song started, Lala's voice arced above, while the surf riffs and Benjamin's voice drove the middle notes. The song had a rhythm like ocean waves. It was definitely Edmund's favorite. As Lala left the stage she stepped out of the tutu and centered it over Benjamin's head and pulled it down to his waist. Benjamin laughed and asked the audience, "Good look for me?"

Everyone cheered in response so he played another song and then played a handful more, and then Benjamin announced the final song, *Purple Devotion*. Violet jostled with Lala and said, "My song!" They ran to the stage and clung to the edge. Edmund was pretty sure blue-tutu-wearing Benny announced the title to bang him over the head with it. The music started out slow. Benjamin leaned down and sang directly to Violet. A love song, a ballad.

Edmund leaned forward and stared down into his drink.

The concert ended. Benjamin's last song had been a love song for Violet. If Edmund had to watch them go home together he would have to throw something—possibly the table. He and Lala and Violet moved to the open floor and stood in a circle chatting, waiting for Benjamin to finish up and join them.

Lala asked, "Wasn't that song the best, Edmund? Well, besides the one I sang. Okay, Violet's song is the second best."

"I love yours," Edmund said, "and I liked the last one very much." He glanced at Violet.

Lala said, "We should have asked you to come up to the stage with us!"

"No, that's okay. I think I would have been in the way." He didn't understand why he said it, and having said it he felt like an ass.

Violet asked, "Why, 'in the way'?"

Edmund pedaled the statement back, "Well, it's a love song, sung by a guy. I'm a guy. It's tough to be in the front row when the singer is crooning about love."

"I suppose that would be awkward, but that would mean I shouldn't rush the stage when Lala sings, and I totally do, usually."

Edmund took a long drink, emptying his glass and glancing around for a place to drop the empty cup. Preferring not to say anything, instead of betraying his feelings. Feelings that right now were swinging between crumpling into a heap, and destroying property.

Lala said, "We love to rush the stage when Benjamin is singing, don't we Cuz?"

"Definitely," laughed Violet with her eyes sparkling. "Especially when they're songs about me!"

Both the girls sang, "Ooooh, vibrate me violet of the rainboooooooow." Then Lala saw someone she recognized in the audience and waved herself away.

Edmund's jaw clenched.

"Wait, Edmund, you're upset."

"I just—this is all so hard. You're here and my brother and —"

"Edmund, Benjamin and me, we're friends. No wait, I love him, but like a brother, like I know he will always be there for me. He's my rock. He's part of my family now, or rather he adopted me, us."

Edmund shoved his hands in his pockets. "If Benjamin is your brother, where does that leave me?"

"You? You're the man I love."

She peered into his face, but he was too shocked and confused to respond quick enough.

She said, "Except now you're just gone."

"You told me to go away. You said you hated me. You told me to."

"I needed you to go away. I had no idea you'd stay gone." A tear slid down her cheek. "I lost everything that day."

"I'm not, I didn't—"

"Benjamin is my brother. You're the guy that I loved." She turned and shoved away through the crowd toward the door.

"Violet, wait! Wait! Violet!" He shoved through the crowd and out onto the street. Violet was leaning against the front wall of the club.

"Violet, I—"

"No, I understand. You had things you had to do. We're both driven by our duty to our family, both of us."

"Yeah, we are." Edmund leaned against the wall beside her. "Yeah, we are."

Tears wet Violet's cheeks, glistening her lashes, she sniffled. "I was so excited when I heard you were finally coming to see us—me. I never understood why you weren't worried about me, wondering about me."

"Oh, Violet." He stood and pulled her up against his chest with a hug, his mouth against her forehead. "I'm so sorry. I wondered about you every day. Every minute of every day. I just thought—I would come if you asked."

"Me? The girl who was carried away by SWAT teams and helicopters? Needed to let you know if I needed you?"

"I guess it sounds kind of crazy if you say it like that."

She leaned up and kissed him softly on the lips. "Seeing you is so much heartbreakingly better than I thought."

He kissed her back more desperately. They kissed and kissed. They kissed for so long that they lost track of time and place. When he came up for air, he had his hand up her shirt on the small of her back, and she had her fingers entwined in his hair. She pulled his body closer and leaned into his.

Her voice was a breathy exhale as she asked, "Where are you staying?"

"A hotel, walking distance."

"Can I stay?"

But he was already leading her there.

* * *

His room was on one of the top floors. In a crowded elevator Edmund leaned against a wall with Violet curled under his arm. His phone buzzed.

Benjamin texted: **Still here?**

E: **Your show was so good Benjamin, so great. You had a crowd to talk to, so I went back to the hotel. Breakfast first thing?**

B: **Definitely. Did you see Violet when you left? Lala is searching for her.**

Edmund showed Violet the text.
She said, "I'm at my studio."

He wrote: **She said she was going to her studio to work.**

B: **Sounds like her. Well we got to see her for a couple of hours, huh? Call me in the morning.**

"Sure little Brother," said Edmund to the people in the elevator. He pulled Violet in tight and kissed her on the forehead as the doors slid open on his floor.

Edmund let Violet into his room and then, still in the doorway, she folded into his arms.

"Hi," she said.

"Hi." They kissed and slowly spun down the hallway colliding with the walls. He pulled her shirt up over her head and left it halfway down the hall. She pulled his shirt off and added it to the pile on the floor. Realizing they were exposed, he laughed, "Stay here, right like this," and ran back to push the door all the way closed.

Running back with a grin, he wrapped her in his arms, and said, "Thank you." He meant, for staying right like this, but he also felt an all encompassing gratitude for her kisses.

They fell onto the bed side by side, and she pulled at his pant's button and zipper while he kicked his shoes off to the floor. She sat up and worked on her boots, taking such a long time that Edmund said, "I used to like women in Docs, but now it's nothing but a hassle."

She laughed as she kicked the last boot off and flung one of her socks towards the bathroom, the other near the TV. Then they stood. Edmund's pants dropped to the ground and he stepped out of them effortlessly, then he peeled hers off and down, and kneeled, wrapping his arms around, kissing along the top edge of her underwear's elastic, before he slowly pulled them down her legs. "They're orange," he said, "I mean, I expected purple."

"There are so many colors, Edmund, and we seriously need to work on your arts education." With her hand on the side of his face she raised him to standing and they kissed and fell onto the bed. The last few moments had been silly and frenetic—laughing and joyful until the last sock hit the wall— and then, bam, naked calm. Time slowed, their eyes were reflective, their fingers searching. A shiver traveled over her body. Their breaths, shallow, caught in their throats.

Fresh and raw, like a first time, this was also intimately familiar, like he and Violet had always been—just like this, his hand running down her waist to her hip, her hand pressed on the small of his back. He closed his eyes to concentrate, to touch and kiss, but couldn't keep them closed. He needed to see—and caught a glimpse of her face as he entered her. Her cheeks were flushed, her lips darkened. The sound on the edge of her mouth was as much a sob as a moan and the skin of her temple tasted of sweat and tears.

He ran his lips down the side of her face as his body reached a rhythm and he lost his way on the map of her shoulder somewhere near the familiar edge of her collarbone. The place that peeked out of her shirts, but now lay exposed and wanting on his hotel room bed.

They made love in a strange room in the middle of a strange city, feeling familiar finally, even though they were almost completely estranged.

* * *

When they were done they stayed entwined together in the cloud of hotel sheets and blankets, wrapped up, yet completely unwrapped.

"God, I love you," he said into her hair.

"I love you too," she said drawing circles on his chest with her fingertips. "I've loved you since the night you came out to the beach and checked on me after I said good night to the sun, and you didn't laugh. You acted like it was the most normal thing in the world. You even thanked me. Not many people thanked me in those days."

Edmund didn't reply. He didn't need to. Edmund had fallen in love with her in that moment too. He tightened his hold, hugging her and kissing her forehead, right at her hairline, soft skin and blonde hair.

"Will you stay the night?" he asked. "I mean, do you need to go work in the studio?"

"Not tonight," she said.

"Good," he said, as they both drifted off to sleep.

* * *

They had forgotten to close the curtains. The harsh light of the morning sun filtered through a one inch crack and fell across Edmund's eyelid nudging him awake. He shifted his arm causing Violet to wake with a "Huh?" The sunbeam fell across her cheekbone causing her to ask in a groggy, barely awake voice, "Good god, is that the sun? Does it get up this early?"

Edmund reached for his watch on the side table and read it with bleary-eyes. "It's seven thirty."

"Oh." She raised her head from the crook of his arm and looked down on him.

He chuckled. "Your hair is pointing in fifteen different directions."

"It's confused because it should still be asleep." She kissed him. "And you're one to talk, morning breath."

He laughed again. "Don't move, don't dress, I'm going to brush my teeth, but you can't move from this spot." He stood up from the bed and then cheekily dragged the comforter and sheet with him and grabbed her pants and shirt off the floor and took them too and wadded it all into a big bundle. "I'm holding all this hostage until I get back." He and his naked buttocks and his armful of bedding disappeared into the bathroom to brush.

When he returned, she was lying naked propped up on an arm. "I can't believe you don't trust me. Why would I get dressed, when I'm counting on more of what we did last night?"

"And that's why I brushed my teeth." He dropped the bundle to the floor and dove onto the bed wrapping her in his arms and kissing her passionately and over-dramatically. He moved up and down her neck and arms to her belly and even her armpit, causing her to giggle. They crossed into giddy— laughed into each others ears and teased with their lips and then made love staring into each others eyes, until the end when all they could do was hold on.

"Whoa," Edmund said after, kissing the end of her nose.

Violet smiled, "Yes, love, true. And I don't mean to change the subject, but is there room service in my future?"

Edmund laughed. "I'm meeting Ben for breakfast, want to come?"

Violet said, "No, I think I'll let you have some time together, besides we have lots of mornings to come, you and I." Violet rolled out from under him and scooped up his shirt off the floor and slid it on and buttoned a button, so that though she was technically dressed, pretty much everything interesting was exposed.

"Nice," said Edmund appreciatively, and then, "So if I was to order room service, what would I like to eat?"

"Probably pancakes."

Edmund smiled nonstop. He flew. While they waited for pancake delivery, he made coffee, naked, and joked that he couldn't figure out the system. To help, Violet disrobed, "Because everyone knows you have to be naked to make coffee."

They laughed and were silly and comfortable and Violet's pancakes were delivered and she ate sitting naked on their bed, while Edmund lay beside her, stealing an occasional bite of her strawberries.

He texted Benjamin: **Are you up yet?**

But the response took a while, so Edmund and Violet showered together, and she dressed in her clothes from the night before, and Edmund dressed in a pair of his jeans and a t-shirt. He was ready for breakfast with Benjamin if the rock star would ever wake up.

He asked, "So no one is worried about you not coming home last night?"

She rubbed her wet hair with a dry towel and then picked at it with her fingertips until curls stood out in every direction. "No, I spend most nights at the studio. I have a couch," she said with a smile.

"I still can't go see?"

"Nope, someday, but not today. When do you go home?" Her attention was more on her reflection in the mirror than on the question, or his possible answer.

Edmund tied his shoes and thought, *home, not really a home at all.* A hotel was kind of like living at the top of a pile of other people's things. He didn't look at her when he said, "I fly back this afternoon."

Her hair-drying towel dropped to the ground.

"Oh," she said. And then, "*Oh.*"

He put his elbows on his knees. "I made the reservations before I knew about us, about this—I could change them, stay longer."

Violet leaned a shoulder against the wall. She watched him for a long, calculating pause, with her eyes narrowed. She had been under the impression that he had come back, had returned for her, and— "No, I think that's for the best."

Edmund shook his head. It wasn't for the best. Leaving was stupid, but she continued, listing all the bullshit reasons he should leave today, like he planned to, though it didn't make any sense at all. "You have all your family business to handle— the lawyers, your estate, your parents, the bed and breakfast— you have to focus on all of that.

"And I have my own thing. I have this big lawsuit coming up. My aunts and uncles and I hired a lawyer and we're going to sue the jerk who stole my home from me, our things. It's going to take a lot of my time, and I'll be busy, very busy. So yes," she said. "Yes."

Edmund looked up at her and quietly said, "I'm sure their things are long gone, Violet. They've probably been carted off to a dump by now."

Anger flashed through her eyes. "I'm not sure how much Benjamin told you, but this asshole bought it from the state, and this owner, this cowardly, anonymous owner, had me arrested and removed from my home. I'm glad he's anonymous, or I'd probably kill him, and they better keep him secret, because I won't stop wanting to." She kicked the wall for emphasis. "We can't let him get away with it, with stealing our property. We can't."

Edmund shut his eyes hoping the pain of the conversation would disappear.

"They'll bulldoze it probably. My home, my mother's home, my mother's burial ground, my grandmother's home. Bulldozed and..."

She broke off mid-sentence and watched Edmund. Her hand had risen to her heart and she clutched a bit of hair that dangled there. She watched Edmund with his head bowed staring at his hands. He wouldn't look at her. She believed he wasn't listening. For a minute she stared, not realizing that his eyes were shut, his hands clasped, because he was begging the universe for help.

She didn't know.

She wanted to tell him all about the day on the mountain. Trying to get the whirligigs back up, solidly into place, while everything under her shifted and rolled and slid and bounced, and her terror, but she couldn't stop—she had to hold it all together. The heart of her mother resided inside after all, her mother, her home. Sliding and shifting while the whole world watched.

She wanted to tell Edmund about it, and she wanted him to say, I understand, you must have been terrified, and, Oh, and kiss the side of her neck, and tell her everything would be okay. And that he planned to stay, had planned to all along, and what could he do for her? And no more. No more. No more at all.

But the whole world had shifted in the months that passed. Shift, shift, roll. He didn't want to hear about that day. His heart broke at the mention of it. His face said it all, he wouldn't. He couldn't. He had caused everything to shift and caused her heart to break. He begged her to stop and caused her to lose her way.

He did that, and now she had lost everything, and now he couldn't even come back and stay. Couldn't or wouldn't, it was all the same. He was gone.

"Yes, it's probably best this way," she said. "Yes, the lawsuit and everything. It was good seeing you, but I'm very busy right now."

She took two big strides to the middle of the room, grabbed her boots off the floor, located first one sock and then the other, and walked barefoot out of the door.

Edmund groaned. Then he fell back on the bed and groaned again. Like a fighter taking punches, he still received the blows. He felt them especially in his gut, so he curled up around his knees and tried to remember a day without so much pain.

He was the owner. Him. He owned every bit of this damage and deserved every second of her ire. He was the asshole that had her arrested. The jerk that possessed her things. Him. The fact that he had just made love to her, was the biggest theft of them all, plain and simple. He was a liar. He had taken everything—and lied about it all.

As always seemed to happen, Benjamin texted right at that moment:

I'll be in the lobby in ten, ready for breakfast?

Edmund texted back: **Meet you downstairs.**

He splashed water on his face. He looked like hell. He splashed more water and practiced smiling. Hopefully the endorphins would kick in and cover his sadness. He checked— his reflection returned a strained, splotchy grimace. He ran his fingers down his shirt and took a deep breath. During the elevator ride down he tried to calm his shaking hands, and practiced a few times, "Hi, Benny-boy, great show last night!" Arriving at the lobby floor, he jogged in place, shook everything out, and breathed deep as the doors slid open.

Benjamin stood in the middle of the lobby in a cheery mood. "Good morning! Too tired to stay for the late night?" Benjamin wore sunglasses in the hotel like a rockstar. In comparison Edmund represented a corporate business-hound, conservative, past-his-hip-coolness. It sucked. He represented the patriarchy and Benjamin the rebellion. It irked him that he wasn't the cool one. He was also pissed he hadn't thought to wear sunglasses to cover up the traumatic loss of love of his life. Benjamin led him to a breakfast place a couple of doors down the street from the hotel.

"I wanted you to have your glory. Your show was great. So much fun. I'm glad I got to see it."

"Me too." Benjamin held the door open for Edmund, and the waitress showed them to a table.

They both sat quietly for a second reading over the menus. Then Benjamin said, casually but using the menu like a barricade. "So why are you staying away?"

"I'm not—"

Benjamin put the menu to the side. "No, you are. Dad's been part of the business our whole life, and he's never needed to attend meetings more than once a month."

"Well, Dad is different, and there's a lot going—"

The waitress came for their orders. Benjamin ordered eggs, bacon, and toast. Edmund ordered pancakes and yogurt.

"A lot going on, huh?"

"Yes. A lot going on."

"I didn't figure you for a money-managing workaholic. You were going to be an environmentalist, the kind of guy who chained his body to a tree."

"I grew up."

Benjamin narrowed his eyes and said, "Well okay. If I can't get you to open up. Here's what's going on with me. I've got this new band. I'm writing songs. We think we're getting in the studio in a couple of months."

"Will Lala record with you?"

"Definitely. What a voice, huh?"

"Beautiful. So how come you guys never got together?"

"I don't know, she's a little sister. And frankly, there's a lot of competition. Boys everywhere, especially when she sings."

Edmund chuckled, "I thought you were talking about *her* competition."

"It goes without saying there are girls. The life of a rockstar is awesome. You talked to Violet last night?"

"Yes. How is she doing now?" Inside Edmund coached himself, *Careful, don't betray your feelings. Don't collapse in your yogurt.*

"Good, keeps to herself, but Lala and I came up with a plan a while back to get her out into the world. Every few days we take her somewhere, to see something interesting or arty. At first we just irritated her, but lately she's putting effort into the planning. I think she's starting to like living in the city."

"Have you seen her new sculptures?"

"No, she won't show anyone."

Their food arrived, and they both tucked into their meal.

Edmund said, "She told me she planned to sue the owner of the land."

"Can you blame her, really? She lost everything."

Edmund nodded. *Don't say too much.*

Benjamin added, "But, of course I wouldn't tell her this, that asshat totally saved her life. She was never going to come down from that mountain. She would have died."

"Too bad she doesn't see it that way."

"Maybe she will someday, with distance."

"Are you bankrolling the lawsuit?" asked Edmund.

"Just Violet's share."

Edmund nodded again and then realized he was sulking. First conversation with his brother in months and he was morose and incommunicative. He checked his watch, he still had a few hours before his flight, so he turned the conversation to a more interesting subject. "Have you been watching the surf contest out of Fiji?"

Part 3
COLLAPSING

CHAPTER THIRTY-SIX
Cleaning up someone's mess

A sky cast with thunderclouds greeted Edmund as his flight descended into the airport in Kingsbridge. A dark afternoon that threatened rain, but wouldn't actually rain. The air was heavy, and Edmund felt achy, not only in his heart but also his joints and head. By the time he arrived at his hotel room, he had a full blown fever. He pulled the curtains and climbed in bed, which was just as well, he couldn't imagine what would be worth getting up for. Not anymore. His emptiness surprised him. This loneliness and its unremittingness. There was no going back to the sunlit surfing days. No going back to his friendship with Benjamin. Their conversation in the restaurant had been forced, the things unsaid too numerous to ignore.

No more Violet. You can't forcibly remove someone from their mother's grave and expect them to forgive you. It couldn't happen. Ever. But knowing it, and living in spite of it, were two totally different things. Better to keep the curtains closed and remain in the dark.

But after a few days he had to go out, he had a meeting with Anderson and Silvers, and he needed something to eat besides room-service food. When he turned on the light of the bathroom and gazed at himself in the mirror his dark-circled stare kind of freaked him out. He shaved and put on a suit, applying a polished veneer over the chipped and broken pieces. He didn't feel better, but the underneath didn't show as much.

Walking home after his meeting he passed a poster in a gallery window with an image of a beautiful painted sunset that halted Edmund mid-stride. He didn't recognize the name of the artist, but then again, he hadn't taken art at school. He was generally uninterested, or as Violet would say, uninteresting, because of his lack of art training. He wandered in the front door.

The gallery blazed white. A young woman sat at the front desk and said, "You're welcome to wander around. If you have any questions..."

Edmund paid no attention. "Sure." He scanned for the painting and bee-lined right to it. It was big. Massive. The sunset began vividly at the bottom and muted toward the top, intricate clouds in a pass through the middle. Edmund stepped to the title card, it was named Set (3) and painted with oil—information that meant nothing to Edmund.

The young woman from the front desk appeared beside him. "Interesting composition, isn't it?"

"I saw it and..."

She nodded, her straight dark hair swung as she talked. "Are you a collector? The painting would be a great investment —"

"Oh, no, not a collector. I only wanted to—do you know where it might have been painted?"

She led him through to a small room lined with books and offered him a chair. She searched the shelves for a book and brought it to him. While she searched for a certain page she leaned a little so her arm brushed his as she read over his shoulder. "This page is about the painting. It's a dialog about beauty and impermanence, but also about the shift between abstraction and realism and the object as—but if you read this you'll see. I'm Emily, by the way, I need to step out and begin closing up, but you can stay for a little bit and read. Let me know if you have any questions."

"Thank you." Edmund scanned the few paragraphs but didn't find any answers to what he really wanted to understand: had it been painted in one sitting, or from a photograph, had the artist watched a real sunset, or invented the image, and how many layers of paint did it take to get such a deep real painting? He was so curious how it happened, how an idea became this beautiful rectangle of sky.

Emily reappeared, "Interesting, right?"

"Oh, yes, sure."

"So, we're closing up now. Are you sure you don't want to buy it? I'm simply an assistant, and if I made a sale my boss would have a heart attack."

Edmund chuckled. "No, sorry, I hope I haven't kept you late."

"Not at all." She spun on a heel and then spun back. "Would you like to go to the restaurant around the corner for a bite to eat? I'm hungry and—not a date or anything, I mean that would be crazy forward of me, I don't even know your name—but I'm going to get some food, and it's dinner time, and..."

Edmund blinked twice, and it might have been the glare of the room, but something obscured his judgment. "Um, sure, I could eat at the restaurant around the corner. I'm Edmund."

"Oh, oh wow. Cool. Okay." Emily spun around and grabbed her jacket and purse and led him out of the gallery to the sidewalk outside. "Do people call you Ed or Eddie sometimes?"

"Nope, nobody does, just Edmund."

She stopped in the middle of the busy sidewalk. "Because this is weird, because you're a total stranger, but, admittedly, in a nice suit—three questions—what is your full name?"

"Edmund Hawkes."

"Local, or stranger passing through?"

"Bit of both."

"Hmmm, any sociopathic or murderous ideations?"

"Never, not once."

"Now me—my name is Emily Cook, I'm a university student, majoring in Art History, I live nearby. Okay?"

"You didn't tell me whether you were a murderer or not."

"I'm an art history major, and I'm like half your size. I think you'll be okay." She led him to a Thai restaurant and greeted everyone who worked there. They were shown to a small romantically lit table and handed menus.

Silence descended. Emily glanced at her menu and tossed it down.

Edmund asked, "What's good here?"

"I let Soon tell me what the special is and order that."

"Okay, that sounds good." Edmund placed his menu on hers.

"So if you aren't an art collector... you are a—let me guess —hmm, a banker or something?"

"I'm in my family's business."

"And that is?"

"Oil, land development, things like that."

"Oh," her eyes widened, "You're a Hawkes? That Hawkes?"

Edmund nodded.

"Whew. Well... So you live around here?"

"I'm staying in the city, near the park, while I work on a project."

"What kind of project?"

"I bought a large piece of property near the coastline, out west, and I'm going to build a resort, high-rises, swimming pools."

"That's so cool."

"Yes, cool. What about you, you love art, are you an—"

The waitress took their order and Edmund continued, "Are you an artist as well?"

"Oh no! I simply love the history of it all, what movements mean in time, and what individual pieces mean in the long view. Like the painting from earlier, it seems like a painting of a sunset, but instead it's a treatise on beauty. Isn't that a better way to think of it? Anyone can paint a sunset, it's art when it means so much more."

"Oh." Edmund spun his drink glass. "Here I thought it was just pretty." He raised the glass and took a long sip. He watched her over the rim of his glass. Her dark hair curtained over her shoulder and shined blue in the low-lights.

"It's so much more. You'd have to ask the artist all the Who, What's, and Where's, but often they can't even answer the big questions, like what it means in the long term. They don't know. Most of the time they don't even consider it. That's my job."

"I guess I never thought about it that way." The waitress delivered their food, one of Edmund's favorite dishes.

"I just met you, and this might be forward of me, but you ought to start collecting. You have the money, you only need someone to guide you to the right pieces. The important ones."

Edmund chuckled, "You're determined to make a sale, huh?"

"I mean it, my boss thinks it will never happen, and I'd love to prove her wrong. But I'll stop, promise. What do you do when you aren't building resorts?"

"Nothing really. My work keeps me busy. How about you?"

"My classes keep me really busy and the work at the gallery. Study, sleep, work. That's pretty much it." They ate in silence for a few minutes and then discussed the weather for a while.

The waitress brought their check and laid it in the middle of the table. Edmund grabbed it before Emily with an, "I insist." Then they were at a loss. What to talk about? How to continue? How to get away?

Emily leaned in and turned the top of her cup around with a swish. The candlelight didn't reflect, but rather absorbed. Her eyes were dark and deep as a night sky. "I bought a painting recently. My first step toward a collection. Would you like to come see it?"

"Your place?"

"Yes, nearby."

"I'd like to," he said without even realizing he would.

* * *

Emily lived in a small apartment in a local brownstone, arts district, expensive. She led him through her entryway and into her living space, an immaculately kept, sparsely decorated room. Nothing out of place and barely anything in a place. Spare. He ran his finger along the rim of a bowl set on a small table. The only decorative element in the whole place.

He watched as she slid her keys into a small silver tray inside a drawer in the table by the door and hung her jacket on a hanger in the entryway closet. She asked, "Would you like a drink?" as she disappeared into the kitchen.

"Yes, whatever you're having," he called and laid his jacket on the back of her couch.

She returned, handed him a glass, and before he said a word, swooped up his jacket and placed it beside her own in the entryway closet. She mesmerized him with the way she smoothed the back and shoulders before putting it away.

"Let me show you the painting." He followed her into the bedroom. "Here it is, my first acquisition." She pointed at a small canvas with painted fruit—grapes and an apple—realistic except the word 'want' had been stenciled across, obliterating it. The painting was spotlit importantly, the only anything in the room except for the bed and a side table with a small photograph of a couple in a frame.

"Do you love it?" She stood very close, her arm against his.

"Tell me about it."

"It's by an important contemporary Dutch painter. He's using a derivative style to juxtapose excess with need. He would say it's about hunger and poverty, but I think the painting in the long run will be about tradition and the creation of culture." She took a small sip of her drink.

"I've learned a lot about art, thank you."

"My pleasure."

Edmund turned away from the painting and took in the scope of the room. Emily's color choices were shades of gray. Her bed was perfectly made, a pewter-colored comforter, smoothed over the thin mattress. Two pillows, also in gray. The side table was a metal cube. "Is that photo of your parents?"

"Yes, their wedding day. I'm not usually sentimental about things, but I like having that one around. They're young and so happy..." Her voice trailed off languidly, but suddenly she grasped his arm, rose up on her toes—and before he realized what happened—kissed him and then laughed. "I'm not usually this forward, would you like to stay the night?"

"Um, yes, I would."

She took the drink from his hand and excused herself to carry their drinks back to the kitchen. When she returned she stepped right up, put her arms around his neck, and arched up for another kiss. He returned it slowly. They kissed for a few minutes, deep and slow. He forgot within them all about the last days and weeks and months. She bit his bottom lip playfully and unbuttoned his shirt. He kicked off his shoes and with his arms around her they fell onto the bed. He kissed her neck and then she kicked off her shoes and they kissed some more with her hands inside his shirt.

Suddenly his phone interrupted with a beep and a vibration. He chuckled through the kiss. "Jeez, Terrible timing. Ignore it." They kissed again. His phone beeped and then beeped three more times. "Crap. I'm sorry, I better check..."

"No, It's okay, it sounds important."

He sat up on the edge of the bed and fished his phone out of a pocket. It was Mike, the head of his construction company. He put his left hand behind him and rested it on Emily's unfamiliar thigh.

The first text read:

Hello Ed, wanted to tell you that the crew has started excavating what appears to be living quarters. We found stuff that seems important. A few of the boxes say, "Mom's China" on the side. Unbroken. Let me know what you want to do with it.

The next few texts were photos:

The china in a box.
The outside of a box that read, "Violet's."
A box labeled, "Mom's photo albums."

Violet's china hadn't broken in the avalanche. The crew had found photos that belonged to her mother. Violet would have them back. "I have to make a call," he said without turning around.

"Hi Mike, what did you find?"

"China, jewelry, clothes, not the usual hoard, this looks like it belongs to the family that lived there."

"Good good. Can you put it all in a container? I'd like you to send me photos for my records, too."

"This is going to slow us down a great deal."

"That's okay, pack it up, and store it onsite. I'll come up with something to do with it. You said the china was okay?"

"Everything seems unbroken."

"Good, take special care of it. And if you find other things labeled 'mom' send photos."

"Sure thing Ed."

"Talk to you later."

* * *

When he turned back to the bed Emily reclined on her side watching him. She asked, "What was that about?"

"The construction crew stopped work because they found things that belong to the family that used to live there."

"You're storing it for them? That's unnecessarily nice of you."

"Well, it belongs to them. I'm sure they want it."

"You'd be doing them a favor by getting rid of it. People don't need half the junk they hold on to." She patted the bed beside her, welcoming him.

"This is different, it's family china, photo albums—"

She huffed. "That's even worse, nothing but sentimental junk."

Edmund stood up. "I'm only trying to get the belongings back to the rightful owner."

"By cataloging and storing and delivering? It sounds like you're cleaning up someone's mess. Make them clean up themselves, or how will they learn?"

During her speech he buttoned his shirt back up. Her eyes narrowed as he made to flee the scene.

He said, "Sometimes the messes we live with aren't the ones we made, but life is like that, messy, and everyone needs help sometimes." He shoved his shirttails into his waistband. "Look, maybe I misled you, but I think you have me wrong." He shoved his feet into his shoes.

She shook her head, "No, I don't think I do, I think you're probably a total ass."

He blinked for a second and said, "Oh, well, yes, I stand corrected." He walked out of her bedroom, remembered to pull his jacket from the closet, and escaped to the dark street, relieved to be headed to his lonely bed inside his impersonal hotel.

CHAPTER THIRTY-SEVEN
You aren't here

He tried to tell himself that what had happened in the city had been normal—only a visit to Benjamin on his birthday, and not a heartbreaking mistake of epic proportions—but it was a difficult sell, because he regretted going, and his heart hurt so much from the aftermath. And then the mistake with Emily—had he become one big epic mistake? He felt like it and had trouble convincing himself otherwise.

He had grown sick and tired of watching the same shows, listening to the same thoughts, lying around doing nothing, so to get his mind off of it all he went to the gym. He attempted a thought-control experiment to forget that he had seen Violet, had slept with her, and had caused her to leave him, forever, by doing so many curls and lunges and squats and miles, that his numbed-mind wouldn't recall it anymore. So far his experiment had not worked though he suspected its implementation was causing him to become one of the most boring people in the world. He frankly couldn't stand to be alone with himself anymore.

Two months slogged by while he waited for a call. He expected it any day now. *What was taking it so long?* He kept his phone waiting on top of the treadmill's console, within view and loud enough to be heard over the deafening music of the gym, just in case. He ran, full pace, covered in sweat when his ringtone crescendoed with notes. Finally. He turned off the treadmill and wiped his face with his towel and answered, "Hello?"

"Edmund, this is Anderson, are you able to get back to Kingsbridge for a meeting?"

"I'm still in Kingsbridge, I'm in the gym, staying at the hotel down the street."

"Oh, I... good." Their meetings were too random to require him being so close, yet he continued on and on and on. Anderson and Silvers had to wonder why he remained. Possibly they even worried about him.

He wondered if he was depressed, like in the Doctor-Gets-Involved kind of way. He had sought his fortune and turned up friendless, orphaned, miserly, a—how did Emily put it?—total ass. Oh yeah, exactly. He counted his money, talked about money, and planned what to do with his money, that was all.

The doubling and tripling of his plans caused the most difficulties—the plans he made with his lawyers, the plans he hid from his parents, the plans he hid from his lawyers, the plans he hid from everybody. *Everything* he hid from Benjamin. He wished there was one single person he trusted, yet he had lost everything that day on the mountain. Now all he had left was a pile of money, a pile of stuff, and lies.

He had forced Violet off for her own good and instead had climbed to the summit. Now he stood there even though the ground kept shifting, threatening to throw him off. He was guard of the summit now.

"Edmund we have terrible news. Remember the crazy girl from your beach property?"

Edmund flinched. "Yes?"

"She's suing you, along with her crazy family."

Edmund said, "Of course they are."

"You aren't surprised?"

"Not really, and that's why I have the best lawyers in the business." He added, "I'll be there in about an hour."

* * *

When Edmund entered their offices, Anderson and Silvers had adopted concerned and sympathetic airs. Edmund attempted to appear confused and worried in reply.

Anderson said, "Here's their suit." He handed Edmund a small pile of documents and then placed a file folder on top. "This is our research, and our side of the case."

Edmund loosened his tie and started with Violet's suit. He had become better at reading legalese now.

After a few hours of perusing the folder he called Anderson and Silvers back into the room.

Anderson said, "We of course recommend fighting it in court. You offered to buy the property from the family directly. We have documentation that proves it. You bought it from the state after the condemning of the property. The timeline is above reproach. We'll win in court."

"I want to settle."

"Edmund you can't."

Edmund ignored them. "This is what the family is asking for all together." He pointed at the number. "Is it possible to break it up into parts, with the family that lived there receiving the largest share?"

"Yes, technically, they're separate suits."

"Well, is that possible—to settle with each individual plaintiff, a separate amount, a separate deal?"

"I suppose, but Silvers and I aren't really in the 'settling' business. We prefer to win."

"I know you do, but here are my construction files." He passed a stack of forms to Silvers, "And here's an accounting of what's left on the land."

Edmund rubbed his hand up over his face and through his hair. He had a flop sweat going right at the moment he wanted to look cool and calm. He had been practicing with the lawyers for months. He should be better at meetings than this.

"I propose we offer to these plaintiffs," he pointed at a stack of fifteen suits, "a chance to come pick up their belongings."

He showed the lawyers photos of the piles that the construction company had made. "We'll send them these photos so they can see the condition of their stuff. We'll create a deadline, if they want their things, they can truck it away. If they don't want their things, I'll divide their settlement up amongst them after I have the stuff trucked away. Either way we do okay."

Edmund put his hand on Violet's folder. "This plaintiff is the representative of the family that lived on the mountain. It was their home. I believe this is a different situation." He pretended to glance in the folder to remind himself of the girl's name. How could he forget her name? The name he repeated to himself, *Violet, I'm sorry, Violet.* Always with an *I'm sorry* in between. Always. "Violet Winslow. It says here that the land belonged to her mother and her grandmother. The construction company has been storing her things, at least what was labeled and recovered, in containers. I propose we settle with Ms. Winslow money for the land, and her things. It's more than I wanted to spend, but we aren't in court and we get to move on. It's still a good deal for us. The land is worth it. I'm certain of it."

Edmund looked around. "Why the long faces?"

"We're sorry, Edmund. You were really excited about this first deal, but sometimes in business things work out like this."

"It was a windfall." Edmund tried to appear and sound nonchalant. "I may have spent a great deal of it, but I still have the land at the end of the day."

"Since you're in town we should discuss the plans for the development. Have you decided what you'd like to do?"

"High-rise hotels, big. Giant swimming pools, or better yet, wave pools. Can we get it zoned for a casino?"

"Your grandfather would be proud." Anderson beamed already forgiving Edmund for his choice to settle.

* * *

Three weeks later, when Edmund was laying in bed watching television, Benjamin phoned, "The owner of Violet's land settled!"

Careful careful, don't sound to informed or too confused. Get the right tone, or better yet barely speak. "Oh really?"

"Yeah, he gave her more than she asked for, and the crazy part is most of her personal things were in storage. He even recovered her mother's china, unbroken, and arranged delivery. Things didn't fare quite so well for her aunts and uncles—they have to use their settlement to help clean up the land, but Violet won.

"She's still worried about what the owner will do with the land. She suspects they plan to develop it, but she's so excited to have some closure!"

"That's really great news, Benjamin. Where will she put everything?"

"I don't know, that will be a challenge, but really I haven't heard her this happy in a long time, or quite possibly ever."

"That's really great. I'm happy for her." Edmund closed his eyes imagining Violet smiling, but it required proximity, desired proximity. He had to be there up close, viewing the edge of her smile, the hum of her giggle in her throat. He wanted to be there to hear it, to see it, to throw his arms around her and say, You won! You beat the asshole that ruined everything! And you're alive and you have your things and you've got enough money now to do something with, something good.

Benjamin said, "We're taking her out to a restaurant tonight to celebrate. It's so weird that you aren't here to enjoy it with us."

"I'll be thinking about you. Where are you going?" Benjamin told him the name of the restaurant. After their conversation Edmund called the restaurant and picked up their tab.

CHAPTER THIRTY-EIGHT
Almost a year

A couple of months later, mid June, Anderson called, "Edmund there's a problem."

Edmund feigned surprise, "Oh really? With the B&B? My parents fortune? My brother's account?"

"No, where are you now?"

"The hotel, down the street."

"Is it possible for you go to the land? It might be a good idea to go—"

"Wouldn't that blow my anonymity? What's going on?" Edmund's room looked out over a park, He watched kids playing on the swings to calm and distract his mind.

"We received a letter from a lawyer for an organization called the Purple Coastal Lizard Foundation."

"Weird, a whole organization for a lizard?" Edmund hoped he sounded sufficiently surprised.

"Yes, they've filed for an injunction prohibiting you from continuing any activity on the land."

"Oh."

"Can you be here in an hour? Silvers and I will have more information then, and Edmund? I'm terribly sorry about this. Environmentalists, you know, don't seem to get how the world works."

"Odd that they want to put the needs of a lizard above development of prime coastal property," agreed Edmund.

"We'll see you in an hour."

Edmund took a long drink of soda and wondered if those kids could keep swinging and for how long.

...

That afternoon the conversation with the lawyers was informative. They had received the injunction and thought there were two courses of action.

Course of action A: Edmund should fight. Anderson and Silvers really wanted to take that course because they were still stinging from being forced to settle over Violet's lawsuit. They were good lawyers; they didn't want to settle, ever. They wanted to fight.

Anderson said, "Screw the lizard."

Silvers said, "Screw the environmentalists."

They wanted to take it to the Governor. Course of action A would take a long time, might take an extremely long time, and might be very, very messy. It would mean hiring a public relations firm and probably losing Edmund's anonymity.

Course of action B: Pay off the environmentalists and threaten them with Course of action A so they would go away quickly. They might do that. It might work.

"If there's one thing animal lovers want more than animals, it's money," said Anderson. "It's the way the world works."

Silvers said, "Everyone has a price, especially Environmentalists."

Edmund thought this charge was untrue, but he let it slide, feeling it safer to agree, "Definitely."

He begged away to consider it for the weekend, but not really. Because he had long ago decided.

* * *

The following Monday, after their usual formal greetings, Edmund began, "I don't like any of the courses of action you presented last week."

Anderson humphed. Silvers said, "Well, I uh..."

"I've thought this all through—" He held his hands up when they began to interrupt. "You aren't going to like it at first, but hear me out, please.

"I received a call the other day from the construction company. The news isn't good. The mound has become increasingly difficult to remove. The parts are so compacted that pulling them apart is difficult work and some areas are impossible. Work has slowed considerably. I didn't want to tell you until I researched more.

He pushed a stack of photos across the table.

Anderson exclaimed, "It's still gigantic!"

"Yes, yes it is. Considering this information, I've decided to give the land to the environmentalists. Let them deal with it. They can run it, work it, or let it sit there. Let it be a sanctuary for the lizard."

Anderson protested, "But Edmund, it's your very first land deal!"

"Sure, but the hill is turning out to be very expensive to move, and well, pardon the pun, developing it is an uphill battle. We might lose in court—"

Anderson and Silvers balked, but Edmund said, "Sometimes it happens, and even if we don't lose, we might lose to public opinion. I don't want my family's company to be the bad guys that killed off the last of a rare purple lizard."

"But Edmund, you've been working on the deal for so long."

"It was a windfall. I'll get the next one right. Besides, when we've given away a giant piece of property as a wilderness sanctuary, don't we get some kind of tax credit? Can we call it a charitable contribution?"

"Well, of course, but such a large amount of money..."

"Yes, but it was extra. The estate is okay. We shouldn't worry about a gamble that didn't pay off. Just move on, right?"

Edmund watched his lawyers as they nodded and shuffled papers and conferred with each other over the next steps. While they discussed they were backdropped by the large painting of a sunset. Edmund had bought it from the gallery, giving Emily full credit for the sale, and gifting it to Anderson and Silvers as a thank you. He didn't know if it would ever be worth what he paid, but it looked stunning in their office.

Anderson looked up from a stack of paperwork and smiled, so Edmund knew he had won them over. There would be no more arguing. They would make it happen because that's what they did—made things happen.

He understood the lawyers well by now, they were almost friends, even with their arms-length formality. They were by far the people he spent the most time with. Two old men who harrumphed and hooeyed over everything and predated him by at least forty years. If friendship grew from proximity and time and shared interests, then they were it, friends. He watched them shuffle papers and talk about forms and percentages and tax shelters, and—maybe they were only acquaintances after all. He regretted lying to them, but it was kind of his thing now. To lie. He had grown accustomed to not telling the truth, and it was easy if he kept everyone at a distance.

He rubbed his hands through his hair and noted the lack of sand on the table in front of him. He interrupted them from across the room. "Speaking of windfall, It's been a long —what's it been?"

"Almost a year, Edmund."

"Wow, that long? I could use a vacation. I think I'll do a bit of traveling..."

"Sure Edmund, we were surprised you were around this much."

"Well, the land deal did seem great, but oh well. I'll go find a beach and stay awhile. When's the next board meeting?"

"Month and a half."

"Good, I'll come back for it. It will be good to see Mom and Dad. Where are they right now?"

"We sent their last money transfer to Thailand."

Edmund stood and shook their hands. It had been a long, very long, almost year.

CHAPTER THIRTY-NINE
Trouble responding

Newly invigorated, he returned to his hotel. He was leaving the city. It had taken many many months, but he had unloaded the land—sadly, a lot of money too—but he had unloaded the land.

It was no longer in the control or crosshairs of his family's buy-it-up, build-it-up, make-it-pay, and then drop-it-away business strategy. He was relieved. He didn't have to pretend anymore to develop it while also protecting it from development. Keeping the two opposing interests oppositional had been exhausting.

The lawyers wondered why he stayed close. Because he had been juggling, and a juggler with so many balls in the air has to stay put. He couldn't walk around when he had to concentrate on catching and tossing all those balls, especially when some of them were on fire.

He opened the hotel's front door and walked briskly through the lobby, almost missing Benjamin, standing by the elevator doors.

"Hi Edmund."

"What? Oh."

Edmund glanced over his shoulder causing Benjamin to narrow his eyes. "Shifty much? What are you looking for?"

"I don't know, you surprised me."

"You see, I wondered what was going on with you, so I called the B&B to see what I could figure out. The person who answered the phones doesn't know who Edmund Hawkes is. Never met him."

Benjamin paused, waiting, then said, "How come my brother, Edmund Hawkes, has been telling me that he has all this work at the B&B?"

Edmund didn't answer so Benjamin repeated louder, "How come?"

"Benjamin, I—" Edmund glanced around. They were in a public lobby and Benjamin's manner and tone were causing people to stare.

"I called Mom and Dad, interrupted their visit to Thailand, and Mom said you were only needed on the family business for a month or so. Dad said Anderson and Silvers told him the emergency had passed. They think you and I have been together, working at the B&B, or seeking our fortune, or somehow both. Why would you be telling them you're with me, and telling me you're working on family business that doesn't exist?"

"Why don't we go up to my room, or head into the bar, or —"

"So you can sit me down and tell me more of your lies? I want you to tell me the truth. What are you doing here? Are you stealing money from the company?"

Edmund's jaw clenched. "No, definitely not. I've had business."

"When you came on my birthday you stayed for less than twenty-four hours. You've barely said a word to me in almost a year. We were best friends. You're my brother. Are you in trouble? What are you hiding from?"

"I'm not in trouble. Look, let's go somewhere else—"

"I'm not leaving right here. Not without answers."

Benjamin glared at Edmund with so much contempt that Edmund avoided his eyes, which pissed him off even more. "Look what you've become. You're nothing but secrets and lies all wrapped up in a tie. You used to have sand on your shoulders, now you're just a pompous fucking ass-hat."

"Ben lay off. You don't know." There were so many people watching now that the odds were high a video of their fight would end up public.

"You haven't been the same since you told me you loved Violet, but here's news, you didn't really love her. You know, you almost convinced me. I felt sorry for you when the mountain fell. But guess what? You didn't love her. You walked away and never looked back."

Edmund had trouble responding. His brother's words, full of truth and equal parts caustic spray, landed on him, wearing him away.

Benjamin pointed at his chest. "When you came to my birthday—I don't know what you said to Violet, but she was depressed for weeks. Weeks getting over it, and you—You. Don't. Care. At all. I'm beginning to think you can't."

"I can't."

"What? You can't? What you can't, you can't love? You *can't?*" Benjamin leaned over Edmund, dominating him, hot, past thinking. He had become a nine year old boy about to fist fight his brother on the playground. Except they were both bigger and more dangerous, and possibly too angry to be in a public place about to throttle each other.

"Because I'm the owner."

"The what? The own..." It took a half second and then Benjamin's mind clicked. He roared, "The owner!?"

"Yes, the owner of Violet's mountain."

Benjamin yelled and threw himself at his brother with his forearm aimed for his neck. He shoved him back against the wall and with his face an inch away growled, "You think it's fun? To be the big powerful man who owns everybody and everything? To buy up homes and bulldoze them down? You make me sick. You stay away from Violet, you stay away from all of us."

Edmund pushed at Benjamin's chest to get him to back off.

Benjamin shook his arms out. "Fine. Be this guy. I don't care. Stop giving me money, I don't want anything from you." He spun in his tracks for the lobby door.

Edmund ran his hands over his face trying to compose himself in front of his audience.

"Ben!" he said as Benjamin reached the handle. "Are you going to tell Violet?"

"No, I want nothing to do with your lies." He rushed down the steps and away.

Edmund went up the elevator to pack his luggage and leave.

CHAPTER FORTY
Wished he could go back

Edmund's flight landed at the same airport he had left months and months and months earlier. He drove to Sandy Shores in a rental car the color of sand.

Despondent and depressed Edmund suffered the same feelings as when he left all those months ago. How had he become so stuck? He hoped surfing would help and working outside, but still he felt as alone as it could be possible to feel.

As he neared the pile he couldn't believe the changes. He had seen photos but seeing it with his own eyes was something all together different. It was smaller. The top four layers had been taken off the tops and sides. The next layers were smaller and compacted and more interesting. Things that had been stacked were now flattened into striations, yet somehow they were still shiny and sparkling in the sunlight.

He craned his head to look out the window. "Whoa." The fence around the perimeter was tall and imposing, but he imagined that if you were a gawking tourist it would add to the mystery and excitement. *That was the mountain of trash, the one that girl almost died on. Did you see it on the news? Photograph me in front of it.*

The whirligigs were gone, delivered to Violet's studio. The piles of stuff had been argued over, sifted through, and checked for anything important. The unimportant things had been trucked away to Habitat for Humanity, or the landfill.

Violet's aunts and uncles received a check with what remained of their settlement. They had many complaints, but when one uncle got excessive about it Silvers threatened to slap him with a fine for unlawful dumping. That fine would have cut into his settlement immensely, so he went away quietly.

With three quarters of the pile gone, the remaining layers were compacted, stratified, hooked, crushed and fused by pressure. Turned into a kind of manmade shale and then possibly, eventually marble or granite. *Wouldn't that be cool? Marble made of household detritus, pressed and shaped by gravity and force?*

He drove up the western side and turned onto Main Beach Road, and like he had so many times before, got out to look back at the hill.

The mountain now measured seven stories tall, an eighth of a mile long. Diminutive compared to its original many, many stories and quarter-mile length size and even smaller still from the length it had become when it had spilled over and all around. There was less of it, making it more manageable, more acceptable. He had a perfect view of the top, yet it lacked Violet. There were no whirligigs, no movement, no life.

His phone rang. His parents were calling and he hadn't spoken to them in months. He leaned against the trunk of the car, on the side of the road, and answered.

"Hello, Edmund."

"Hi Mom. Where are you guys right now?"

"We flew back home, arrived last night. Are you nearby? We'd love to see you."

"No, actually I..." He looked over his shoulder down Main Beach Road toward the ocean and then turned back to his hill. "I'm seeking my fortune again."

"Oh, good, is Benjamin with you? He called us the other day. He acted very strange, and asked a lot of questions about you."

"He's not here. I decided to go in a different direction."

"Oh, okay. Well, when you see him tell him we're back from our travels for the time being."

"Mom, I need to tell you about... About what I..."

"We know, we know. You hired a management company to run the B&B." Michelle laughed a high twinkling laugh. "We were very surprised when strangers greeted us in the lobby, but the truth is they are very good. Your father and I are very proud. This is the best B&B we've overnighted in, and we've stayed in a lot. Here, your father wants to say hello."

Edmund's father came on the line, "Hello Edmund, we're back from our world travels. We have thousands of photos. When will we see you?"

"I'm not sure... I..."

"Good, good. Here, let me step out of the room." Edmund heard rustling and jostling and his father's voice again, "I didn't want to speak in front of your mother—I know we burdened you with running the Bed and Breakfast. Come to find out it's not as easy to run one as we originally thought. And I would never say this in front of your mother, but it's not really her skill set. She is a wonderful woman, but the effort exhausted her, and it took months and months of vacationing to get over it."

Edmund ran his hand down his face. "Of course Dad, that's why I hired the company to do it."

"Yes, you did great. It's been a big responsibility running everything, controlling things for the people I love. I have been so responsible for so long, that I have to admit, I'm glad someone else can be in charge now. I can finally sit back and relax. Thank you."

Edmund had been wondering where this line of reasoning would end up, so his father surprised him when he concluded in gratitude. "Oh. Thanks Dad. I mean, you're welcome."

"Good, good. I'm passing the phone back to your mother."

"Hello, Edmund, if we don't get a chance to talk to Benjamin before we leave for Ireland will you tell him we love him?"

"I will, but he would probably like to hear it directly from you."

"We'll call him when we hang up."

"When do you leave for Ireland?"

"The end of the week after we deal with everything here."

"All right, safe travels." He wanted to keep them on the phone. It suddenly dawned on him that they were all he had left. He wished he could go back, check into the B&B that contained his childhood bedroom, and go to Ireland with them. He hadn't ever been to Ireland. His parents were bustling around unpacking their clothes into a familiar drawer. He could picture it. But then again he couldn't, now that the room had been redecorated in B&B style.

His parents had become unconcerned and carefree, and Edmund had helped them achieve that state, and surprise, surprise, they had thanked him. But they were also going away, and the call ended leaving him alone again. Or still. A tumbleweed rolled across the road and halted on Edmund's shoe. He shifted so that it continued rolling on by.

CHAPTER FORTY-ONE
Becoming unrecognizable

He checked into Sandy Shore's hotel. Then he walked to the local surf shop, bought a long board and a short, and surfed that afternoon. The waves were good. He caught wave after wave and tried not to think about how much he missed Benjamin. He walked to shore and right through the campground they had stayed in together so long ago. *Feels like a totally different time, instead of only months ago. Like ages. Ages and ages.*

His hotel room resided on the ground floor, which meant sand covered its small deck. He leaned his surfboard on the railing and in a kind of daze turned and wandered up Main Beach Road to the mountain. The sun was setting and burnishing the hill—rust and glitter and silent stillness. He walked to the edge of the town, where the buildings ended, and stood in the cool evening air with his towel wrapped around his back, watching the mountain, imagining Violet saying good night to the sun.

* * *

Edmund met with Mike, the construction company owner, and received a final report about the sturdiness of the hill and whether it had stabilized. It had. He found a lizard expert from one of the local universities to decide if the substrate was acceptable. It was close enough. He learned so much and had absolutely no one to share it with. Whenever he had an interesting conversation, learned something new about the lizard or the hill and wanted to tell someone, he would go hang out at the pub restaurant and start conversations with the waitress about his day. Their exchanges were short though; she simply wanted to take his order after all. She only had enough time for niceties.

After a week he moved into a small vacation rental house. The house had clapboard sides, originally blue, but now sand-sprayed gray, and it looked over a sandy stretch, a small dune, and beyond to the ocean. He sat out there for hours every day, reading some, but mostly watching the waves and thinking about things.

Over time, he was so quiet and introspective, that it seemed like his senses heightened. He became really good at sensing the weather and the approaching ocean swells. He heard cars coming down the sandy road, for instance, before he ever saw them. That was one of the cool things about being alone. One cool thing. The bad parts were impossible to keep track of, like he wanted to talk to Benjamin about the waves.

He quit carrying his phone because didn't need to talk to anyone. It was lonely work even so, but Edmund was growing used to that. One day, puttering around in the parking lot of the mountain he stopped and watched a circling hawk in the sky for twenty minutes and then slowly shook out of it and didn't remember what he had been doing before. He drove home, unsurprised by his lapse. His gait slowed, and he wondered if he might be going a little crazy. Maybe a lot crazy.

He let his beard grow, becoming unrecognizable when he caught sight of himself in the mirror. He tried not to look. He didn't like to look himself in the eyes. He looked like the liar he had become.

CHAPTER FORTY-TWO
She's kind of a mystery

A couple of months after he arrived, well into this routine, Edmund was lounging on his wicker love seat staring out over the railing at the ocean when a truck wheeled into his sand driveway and skidded to a stop. His truck. From a year ago.

Edmund set his jaw. Had Benjamin come to carry on again? He had been enjoying a soda and watching the waves, and did not want to deal with this drama. He was pissed that he hadn't been given a heads up, though truth was, he hadn't checked his phone for a while. His anger was illogical, but *still*.

He decided to stare straight ahead and watch peripherally. The truck door slammed and footsteps climbed to his porch and then, not Benjamin, but Lala leaned on the deck railing.

"Eddie, you have a beard."

"Lala? What are you doing here?"

She glanced back at the truck incredulously and said, "Um, I drove to come see you." She was wearing a tight fuzzy pastel blue sweater, jeans cut off at mid calf, and on her feet two different shoes—one a pink high-top, the other a low profile blue sneaker. Edmund decided not to ask.

"Last I heard you didn't drive."

"Well, I don't usually, and not well, but how else would I get here?"

"I'm surprised Benny let you take the truck."

"Well, I... Since I spent my teen years on top of a mountain—so you know, I stole it. I've a right to some rebellion."

Edmund chuckled. He had been set for conflict, but welcomed this, an ocean breeze of relief, until—

"Eddie I know."

He looked at the bottle in his hand, "Know what?"

"I know you're the owner of the land."

"Did Benjamin tell you?"

"No, I mean, yes. I figured it out a while back when Violet got the settlement. There was something off about it. It was almost personal, like a gift, *nice*. It didn't jibe with how we expected the owner of the land to act. Violet and Benjamin brushed it off, but you had dropped out of our lives that day, and I guessed. Call it a hunch."

Edmund chewed his lip. This sounded like a more dramatic conversation than he had wanted to have, and on his own porch so he couldn't get away. He felt trapped, forced to discuss things. Now he wished he had used his phone, used it as a shield. He could have sent her to voicemail and answered in texts.

Lala walked to the love seat and perched on the edge facing him. "When Benjamin came back from seeing you he was furious and depressed and totally obnoxious, so I finally cornered him and asked him what happened. He tried to hide it, but like I said, I had already guessed."

Lala's eyes drilled into the side of his face, he leaned forward, under the guise of putting the bottle on the ground and remained with his elbows on his knees staring at his sandy feet.

"Edmund, I am so sorry. For you to do all of that, it must have been so... Oh my god, I can't imagine what you must be going through, and we all deserted—"

Edmund pressed his thumbs up against his tear ducts trying to stopper the flow. "Lala, don't..."

"We deserted you, Edmund, we did, and it's been months and months, and we moved on and started living our own lives, and you were still there, on the mountain."

Edmund's shoulders shook, and he tried to suppress his tears, but liquid and salt rolled down his nose anyway. Lala put her arm around his shoulder which made it worse. He moaned, so she pulled his head over to her lap.

He held on to her thighs and cried there, waves of sadness washing onto his shores.

Lala said, "I know."

And then she said, "I'm just so sorry."

And then she said, "All of this, so much. Too much to do by yourself."

Lala folded over his head and held on while he cried.

* * *

A long time later, after the waves abated, he asked from his huddle in her lap, "Does Violet know?"

Lala stroked his back. "No, Benjamin and I talked it out and didn't want to tell her until we talked to you first. We wanted to make sure it was as bad as we guessed."

Edmund leaned back up into his seat and nodded and asked, "Is it as bad?"

"I'd say worse."

He recovered a bit and caught his breath. "I'm not sure why I'm carrying on this way."

"I understand, and you don't have to worry about it. You're family. You should be pissed at us for deserting you."

"I lied to everyone. Come to find out I'm good at that."

Lala put her arm around his shoulder and kissed him on the cheek. "I honestly wouldn't blame you if you didn't forgive us, but we need you to."

He gave her a half-smile. "Yeah. It's all good."

Lala cuddled in and put her head on his shoulder. "What's going on with this chair anyway?"

"This? My wicker love seat?"

"It's up on blocks." She motioned to the wood that elevated the legs.

"Oh, the wooden *blocks*. It's so I can see the ocean. Some idiot built the railing at my eye level."

"Uncle Bruce would hate this."

Edmund smiled again. "So what now?"

"Well, since I'm visiting my big brother Eddie for the weekend—" She was so easy and cheerful, the fresh ocean breeze had returned. "Will you teach me how to surf?"

Edmund stretched out of his slump and said, "Definitely sis, no time like the present."

* * *

Edmund gave Lala a lesson in the sand and then pushed her into the shore break for a few waves. She giggled a maniac-style giggle the entire time. When she came up for air after her third big splash-tumble she said, "I'm ready for the big waves now, let's go!"

He looked over his shoulder where the ocean glistened in the sun, quiet and barely swelling. "Well, the waves aren't really..."

"Let's at least paddle out to where you and Benjamin sit. I want the whole experience." Edmund ran for his board and they paddled out farther from shore. Edmund sat on his board, and Lala laid on hers, rocking and jiggling and barely keeping afloat, capsizing whenever she spoke. "You make it seem easy!" She giggled as the board spun up and over her.

Edmund laughed and flung water out of his hair. "It's been a long time since I laughed," he said when she came up pretend-gasping.

"You can tell, it's awkward looking, but at least your beard covers it up." She splashed him jovially with water.

"So how is Benjamin?"

"He's better. He understands now at least. The lies, and why. He's still sore because you didn't trust him. Truth be told, he's a little embarrassed about how he acted. He'll come around. I'm working on him."

She turned her board to face the shore and the hill beyond. "So the hill is smaller. Strange without the whirligigs. I saw signs all over—it's a sanctuary now?"

"For your favorite lizard. My company gifted Violet's Mountain to the very grateful Organization for the Preservation of the Purple Coastal Lizard. You should have seen their thank you letter. So gracious."

"Violet's Mountain?"

"That's what the OPPCL calls it."

"You mean, you."

"Yes."

"A long time ago, when the Hawkes brothers started coming around, me and Violet joked that you were predatory birds circling around trying to carry us off, but you aren't really like that at all."

"Except we kind of did."

She laughed and said, "I guess you did."

"So we should go in. It's nearing sunset and I usually walk to town and grab a bite to eat after."

"Sounds perfect."

* * *

Edmund excused himself while Lala washed up. The road beckoned him to his evening ritual—watching the hill reflect the sunset from it's protected habitat land. The summit was empty now, but it hadn't always been. He remembered it like it was yesterday.

The sunlight washed red over the mountain. After a half hour Lala joined him, pink cheeked, with wet hair. She wore a little sundress and flip-flops and laughingly put her arm through Edmund's and asked, "Where are you taking me for dinner?"

He said, "Well, there are only two places. One is not so good. The other is better, and I've been driving the waitress a bit crazy by my lonely, excessive, pay-attention-to-me talking. She'll probably be relieved to see me with a friend."

"I cannot imagine you talking too much."

"I swear last time I ate there she rolled her eyes."

"Seriously? Okay we'll go, and I'll hang on your every word. How dare she!"

He paused for a second taking a last look at the hill. "I love it like this, about dark, the sky behind glowing deep blue."

"This is a view I didn't really ever take."

"When Violet lived there it was glorious. She stood at the tiptop, up about there," he pointed above its height. "The whirligigs would spin and turn and sparkle. Once the sun set she would start welding. God, she was beautiful up there."

She tightened her grip on his arm as they walked to the restaurant.

"How about tomorrow we go, and I'll show you around?" He held the front door of the restaurant for her.

"I'm not sure—" Edmund followed her to the table and held out her chair. "I actually—I have nightmares about that night. It's kind of freaking me out to go there. I didn't even look at it as I drove by. We could have been..."

"I know," he said, "but I fixed it. It's better now."

They ordered their meals and Lala asked, "Have you gone out with anyone?"

"Once, it didn't stick. And perhaps you haven't noticed, but I've been working on my Reclusive Hermit Persona. At the hotel in Kingsbridge I considered wearing a monocle and pretending to be a mysterious industrialist. I don't think anyone would have noticed though. I was alone in the morning, alone in the evening, coming and going. All I did was workout in the gym, sit in the park, and watch TV in bed. It's been a long year. See there I go, excessive talking. Who knew that would be a side-effect of living the hermit life?"

"Who knew?" Lala said with a laugh.

He asked, "How about you, dating anyone?

"Totally. I have a guy who's completely sweet on me, Doug."

"*Doug?*"

"Yeah, he's a little death metal, but I don't hold it against him. Whenever he comes by you should see Benjamin strut around and bow out—huffing and puffing. He doesn't think Doug's good enough for me." She rolled her eyes.

The waitress sidled up for their order. "I'm glad you have a date Edmund. You spend too much time fussing with that mountain. Though we are really glad of it. Now we have a wildlife sanctuary *and* a tourist attraction."

Edmund ordered their food, and when the waitress left harkened back to the prior conversation. "I wholeheartedly back Benny-boy's stance on this guy. This Doug character is definitely not good enough for you."

"You haven't even laid eyes on him!"

"I know all I need to know in these three things: One, his name is Doug. Two, he likes death metal. Three, before you met him you didn't steal cars."

"Hey, you caused my grand theft auto."

"Speaking of which, you're leaving tomorrow?"

"Midmorning."

"Maybe I should drive you home and rent a car back or something."

"Are you kidding me? I totally did the coolest thing ever— heard that Edmund was sad, stole a truck, and drove six hours to go check on him. Now imagine if you drive me home after I check on you? The story loses all of its drama! I mean, come on."

"I suppose that makes sense. Though I can't believe I'm listening to the logic of someone who likes Death Metal *Doug*." She swiped at him with her napkin.

They ate a big dinner and talked all the way back to Edmund's house. He gave her his room, because he hadn't furnished the extra bedroom yet, and he slept on the couch.

"Good night, Lala. Thank you for coming."

"Anything for you. G'night, Eddie."

. . .

The next morning Edmund took Lala to breakfast and then to the mountain. He had already removed the fences because of the hill's stability. He pulled the truck into the parking lot beside the parked condor.

"So all the other equipment is gone?"

"Part of the deal with the construction company. They got to keep it for cheap. The money is in Violet's account now."

They walked to the condor's basket while Edmund explained, "The top layers of the mountain compressed these bottom layers. They've formed almost a shale." They climbed in and ascended the side. "See this?" He pointed to an area with stratified colors. "Those were clothes. If you rub the edges they're fuzzy like felt. See that, it's *boxes*, rained on and compressed so much they've become stiff and connected to the layers of paper under them." He pushed the button to ascend some more.

"I have plans to build a wooden path that will spiral up the side and end in a deck at the very top, but that will have to come later." He continued to point to parts of the mountainside—appliance corners poking out and fragments of rock-ified things—quilts and clothing and shoes. "I like this, there, that's a television, right there."

"These are newspapers?"

"Yes, beautiful, huh? If I knew they'd end up like this eventually, maybe I wouldn't have forced Violet to get rid of them that day."

"It was a crap-load of newspapers. And how much would you have to put on top of them to get them to congeal like this? You did what you did because you had to. You *had* to."

Edmund clenched his jaw. It was comforting to hear someone say that, but he still felt raw. His decisions that day had been so primal, reactionary, he always wondered if they were the right ones. What if he had given Violet time to say good night? Would she have left on her own? Would he be there with her right now? Instead of here, now, alone, protector of the mountain?

"It's so beautiful. I can't believe this is common everyday stuff."

"Stuff condensed, rained on, pressed and forced."

"And our grandmother's house is like this too, compressed and transformed underneath?"

"Probably. It's buried though, forever, and that's a good thing—hey, look right here, by my hand, one of the lizards."

"Ew."

"They poke in and out of the holes but don't head out into the open much anymore."

They reached the summit and Edmund brought the condor basket to rest at the landing point. "The flat part is over here." He scattered sea gulls in front of him.

She said, "You need the whirligigs back."

"Without them I'm not sure the lizard survives. And if the lizard doesn't survive then all of this is for nothing."

"It's not for nothing, Eddie."

The wind blew in gusts, pushing the clouds away, creating a long and brilliant view. "It is so beautiful up here. I didn't go up very often before. It was big, so big, but this is good. As long as I don't go to the edge."

"I think the deck would be right about here, with a railing so people can come up and see the view."

"You should do that. What's holding you back?"

Edmund's hands were stuffed in his pockets. "Well, this is embarrassing. It's money. I spent a lot this year and find myself in an in-between. In a few months I turn 23 and I'll have my trust, but until then I have to budget."

She shook her head. "So let me get this straight, you did all of this until you were broke?"

"Well, I'm not broke. I just have to..."

"I want to pay for the wooden path and the deck."

"You don't—"

"Violet gave me my own account, with a ton of money in it. To do whatever. I want you to build a path and deck with it up to the top of the mountain."

"Don't be ridiculous, Lala. I'm not taking your money."

"Well, first, it's kind of your money." Edmund balked and shook his head.

Lala looked at him for a minute. "Don't you think Violet would love a deck up here?"

"Well, that's a complicated question, but yes, I kind of do."

"She gave me money, and her birthday is in a few months. I want to buy her a deck and a path. I'll pay extra for a plaque with her name on it."

"Her name's already on the mountain. I named it after her."

"Well, I want the plaque to have birthday wishes on it. You have to let me. It's your first charitable contribution—besides, of course, the ones you made yourself."

"Okay, okay," Edmund laughed. "Okay Lala. Okay."

* * *

They returned to Edmund's house. Standing beside his truck for a farewell, Lala wrote Edmund a check. Then she scribbled a message on a piece of paper saying, "This is what I want the plaque to say, the birthday plaque, okay?" She folded them together and handed them to Edmund, who stuffed them in his pocket.

"I'm glad you came."

"I had to, I know what it's like to be left."

Edmund pulled her up in a hug and kissed the top of her head.

She returned his hug and said, "Thank you for teaching me to surf."

"You need a lot more lessons."

Edmund rubbed the palm of his hand along a scratch on the side of the truck, checking for a dent. But why was he checking, for what purpose? He turned his back to the truck and leaned. He was self-conscious, because though her visit had fixed so many things, there were still big broken pieces lying around tripping him up. He asked, "What about Benjamin?"

"Benjamin will come around. He's hurt, but I don't think he can stay that way once I—" She let her voice trail off.

Edmund nodded his head. He had hoped to be the kind of guy who held it all together, but he was really openly dropping things, collapsing like a big, giant, too-tall hill. She would talk about it to people, tell them. They would pity him and feel sad about it.

It sucked because he wanted to be the guy who had solved it all. The superhero who saved the girl and restored a mountain. Instead he was the weak guy, all alone and sad.

"It'll be okay. I'll tell him," she said. "And you have to forgive him too, he's taking really good care of us."

"Yes, of course."

She lingered.

"I'm going to talk to Violet too."

Edmund chewed his lip. "How do you think she'll take it?"

"I don't know, she's kind of a mystery sometimes."

Lala climbed into the truck. "I'll call you when I get home, tell you I'm safe, but then it might take awhile. I don't want you to get your hopes up. It might be awhile."

"I got you, no worries." Edmund closed the driver side door and watched Lala back his truck out of the driveway. She turned out and spun the tires in the sand blowing a dust spray into the sky. Edmund raised his hand farewell, as her brake lights lit, and she kept going away down the street.

Edmund had been thinking that weekend—during the laughter, the friendly zings, the teasing, and the planning—that things were better now. That the moment Lala spun wheels into the sand of his driveway she had fixed it all. But watching the dust cloud of her departure was eery and lonely and final. The quiet sand sifted back down, and with just a very minuscule second of time he found himself alone again. Possibly more alone.

He turned, taking in the quiet beach town road. The houses were vacation rentals. It was almost September so most of them were vacant, shutters pulled, drives empty.

He turned to the dunes and looked out over the ocean. It surged. The wind had come up today. The calm lake of yesterday's surf lesson had been replaced with a rolling whitewater mess. The sky had turned the color of the sea and the foam sprayed to the sky, mimicking the cloud of sand from a minute earlier.

Edmund turned to his house, quiet, blue-gray, adorned with white details. He walked to the porch and slumped into the wicker love seat and waited to see what the wind would bring.

CHAPTER FORTY-THREE
So happy for her

Monday evening, thirty-six hours forty-two minutes later, Benjamin called. "Hi Edmund."

"Hi Benjamin."

"I've been talking to Lala and I'm really sorry about our fight, about all of it, everything."

"Yes, me too, all of it."

"I was so mad that you were keeping things from me, but I get it. You couldn't tell me. There's no way I would have been able to keep it quiet and—I get it. You did what you had to do. I get it."

Edmund worried that saying anything would cause a torrent of tears, and that would be unseemly. He was a lonely hermit, didn't want to be the unhinged guy too. Better to simply nod, even if over the phone a nod didn't translate.

"Can we have a do-over? You don't keep secrets and I don't act like a jerk?"

Edmund chuckled, "Yes, we can have a do-over."

"What are you doing right now?"

"Me? I'm looking out over the ocean. Wishing the waves were rideable."

"Too small?"

"The wind is all over them. We have a swell and a tropical storm coming up from the South, so I think tomorrow morning will be better."

"I have shows next weekend, but I think I can come on a surf trip the last week of this month. I want to come for a whole week, really hang out. Would that be okay?"

"That would be great." In his recent past he would have pretended to look at a calendar first, but he was putting that behind him. He wasn't pretending to be busy to keep them at arms length anymore. "I'll make sure I put a mattress in the spare room for you."

Benjamin said, "Okay that sounds good." He was about to hang up without mentioning Violet and whether anyone had said anything to her. Edmund felt like he was suffocating. The weight of the question pushed down on his shoulders. His wicker chair was up on blocks, but he was sunken so low that he couldn't see the waves again.

"I'll call you later in the week." Click.

Edmund wondered if he would collapse in on himself and turn into a black hole of nothingness, invisibility. The inverse of invisibility, completely gone. Gone, Like Violet had accused him of being. He wasn't gone though, he was left.

The next morning Edmund went for a surf, a four hour surf. He was exhausted when he came back, but he had plans. He planned to go to the mountain and design the decks, but needed to find Lala's check. He searched his jeans, grateful he hadn't done laundry in a few days, and then two pairs of shorts before he found the folded check. He unwrapped the surrounding note. Lala had written:

Please have my plaque say this:
Thank you Edmund,
Love Lala

* * *

Edmund was standing on the mountain when Lala phoned, "Hey, Eddie. You talked to Benjamin, right? It's all good?"

"It's all good."

"I'm so glad, really glad. I plan to talk to Violet. She worked in the studio all weekend when I got back, and—Guess what?—She showed us her sculptures last night! They were so —they were so amazing. She had a collector and a gallery owner and all kinds of people come to her studio for a whole meet and greet, and she's taking the sculptures to New York and installing them in a gallery. She leaves tomorrow morning for the first phase. She's been working all night getting things ready."

"That's awesome Lala, I'm so happy for her."

"I know, me too."

"You saw the sculptures, what did they look like?"

"Beautiful miniatures. I took photos. I'll send them or a link to them, or I'll figure it out, my phone is acting weird. She'll be back next week, I'll talk to her then, okay?"

Edmund ran his hand over his eyes and said, "It's not that big a deal. Don't worry about it."

Lala sighed, "It is a big deal, and I'm going to talk to her."

"Sure," said Edmund closing his eyes. He was imploding. Possibly exploding. He definitely needed to throw up some barriers, or the shrapnel would put out everyone's eyes.

"I've got something I need to do, Lala. I'm really busy, okay?"

"Okay Edmund, I'll send the photos."

CHAPTER FORTY-FOUR
A different low view

Edmund checked his phone constantly. He checked the texts, his emails, the junk mail folders. He went on the mail server and checked the mail, the junk folders, the trash. He called technical support too, totally wasting his time.

He didn't want to ask Lala. He didn't want to sound desperate but thinking about Violet's artwork being displayed for the public without him—when he hadn't even seen it, everyone else had but him—was as final as a door slam, and he couldn't believe he stood on this side of it. Alone.

He had some last things to accomplish. The decks needed to be built, but then he would be finished and then what? He should leave. He had been in the shadow of this mountain for way too long. He couldn't imagine leaving, yet soon there wouldn't be one reason for him to stay. What would he do? Where would he go? He had been working to this goal for so long that the finish line felt like a cliff's edge.

* * *

On the third day of waiting an email came from Lala. It linked to a photography sharing site that Edmund had to log into. He created an account on his phone, and then realized the pictures wouldn't load, so he drove to his house and logged

into the account on his Mac. The first photo loaded and—
Violet.

She stood in the background talking to a strange man in a
suit. A well-fitted suit. The foreground contained a diorama of
her mountain, small in scale, though massive in its layout,
about 20 feet by 20 feet. In miniature form, though almost—
what was it, about six feet tall, maybe more? Edmund couldn't
see the specifics because of the angle, but it looked perfect, a
perfect replica of the hoard. Shiny and shimmering, a model of
a hodgepodge of excess junk.

Edmund tried to focus into the photo, but the details were
blurry. He clicked through to the next view: the top of the hill.
There were whirligigs, replicas, but really really small. Edmund
figured they must spin because one looked blurred. Tiny
spinning whirligigs.

Violet had painted or sculpted the model to look exactly
like the real-life mountain, including everything from
refrigerators to taxidermy, bright colors and reflective bits,
wooden pallets and doors, all to-scale and perfect.

The next photo stepped out a bit and took in the whole
mountain from the back. A parking lot containing small
bulldozers, trucks, cranes, and a little condor. It looked like she
had hung a bird from the ceiling. A teeny tiny seagull? Edmund
clicked around until he figured out how to focus in and
realized that a spinning mobile hung above the mountain
dangling a teeny tiny, circling hawk.

He smiled.

Lala had photographed a different low view from the
front: the ground in front of the hill, a small road, and pulled
off to the side, a miniature replica of Edmund's truck, and
standing beside it, the only person in the whole diorama, a man
looking back at the mountain top.

Edmund spent an hour flipping through photos, focusing in, focusing out, trying to make out details and investigating the studio visitors standing in the sides and backs. He especially studied the blurry photo of Violet talking to strangers.

He googled her name and sifted through all the news stories from the day of the avalanching mountain and found an announcement of her upcoming gallery show.

He looked through the photos again. He had no idea if he felt better or worse that she was still stuck on the mountain too.

CHAPTER FORTY-FIVE
She squinted at the sun

A week and a half later Edmund climbed the mountain. It was late afternoon and he had been loading and piling lumber all day for the beginning of the deck. A construction crew had been hired, but to cut corners he would work with them. He even bought tools for the occasion though the crew would probably make him carry lumber the whole day. He still looked forward to it, and hoped he wouldn't make a fool of himself. Though without a doubt he would.

He ascended the side of the mountain in the condor, taking a different trajectory to investigate new sections. This time he saw a box of gift wrap and ribbons, formerly square, now compressed and flattened and congealed. He stopped and looked at its glittering shiny beauty, and noticed the edge of an ornate frame. He couldn't decide if it once contained a painting, or a mirror, but it was a gilded gold part of a mountain now. In one spot, a bit of cardboard flaked away from an edge exposing a block of brightly colored and patterned cloth. Edmund poked at it and realized it was formerly quilting squares, very old quilting squares, turned into something else entirely though pressure and the elements.

What would happen to this mountain after years and years? Would the top layers peel away, eroding, and diminishing in size? Or would the winds pile up sand and rock, the mountain growing in size and shape? Changing or further stabilizing? Edmund had no answers, but it was time to let nature steer its course, instead of lonely humans adding and taking away.

He finished the climb and exited the condor. The seagulls swirled and twirled through the air in front of his advance. He chased them back and forth for a few minutes, watching them wave and spin and arc and crest. Then he walked up and over the uppermost point. He adjusted to the wind, which had calmed from earlier in the week, but still gusted, especially at this altitude. There was always a moment when he wondered if it might push him off.

He thought about Violet crawl-walking across the top while the helicopters hovered. It must have been terrifying. What had she been thinking at the time? About the whirligigs, or the lizards? Or simply trying not to change, not to bend with the wind, to not alter from the course?

She had a new course. She had made a good change of direction. And she still made art. What had the miniature of himself meant in Violet's sculpture? Why was he there?

He had never realized that she saw him or his truck from her hilltop. Had never considered that she knew he stopped and watched her from far away. Now she built little worlds containing him, the only figure. The only little teeny tiny creepy stalker-y character. Watching the hill. Guarding the hill. Him. What about the hawk? Was that him too, circling above?

He walked to the center. It was almost sunset. He wouldn't make it down to the road in time, so he would have to stay here. *Change of perspective might do me good.* He sat down cross-legged in the middle and took stock—the expanse to the Southeast, days away, lay his former home, in front of him the coast, the beach town nestled in the dunes, the North through and beyond, and way beyond by five hours, the city. Way out there, far away, a blurry Violet created art and met with well-fitted suits, planning her future. Which really, wasn't that the whole goal after all? The point of everything?

A truck drove south on Coastal Highway towards the mountain. It wasn't really that big of a deal, with Edmund's construction projects and the occasional deliveries for the town, but this was a big truck, and he wasn't expecting anything. He wondered who in town might be. Who would need supplies delivered? He couldn't think of anybody working on a project that required a semi truck.

Oh well, the driver was probably passing through. He returned to the view, but in his periphery the truck disappeared behind the mountain's northern edge, and didn't reappear. The only other place for it was into Edmund's parking lot.

He walked to the edge and peered over as the truck entered and parked right in the middle. The driver made some movement and then opened the door and—not a stranger but Violet—backed down the steps to the ground. She stood and took stock of all the empty spaces, Edmund's vehicle, and the piles of wood in the parking lot. Her boots planted firmly, blonde hair wild, pointing in all directions. She arched and turned to the top of the mountain. Edmund almost flinched, almost ducked and hid. What was she doing here? Had she come to fight?

The pause was long and curious—he looked down at her, she looked up. He held up a hand in greeting, but she didn't respond. She ducked into the condor cab—and before he had a second to think—started the basket, so that it moved down and away from his place on the mountain.

How would he get down now? Did she plan to leave him stranded? But that wouldn't explain the truck. As the basket descended Edmund grew more nervous and agitated. Should he stand here and wait, and for what, staring at her?

She decided for him by stepping into the basket and rising to meet him. Edmund glanced around. His brand new tools were scattered everywhere; should he tidy up? He put them into his tool bag and stood awkwardly with his hands in his pockets. But that seemed weird. He went back to the edge and looked over. She was two-thirds of the way up, focused intently on the surface of the hill as she rose. He ducked back and pretended to be interested in the corner of a box that flapped a little in the wind.

He couldn't pretend like she surprised him, because he had already waved, and now that seemed like the dumbest thing in the world to do. Waved, like a chump.

The basket arrived at the edge, and Violet stepped onto his planet. Which after all had been hers; she had planted the flag long before.

"Hello Edmund," her voice was cold, she walked by and past and stopped with the west reflected in her eyes.

Edmund closed the distance. "Lala told you?"

"Yes. She told me." Her eyes misted. She squinted at the sun, damming the deluge. "I don't know if I get to, but may I be alone? I drove straight through hoping to get here in time. We have a tremendous lot to talk about, you and I, but first I need to—"

"Of course. Absolutely. Yes, of course. Um, wave when you want me to bring the basket back for you." He crossed to the condor and rode it down the mountain. He had trouble catching his breath. The pink light of the setting sun had been reflected in her eyes and he had forgotten to breathe, not wanting to alter the breeze or the light or the sounds in any way. She had asked him to leave, when he wanted to be back there more than any other place, not in front of the mountain, not on top of the mountain, but beside Violet, saying good night.

CHAPTER FORTY-SIX
Nothing left to lose

The sun set. Violet waved over the side and Edmund traveled back up to collect her. She said, "We should go somewhere so we can talk."

"We could go to my house."

She said, "Only if there's food."

"Sadly not really, but I have a long-standing deal at the restaurant, they feed me and I pay them."

"The restaurant it is."

The sky was a deep black and blue. The air cool, the night breezy. He grabbed his tool bag, and they traveled down in the condor basket, barely speaking. Until she said, "You own tools?"

"The construction crew is coming tomorrow to build a deck, and they're letting me help. Everything is brand new, which I'm sure they'll tease me about mercilessly."

When they reached the bottom, Edmund swung his tool bag into the back of his new truck and asked, "Do you need to gather your things? What's in your gigantic truck anyway?"

"Lala told me there were lives on this mountain that needed rescuing, so to that end I'm delivering a truck load of whirligigs. And yes, I need my suitcase." She climbed into the cab of her truck and passed down a bag. "I didn't make a reservation at the hotel yet, hopefully they have rooms."

His forehead furrowed, irritated. She planned to stay at the hotel? "I have room, Lala stayed when she came. I slept on the couch. I plan to get a bed in the spare bedroom, I just—"

"Sure, that would be okay." Her voice was so noncommittal he thought his heart might break. They climbed into Edmund's truck and countered every movement with stiff politeness. After you. Why thank you. Are you warm enough? I'd like the windows down, please.

They rode in silence until he turned onto Main Beach Road. Violet's hair was down loose, big and spiraling. She was wearing a simple gray v-neck t-shirt and old faded tight jeans and her boots. Staring straight ahead she said, "It's smaller."

Edmund gripped the wheel tighter, "I tried to leave as much—"

"Yes, I know." Her voice sounded so tired it barely rolled to his ear. She balanced her chin on her fingertips, turned away, staring out the window as the landscape slid by and the first buildings of the little town of Sandy Shores appeared. Violet's stomach growled as Edmund pulled up in front of the restaurant.

* * *

His favorite waitress greeted him, "Hello Eddie, long time no see," though he came four times a week, sometimes more. She led them to a table.

As she handed them their menus, she said, "Wait a minute, you're Princess Violet, aren't you?"

Violet timidly nodded. "Well, Honey, how are you doing? We've been so worried about you!" She waved to the other dining room staff and as they gathered, announced, "This is Princess Violet! I'm so glad you're okay, Honey."

She beamed at them both. "And you're with Eddie. That is so nice. Eddie here has done such a nice thing with your mountain. Isn't it lovely?"

Violet said, "Yes, it is."

"It only needs your whirlie-sculpture-thingies."

"I brought them. We'll install them soon."

The waitress clapped her hands together and said, "That's wonderful! Where are you living now?"

Violet said, "I live in the City. I'm an artist there."

"Well, that is wonderful." The waitress paused and regarded her proudly and then said, "Okay, signal when you're ready to order." She turned away and the small crowd dispersed.

Violet ducked behind her menu, "That was so incredibly awkward."

"You were on the news, the closest thing to a celebrity that they have. And your story and mountain bring in a lot of tourists."

"Gawkers."

He put his menu aside and leaned forward and said, "So, I really want to explain—"

"No," she shook her head, "we can't talk here. They *recognized* me. I might cry and... and it might get..."

She looked like she might cry anyway. Splotches appeared on the side of her cheeks, so he flustered and said, "Of course. Absolutely." He busied himself staring at his menu though it had been long ago memorized. He was on the verge of a cry himself. One big raw nerve. He needed protection and the menu wasn't enough for the amount of exposed he was.

He had ripped off all the layers leaving only sensitive hidden secrets. He had been outed. Yet she responded with silence, steaming silence. Was he being punished? Because this

kind of felt like it. The worst punishment he could think of—
sitting across from Violet and not being with Violet.

He had to do something to protect himself and short of
running from the room he decided to stay and try to recover
some good feelings. Because it might be their last meal
together, and wouldn't he be angry with himself if he spent it
sullen and glowering?

He took a deep breath, and lowered his menu. "I'm
thinking about having the fish. Any thoughts?"

She smiled with relief. "I am totally not that kind of
person anymore, what a control freak."

She disappeared behind her menu. "Get whatever you
want. But if you're getting the fish, can you get it pan-seared,
with garlic mashed potatoes? But only if you want to. And the
steamed veggies."

The waitress returned and Edmund ordered everything
exactly as Violet had asked.

Violet ordered a small salad and then said she wasn't very
hungry and ordered the Volcano of Chocolate cake. "All at
once please."

After they placed their order and the waitress took away
the menus, there was a long and oh so complicated pause,
where Violet stared at Edmund causing him to look down at
his hands. Her gaze intruded in his pretend calm. This was all
so awkward and troubling and difficult.

"What is this?" she asked, gesturing toward her chin,
meaning his beard.

"Part of my new persona," he said. "Hermit-style"

She looked at him thoughtfully. "I like it. It fits you. Last
time you were too clean and dressed-up, like you owned the
world."

"I could use a shower. I went surfing and I've been moving lumber."

"You forget I was used to you after a long day's work. It's been a while."

"It has, it really has." He had slumped under her gaze so he gathered his height again. "So tell me about your art show. Did you know Lala sent me pictures?"

"She told me a couple of days ago when... it... she told me she came to see you."

"I'm grateful to her."

"Me too." Edmund's heart skipped a beat at her words. What did she mean?

She moved on, "My show is at the Armory in New York. The work is moving there right now and will be installed over the next few weeks and I go a few days early to make sure it's all perfect. I'm really nervous about it all. I mean these are bigwigs in the art world, and there's a—"

Edmund watched her tell him all about her life. She gave him the details. The thoughts behind the details and her feelings about the thoughts behind the details. All of it, in proximity, eye level to eye level. He wanted to pay attention to every detail, but he also got lost in her voice and her breaths and the little shifts and movements of her body. He desperately wanted to hold her hand as it fiddled with the bottom of her soda glass while she explained how much her life had changed without him. He needed to hold on to stay on the trail before he lost his footing.

Their food arrived and while they ate she tried to spear his fish and he tried to ward her off with his spoon. They both laughed and their mood lifted by degrees. They had stuffed all that needed to be said down deep for later. They floated above the deep hidden dark and playfully sparred over food, yet no matter how he protected his plate, she always managed to get the bite she wanted. Probably because of the fluttering edge of her eyelash or the bit of a smile caught in the corner of her mouth. Finally he put his fork down and looked at her, his breath like a sigh.

She said, "We have a lot to talk about you and I."

"Yes, we do."

Violet speared his last bite of fish.

"Hey, you distracted me!"

Through her full mouth she said, "You totally deserved that by the way." She took a big bite of cake and a big bite of salad. "As Bruce says, the fitness of your constitution is dependent on a healthy gratitude for what you're given. I'm not sure that applies." She speared his last bite of garlic mashed potatoes.

She put her fork down and crossed her hands over her plate and leaned them against her lips, as if trying to suppress her movements, her thoughts, and her voice all at once. She shook her head, stared deep into his eyes, and said, "I have been so fucking mad at you for so long."

He said, "Violet, please, God, can we go home and talk? Please?"

She stared into his eyes for another moment and then nodded and slid out of the booth, headed for the door.

* * *

They drove the block and a half to Edmund's house and pulled into his sandy drive, about where Lala had pulled back into his life a month ago. "So there it is," he said, leaning forward over the steering wheel and looking at the side of the house.

In answer, Violet opened the truck's door and walked to his porch.

He opened the door for her and followed, dropping his keys in a tray. She ran her fingers along the table, looking from side to side. "Does any of this belong to you?"

"No, almost everything you see came with the rental."

"I thought so. It didn't seem like you, but I barely..."

He said, "I need to use the bathroom really quick."

"I'll sit on the porch?"

"That would be great. Please make yourself at home."

He stepped into the bathroom and stood holding the doorknob, breathing heavily. This was so much harder than he had thought. Juggling had failed and flying objects were crashing down around him. If only he hadn't juggled flaming swords and activated chainsaws; there was no way he made it out of this unscathed. He considered, for one disagreeable moment, locking the door and escaping through the bathroom window. Anything to miss their looming conversation. He walked the two paces to the sink and leaned on it, resting his forehead against the mirror's cold glass.

Grab a hold of yourself, Eddie. She came to talk and he had nothing left to lose because she was lost—lost to him the day he ordered her removal from the mountain. She deserved to be able to ask questions, and he needed to answer them. It was the next to the last thing he had to do. Then the final thing would be to ask for her forgiveness—to beg her to forgive him—so he could get off the mountain for good.

CHAPTER FORTY-SEVEN
Ocean-facing

Edmund stepped onto the porch and abruptly said, "I need to explain some—"

"Your house is west-facing." She stood at the porch railing, wrapped in a blanket from his couch, looking out over the dunes at the sea. The top of her hair blew in the wind and glowed in the spotlight of a small lightbulb that hung from the porch's ceiling. It danced, while she remained still. And far away.

Their distance infuriated him, tested his calm. He stood steps away from Violet, but a chasm of his lies lay between them.

He slumped into the wicker love seat, but his feet didn't rest because of the blocks. They dangled. He needed his fucking feet to touch the fucking ground.

He stood and raised the left arm and kicked the blocks out from two of the legs. *Why did I do it?* He lifted the right side and kicked the blocks out from under the last two legs and dropped the love seat back down. He slumped into the seat. *That was better.*

Violet watched his frantic movements curiously. "What was that?"

He gestured at the railing beside her and the ocean beyond. "When I sit on my rental chair, on my rental porch, I can't see the only thing that I wanted this house for.

"Because honestly, It's not west-facing, it's *ocean*-facing. Of everything that I've done this last year, picking this house was the one thing I did without you in mind." He sounded surlier than he wanted, but it was also true. The first step in dispelling the lies.

She said, "That's probably what I like best about it."

He leaned forward with his elbows on his knees and said, "Violet you need to know. I need you to know—that I didn't plan any of this. I mean, I didn't arrive at the mountain wanting to take you off it, or wanting to buy it, or wanting any of that to happen. None of it was premeditated."

He had his hands clasped and stared at his thumbnails trying not to break his concentration. "I mean, I loved you, I just didn't understand how any of it would work. The morning after we... the morning of the avalanche, my parents called. My mother told me I had to come home because of an emergency.

"So when you sent me away, I had to go home. The whole way home—the airport, the newsstands—were stories about you and the mountain. That you were going to die, probably, die. They said it was only a matter of time. I had to meet with my family's lawyers and found out that I had enough money and power to buy you off. I did it without really thinking. You were on the TV and I just did it."

His hands shook. "Everything else has been me trying to fix it. Or at least stabilize it. Everything has been in reaction to that day." He curled forward, head in his hands, almost between his knees. His thumbs were on his temples. His eyes covered. So he didn't see Violet approach until she edged herself between his knees and the coffee table and sat down knee to knee.

She put her hands on the sides of his thighs. "Eddie?"

He raised. She was close, too close, so he slumped back, leaning his head on the rest behind. She leaned in and took his hands in hers. "Eddie I want you to listen to me, Okay?"

He nodded.

"I wanted to leave the mountain for you. The night you came to my room, I knew that I would, I only had to figure out how.

"Then the avalanche started, and all I thought about was fixing it. I had to stop everything from falling. I blamed you, and I was terrified. Terrified that my family wouldn't forgive me, that I let everybody down, that I couldn't stop everything from wrecking even though I tried. I felt so responsible. I wanted to die. That's all I knew, and all I believed I deserved. I wanted to die." She peered into his eyes and let that echo for a second.

"Eddie, I wasn't ever going to come down. Ever. Not on my own. Not without help."

He nodded. "I didn't want you to die."

"I know."

Using his thighs and shoulders she climbed his body and straddled his lap—pinning him. She held his chin. He tried to look away, but she forced him to look up at her. The lightbulb backlit her hair, haloing her face.

He averted his eyes, "I don't..."

Violet leaned back, lording over his lap. She gestured out in a incredulous shrug. "You don't? Don't? Don't want what— to look me in the eyes? You like staying gone? Is that what you really want?"

"It's not like that..." He made an effort to look up.

"I know exactly what it's like, and I'm not going to let you stay gone. I'm deciding for you, just like you wouldn't let me stay on the mountain. Now it's my turn to decide. My turn. Do you hear me? My turn."

"Yes, okay."

"I'm so tired of being angry. First, I wanted to kill the owner of the land. Then you jilted me. And you turned out to be the same person? I hated you. I wanted to find a way to continue hating you."

Edmund groaned.

"But then Dad left me this note beside my cereal box." Violet searched around in her front jeans pocket and pulled out a folded piece of lined paper, torn small, and handed it to him.

Edmund read in the faint light.

Violet,

Seems to me the brooding boy from the mountain is writing you love poems, perhaps you need to take a deep breath and listen?
Love,
Dad

He dropped the note to his chest.

Violet's voice calmed. "It was like the story I had heard, the one where you were the owner, became altered into something else. Same story, completely different script. I sat in a chair with an empty bowl in front of me staring at the wall. Benjamin and Lala found me like that and asked me if I wanted to talk—if I had any questions."

Edmund ran his thumb along the seam on the outside of her thigh. Touching her was a technicality, he needed something to do with his hands and she sat on top of his body. "Did you?" His voice was faint.

"I asked about when Benjamin went to see you. He told me about the hotel lobby and that's what I couldn't believe, you had been living in a hotel? The whole time? I asked Lala about her visit here, and she told me about the habitat signs and the mountain and about its name, and I understood everything, logically, finally."

She leaned her forearms onto his chest and gently placed a hand on each side of his jaw. She stroked the left side of his beard along the jawline and then pushed a bit of hair behind his ear.

"I needed to forgive you. I wanted to. But I honestly couldn't figure out how. Everyone always says, open your heart, but when your heart is wounded, how do you open it up? Every time I'm with you my world shifts dangerously. Terrifyingly."

Her face hovered inches away. So close that Edmund felt her breath, slow and deep. "So, I was sitting at our kitchen bar, you know the one?"

"Yes, I sat there once."

"Benjamin and Lala were carefully keeping me calm and my anger from blazing again. They answered my questions and tried to champion for you without being pushy, but that wasn't what I needed. I needed to figure out how you were safe. Does that make sense?"

Edmund nodded. She stroked her fingers down his cheek.

"After talking for a while, Benjamin got up and made me lunch. He's so kind. He and Lala were talking about the lizards, but I don't remember what they were saying, I was thinking about Benjamin. How he had been loyal and trustworthy since the day I met him and about how he had become a part of my family now, and you ought to be too, and why weren't you? And wasn't it time? Somehow, watching him putter around our kitchen, humming his rock star songs—I just loved you. I had to come get you."

She leaned in and kissed him, but he wasn't receptive yet, still a second behind.

"Me?" he asked into her parted lips.

"Yes, you. This is me coming to get you, and don't forget, it's my turn."

Edmund wrapped his arms around her and pulled her close. They kissed and kissed, her fingers entwined through his hair.

"God, Violet, you are always unexpected."

She kept her lips on the edge of his as she said, "I know, Eddie, and it's going to be okay."

She pulled higher up his chest and kissed him more deeply. She kissed his eyelids and the edge of his cheek at his beard and then more kisses until she pulled away.

"So I rented the truck, and Benjamin and Lala helped me load the whirligigs, and here I am."

"Here you are." He pulled her arm forward and brought her face in for another kiss. This long kiss was a savoring kiss, a forgiving kiss, a life-changing kiss.

Pulling a breath away, he asked, "What now, Violet?"

Still astride his lap, she said, "You take me to bed, and I spend the night."

He wrapped his arms around her in a bear hug and stood —lifting her and carrying her into the house through the living room and into the bedroom, lowering her feet to the floor by his bed.

"You're barefoot," he said into her ear.

"I took my boots off while you were in the bathroom."

He smiled, "You knew this was how it would go?"

She dropped down to the bed and said, "You love me, I love you. How could it go any other way, Edmund Hawkes?"

He dropped down beside her on the bed and pulled her shirt up and off and then pulled off his own and nestled into her breasts. Kissing and caressing. She unbuttoned his pants, crawling down his body and kissing on her way back up. Then he unbuttoned her pants and pulled them off, exposing her bright purple underwear. He chuckled to himself, and looked up at Violet, who nodded with a smile. They were naked together again. This time was different though—without the desperate sadness of their first or the lie-shrouded laughter of their second—this time was different. Edmund and Violet made love, slowly, on a bed in Edmund's rented house on the shores of the Pacific at the base of their mountain.

At the end Edmund rolled to his side and Violet cuddled in, her back to his front, his arms tight around. Her body the radiant curl, his body the enclosing shell. His breath in her hair, her ear, along her neck.

His eyes were closed, ten breaths away from asleep. Her eyes were open, not wanting to miss one single detail. "Tell me about the mountain after I left."

His voice was low and resonating. "I watched it from a leather couch in my lawyer's office. When you were gone, it was silent and lifeless."

"Did Benjamin call you?"

"Yes, he told me that you were going to jail, and that he would follow you with Lala and Bruce."

In the quiet and dark room, their voices were small, waves rushing from mouth to ear. "And what did you say?"

"I said, good. And I told him to hire you a lawyer, and then I walked to my hotel and went to bed."

Violet curled her hands up into his hands, so that she was within every part of him. Nestled protected. Her heart hurt because of the spaces in between his words. "Did you come back here?"

"Not while I was the owner. I met with the construction company and they sent me photos, but I didn't come and see. I couldn't."

"Did you talk to Benjamin?"

"Sometimes." Violet kissed the palm of Edmund's hand.

"Would he tell you about me?"

Edmund's voice had gotten very quiet and slow—two breaths from sleep. "Only sometimes. If I was lucky."

They lay in the quiet darkness, and Violet felt Edmund grow still and heavy. She whispered, "I think my mother would have liked you Edmund, and sometimes, when I believe in magic, I think she may have sent you to me."

He mumbled, "I wu—um—"

"Good night Eddie, Sweet dreams."

CHAPTER FORTY-EIGHT
We have plans

"Good morning." Violet turned to her back and raised an arm, presenting her full naked pale side, long and lean. Edmund pressed up against, beside and along, and nestled his mouth into the softest part of the side of her neck and held both of her hands above her head and ran his fingers down the length of her chest causing her to shiver.

"Good morning, this is early for you." His voice was lost in her hair, the vibration tickled the edge of her neck.

She said, "I wondered about this strange light, and I'm almost convinced those are birds."

"You can go back to sleep if you want. I'm never leaving this valley, right here." He kissed her right below her ear.

"You can't stay here doing this, we have plans, Eddie, plans." She used her cheek to raise his lips to meet hers. They kissed slow and soft.

He kissed her lips, her cheeks, her throat. "Plans? And they don't include this? But then again, I love a good plan, as long as I can come back to this spot sometime later today." He kissed the pulsing spot on her neck again.

"You can, I promise."

"So what's our plan, Violet?"

"Today I help you and the crew build decks, and the day after that and the day after that, and on and on and on until we've finished. Then I'll install the whirligigs and you can help."

He leaned up on his elbow and watched her lips as she laid out the life before him. She said, "On our first day off—when do you think that might be by the way?"

"Saturday? But I think we get to take the day whenever we want, your name is on the mountain after all."

"About that, can we name it after my mother instead, Elizabeth's Mountain? I think it should really belong to her."

Edmund nodded and said, "Yes, I think that's perfect."

"Me too. So, on Saturday, I'll lower that blasted porch railing so you can see the waves."

"Nice. You came up with all of this while you were sleeping?"

"While you were sleeping." A smile shimmered at the edge of her lips. "And then I'd like you to come with me to the city. I have an art show in a few weeks and I want you to be there. I know, I know, it's hard to leave the mountain, but it will be good for you. I didn't believe it could be, but come to find out..."

"Let me make some breakfast."

"Sounds good Eddie. I think I'll go to the porch to say good morning."

THE END

ABOUT ME, H.D. KNIGHTLEY

Three things I love:

1. watching sit-coms
2. eating shrimp, cheese, and cabbage burritos smothered in cilantro sauce
3. writing on my Ipad at the edge of a fire-pit on a beach-adjacent campground in Southern California after everyone else has gone to sleep.

I love writing romances with a twist of magical-realism, which is like fairytales for grownups. I write about young women who are badass and the hotties who adore them. Usually their world is falling apart with droughts or light-polluted night skies or rising seas and everything is awful, except they rescue each other and kiss in the end and then it's all good.

When I'm not writing, I'm usually hanging out with my family in Los Angeles, as close to the beach as we can be.

ACKNOWLEDGEMENTS

This idea, a young woman living on top of a mountain of things, sat with me for quite a while. Then in a coffee shop one day R.C. Hwang was talking to me about how women artists will never get to the same level of celebrity as their male-counterparts until women start receiving crucial day to day support. Like meals and laundry. Little did she know that our conversation would turn the beautiful and lonely Violet into a badass sculptor and introduce her helpmeet Lala and then their adopted-brother Benjamin and finally everyone's rescuer, Edmund. Thank you R.C. that was just what the story needed.

I really wanted to explore the idea of a princess who didn't want to leave her tower, and had to be rescued in spite of herself. And whether she could forgive the person who rescued her. And while writing, some days, I wondered if it was impossible. But I believed I accomplished it when, at the end, Violet rescued Edmund—who had become her mountain after all. Thank you Mara for being a first beta-reader and agreeing that I was successful.

Thank you Melissa Scholl for telling me you loved it and that you wanted more more more of Violet and Edmund. I added more, because you were of course right, and now I think there needs to be a whole series. I just love the two of them. Maybe they go thrift-shopping? Okay, I'll keep thinking.

Thank you to Heather Hawkes and family for letting me borrow their last name for my heroes. It was exactly what I was looking for.

Thank you Jodie Jiminez and Mel Legget for reading and advising and complimenting. I so appreciate your time. Every suggestion made the book better and better.

Thank you Fiona for reading and telling me it was the best ever. You always say that and you're always right. And I think you're the best ever.

Thank you Isobel for reading and giving me pages and pages of notes. Every single one of them was perfect and necessary, as are you.

Thank you Kevin for being my resident surfing-hottie advisor and listening to me go on and on. And to Ean and Gwynnie, for inspiring, cheering, and advising, even though you didn't get to read it—yet.

And to my dad, David Cushman, thank you for editing. You've always been a strong supporter of my—everything, the best dad ever for a girl like me, full of dreams and ideas. And thank you for the beautiful poem.

And finally, thank you to my mother, she wanted to keep every memory to share with me someday. She loved to share and teach and lived on her mountain with grace and generosity. I write to keep her laugh here.

MORE BY H.D.KNIGHTLEY

Subscribe to my mailing list:
hdknightley.com

Chat with me:
facebook.com/hdknightley

twitter.com/hdknightley

goodreads.com/HDKnightley

Please remember to leave a review at your favorite retailer.

Made in the USA
Middletown, DE
18 January 2019